Hesba Stretton

Highway of Sorrow at the Close of the Nineteenth Century

Third Edition

Hesba Stretton

Highway of Sorrow at the Close of the Nineteenth Century
Third Edition

ISBN/EAN: 9783744791335

Printed in Europe, USA, Canada, Australia, Japan

Cover: Foto ©Andreas Hilbeck / pixelio.de

More available books at **www.hansebooks.com**

THE
Highway of Sorrow

AT THE

Close of the Nineteenth Century

BY

HESBA STRETTON

"WIDE IS THE GATE, AND BROAD IS THE WAY; AND MANY THERE BE
WHICH GO IN THEREAT."

THIRD THOUSAND

CASSELL AND COMPANY, LIMITED

LONDON, PARIS & MELBOURNE

1895

PREFACE.

I have written "The Highway of Sorrow" in collaboration with a well-known Russian author, now an exile in England, who has supplied me with the outlines of the story; especially with the prison and Siberian incidents, which he assures me are founded on facts. It would have been impossible for me to have done this work without help as complete as that which he has rendered.

For information about Stundism, its simple tenets and humble organisation—for it is embraced only by the peasants—I am indebted to an anonymous pamphlet, entitled "The Stundists," opportunely published by the proprietors of *The Christian World* just as I was beginning my task. It seems to me that this poor and persecuted sect approaches more nearly to the

Christians of the Apostolic age than any other existing church. They have as yet no systematic theology, and no formal ritual. They have neither churches nor clergy. The New Testament is their code of. religious, moral, and social laws; and they interpret its precepts in a very literal and child-like manner. The first duty of a Stundist is to learn to read, that he may read for himself the words of the Lord Jesus Christ.

These primitive Christians are suffering persecution for conscience' sake, as flagrant and unrelenting as that which in the same country is pursuing the Jews. But the Jews have powerful friends among the great philanthropists of their own race; whilst the Stundists, themselves Russian peasants, are persecuted by their compatriots, with no one to plead their cause before the world, and appeal from Russian bigotry to the tribunal of public opinion. They are dumb, as our Lord was when He was oppressed and afflicted.

It is for the purpose of making their sorrows and martyrdom more widely known that the facts of their history have been woven into this story. There has been no exaggeration. The worst has not been told.

HESBA STRETTON

CONTENTS.

CHAPTER	PAGE
I.—Anno Domini 1888	1
II.—A Stundist Service	13
III.—Yarina's Garden Party	24
IV.—Testing the Future	48
V.—Panass	59
VI.—Loukyan at the Fair	66
VII.—An Iconoclast	77
VIII.—Father Vasili	90
IX.—Strongly Tempted	102
X.—Matchmaking	111
XI.—Arrested	129
XII.—Batushka and Matoushka	143
XIII.—The Pannotshka's Grave	154
XIV.—Halya's Betrothal	172
XV.—Inquisitors	185
XVI.—In Deep Waters	199
XVII.—The Lowest Depths	210
XVIII.—Stepan's Outbreak	226
XIX.—Safe Home	239

CHAPTER	PAGE
XX.—Valerian the Agnostic	254
XXI.—What is True?	270
XXII.—A Funeral Service	280
XXIII.—A Disastrous Winter	288
XXIV.—A Sign and a Dream	300
XXV.—The Patron Saint's Day	314
XXVI.—Exorcising the Stundists	326
XXVII.—Paul's Defence	339
XXVIII.—A Miracle	352
XXIX—Another Martyr	371
XXX.—A.D. 1892 O.S. 1893 N.S.	391
XXXI.—"Would God It Were Morning!"	410
XXXII.—Via Dolorosa	424

THE HIGHWAY OF SORROW.

CHAPTER I

ANNO DOMINI 1888.

OLD KARPO, the richest man in Knishi, sauntered out of his cottage, where he had sheltered from the scorching heat. Humping his shoulders peevishly, he set to work to make a new handle for his plough; but moving slowly and listlessly, as if he took no pleasure in what he was doing. True it was a Sunday, a day when no labour should be undertaken; and it seemed only half a sin to work lazily. He knew that properly he ought to sit on the turf seat against the cottage wall, and stare into vacancy; as he was not fond of gossiping with his neighbours. Occasionally, on a Sunday evening, he would obey his conscience; but he was never happy without his work, unless his daughter Halya sat beside him chatting or singing her pretty songs.

Halya was not at home, for early in the

B

morning, whilst it was still cool enough for
the walk, she had gone to spend the day with
Yarina, her old friend and companion. Old
Karpo—he was not more than fifty years of
age, but, being the head of a family, he was
always called old—had found the long, hot
hours terribly dull. There was nothing to do
but to watch his grey-haired, hard-featured
wife, Marfa, fussing about her household duties.
She was now cooking the supper, and the heat
of the stove would soon be as bad as the heat
of the sun. It was more pleasant to be out
of the way.

Knishi was a small village in one of the
Oukrainian provinces, scattered over a slightly
rising ground. A new life and movement began
to appear in its wide, grass-grown street. The
cattle lowed, and the barn-door fowls cackled.
The children turned out, and set to play at
ninepins. Here and there the heavy cranes
were made to draw up water from the deep
wells, to allay the thirst of the suffering beasts.
The dead stillness of the suffocating summer's
day was at an end.

The June sun had just set below the distant
and level horizon. Every living creature had

sought shelter from its scorching rays. But
now the long, uneven shadows of the hazel
coppices glided upwards from the meadows,
and, as though melting in the cooler atmosphere, filled it with a faint duskiness. The
heavens still burned with the flaming sunset,
which suffused with crimson and gold the
feathery clouds floating on the dark-blue vault
of the sky. The cross of the village church
glittered like a star against the deep blue.
Even the roofs of grey thatch seemed touched
with a rosy mist; and the great wooden cranes,
black with age, which stretched across the
wells, for a few minutes looked bright in the
golden light.

On the turf seats before the whitewashed
cottages the villagers were sitting; men and
women chatting over their affairs. An air of
sweet tranquillity and peace reigned. The
merry cries of the children at play hardly disturbed it.

All at once, from the last cottage in the
village, came the sound of soft, harmonious
singing. It was choral singing; but the tune
was so solemn it could not be an ordinary
song. Neither could it be church music, for

B 2

clear female voices were distinctly audible;
and women do not sing in the Greek Church
choirs. Indeed, this song, which floated so
softly through the rosy twilight, bore no resemblance to any monotonous ancient chant
of the Church. There was something quite
different about it—a special peasant character
—reminding one, now of the Kossack ballads,
and now of the mournful strains of the blind
minstrels, who sing for alms on festival days
in the porches of the Russian churches.
The voices were fresh and pure, and the
singing was so full of deep emotion, and so
touchingly simple and devout, that even old
Karpo was softened in spite of himself.

"The heretics sing grandly," he muttered
to himself; and although he kept on with
his work for the look of the thing, the movements of his arms grew slower and slower;
the hatchet rested on the block of wood, and
old Karpo very nearly stopped to listen. The
words were not distinguishable at this distance.

"Stop your noise there, you young limbs!"
cried Marfa, coming to the door and calling
to the children, who paid no heed to the
singing, but went on vehemently shouting

and knocking about their wooden ninepins. The gossips on their turf seats ceased from chatting. But for fear of the priest's anger, a little group of village people would have collected round the cottage where the Stundists were holding their Sunday prayer-meeting. The Oukrainian peasantry are passionately fond of singing, and this was different at once from church music and from village songs.

"It sounds as if it came down from heaven," muttered Marfa, not loud enough for her husband to hear; "but it will bring trouble to Hälya if Paul goes hand-in-hand with them."

There were not many Stundists in Knishi, and the heresy was still almost a new one. There had been living just beyond the village a bee-master of the name of Loukyan, who had earned a good living by selling wax and honey. He was a peasant like all the rest, untaught and ignorant, able only to read, scarcely able to write. But from his youth upwards he had been much given to church-going, and wonderfully fond of reading the Bible, the words of which were deeply impressed on his memory. Father Vasili, the

village priest, was often perplexed and annoyed
by the questions of his devout parishioner,
though he felt proud of him as a good Churchman. The peasants of all the country round
had learned to look up to Loukyan, both for
his book-learning and his good, honest life.
Though he was not one of the rich farmers
like Karpo, his voice had more weight in
the Mir than theirs, and his counsel was
sought for by any of his neighbours who
found themselves in any kind of difficulty.
He was getting on in years now, and had
been looked upon as a father by the whole
parish until about two years ago. It was all
changed now. The change had come so suddenly that the people in Knishi said the poor
old fellow had gone clean off his head!
Father Vasili encouraged this opinion. Loukyan had taken his honey and wax to sell in
the Kherson province; his ordinary business.
But the very day after he came back from
his journey, when his fellow-members of the
Mir came to visit him and to hear all the
news of the outside world, what did they see?
It was just at the beginning of the long fast,
the forty days of Lent; and there upon

Loukyan's table stood bowls of ordinary soup, and milk, too, and he and his nephew, Demyan, with his young wife, were sitting at dinner as if they had forgotten Lent.

"Why, Loukyan! have you lost your senses?" they asked in amazement.

"No, no! I have not lost my senses!" he answered, with twinkling eyes; "it's you that have never come to yours. Why should we fast for forty days? Our Lord says in the Scriptures: 'Not that which goeth into the mouth defileth a man, but that which cometh out of the mouth. For from within, out of the heart, proceed evil thoughts, adulteries, fornications, murders, thefts, covetousness, an evil eye, blasphemies, pride, foolishness; all these things come from within, and defile the man.' Let us fast from these, and all will be well with us, both in Lent and out of Lent."

But that was not the sort of fasting that suited them. They could not answer him, however; and they went away perplexed and discontented.

The next thing was that Loukyan left off going to the parish church, where, for forty

years or more, his familiar face, full of serious
and gentle thought, had never been missing.
Soon after, the village gossips told one another
that he had taken down the sacred icons from
the shrine in his cottage. He had bought
quite a number of them, and some of them
were good ones, for he never grudged his
money for them. But now he broke up some
of them into splinters, and gave the rest to
his niece to cover the milk-pails.

"They are vain idols," he said to the
people who asked him the reason of this
conduct; "does not the commandment tell us
that we are not to make them, or to bow
down to them? Must we not obey the voice
of the Lord our God? We have all of us
bowed down to these idols; but now I am
going to worship God, and Him only."

By-and-bye, very quickly indeed, all this
reached the ears of Father Vasili; and he
came to Loukyan's cottage in his vestments,
and bearing the crucifix with him. It was a
ceremonial visit, almost as if there was going
to be a funeral in the house. Though Loukyan
was a troublesome parishioner, full of notions
and knotty questions, the priest could not bear

to lose him from among his congregation. But Father Vasili was no controversialist; and all he could do was to hold the crucifix solemnly before Loukyan, and command him to resume his habit of going to church.

"Father Vasili," said Loukyan, "your church is no House of God. It is a place of buying and selling, as if a man could buy salvation, or a priest sell it. I cannot worship God in it."

"Look on this, and be ashamed, poor sinner!" cried Father Vasili, pointing to the crucifix with one hand, as he held it at arm's length with the other.

"I see it," said Loukyan; "it is an image of the cross, and our Saviour nailed upon it. But it is only an image, father! It cannot see me and it cannot hear me. It is only a bit of wood. But I pray to Him who died upon the cross; and I know in my heart that He sees and hears me. I can never bow down to that again. It would be an offence against God, who has said, 'Ye shall not make gods of silver; neither shall ye make unto you gods of gold.'"

"And you have profaned your icons!"

exclaimed Father Vasili angrily, turning towards the desecrated shrine. " We shall see what the authorities say about it."

Some days afterwards two policemen came to Knishi, and carried Loukyan away to a town at some distance, where he fortunately had a few acquaintances, who had often done business with him, and were favourably inclined to him. Loukyan was put into prison, but was not on the whole harshly treated. From time to time he was put under examination as to his opinions; but as the questions asked him were principally political, he could answer them satisfactorily. The new heresy was scarcely known in the province; and the head officials did not as yet trouble themselves about it. They could not see the full importance of Loukyan's insignificant change of religion; and after an imprisonment of six months he was released with a caution to avoid offending his parish priest again.

Loukyan came back to Knishi; and with the ardour of a messenger with glad tidings, began to spread about his new doctrines. His nephew, Demyan, and his wife, who lived in the house with him, were his first disciples.

Next to them came Ooliana Rudenko, a widow with one son, who were the richest people in Knishi, next to old Karpo. Like Loukyan, Ooliana had been one of the most regular and devout worshippers in the village church, giving liberally of her substance to the maintenance of Father Vasili. She and Loukyan had often talked together on religious subjects; and now she studied the New Testament with eager intelligence; soon adopting the new views, and carrying them out conscientiously. After Ooliana others joined; until at last ten families, who became the most steady and sober and honest of the villagers, had formed themselves into a little religious community, who worshipped God after their own consciences.

Father Vasili, disappointed with the action of the police, confined himself to cursing the Stundists from the pulpit. The Mir, which had treated Loukyan indulgently as long as he was alone, looking upon his conduct as a kind of madness, began to be angry. The peasants were not very jealous for the Orthodox Church, the dues and fees of which were heavy; but it irritated them that these

people, ordinary peasants like themselves,
should set themselves up to be better and
wiser and holier than their neighbours. The
Orthodox religion had been good enough for
their forefathers, and was good enough for
them. The Stundists were a perpetual vexation
to the members of the Mir,' for their piety,
and thrift, and sobriety; and also for the very
patience with which they bore jeers and injuries
from their neighbours. Old Karpo was specially
infuriated. Ooliana's son had long been in love
with his daughter Halya; and no match could
be more suitable. But if Paul joined the
new religion nothing should prevail upon him
to give Halya to him.

The little Stundist community lived in an
enemy's camp, as it were. Any day might
find them exposed to a furious attack. These
men and women, whom they had known in-
timately all their lives, with whom they had
held friendly intercourse, rejoicing with them
and weeping with them, now looked askance
at them, and held themselves aloof from them.
There is no hatred like the hatred arising
from religious differences.

CHAPTER II.

A STUNDIST SERVICE.

Now, in the darkening twilight of that fair evening, a little band of Stundists had met together for prayer and the study of the Bible. There were from fifteen to twenty persons present, grave and quiet-looking men and women, who asked for nothing but to be left to worship God, none making them afraid. The slight persecution they had so far met with had only tended to draw them closer together, and to give them that fervour of spirit which seems the special gift of God to those who suffer for righteousness' sake. How often did they say one to another, " Blessed are ye when men shall hate you, and when they shall separate from you, and shall reproach you, and cast out your name as evil. Rejoice ye in that day, and leap for joy; for behold! your reward is great in heaven!" Their grave, quiet faces shone with an inner light; and their voices took a tone of exultation. It was a great thing to endure persecution!

It was this persecution which had at first
driven Paul Rudenko into the band of Stundists.
He was indignant and hurt at seeing his
mother, the best woman in Knishi, avoided
or molested. Was she not always ready to
help anyone who was in trouble? How often
had she sat up all night nursing the sick
and dying! Her house had never been closed
to a neighbour. Yet now, because she chose
to pray in another fashion from theirs, she
must be insulted and injured, and banished
from the society of her old friends. It
must be a poor cause which needed such
weapons.

But for a long time, half unconsciously,
Paul's love for Halya, old Karpo's daughter,
hindered him from definitely adopting his
mother's religion. Halya and he had grown
up together, the one the only son, the other
the only daughter, of the two richest farmers
in the district. There had been no formal
betrothal, for they were both young; and
Paul's father had died not two years ago.
But everybody knew that Paul and Halya
were intended for one another. The course
of their love had been smooth enough until

Ooliana, Paul's mother, had openly joined the Stundists. Ooliana had been insulted and abused both by old Karpo and his wife Marfa. Paul was threatened that he must give up Halya if he followed his mother's example and attached himself to that old fool Loukyan. There was a deep and terrible conflict in Paul's heart between his love for Halya and his love for his mother, and the irresistible dawning of light in his inmost soul. To please his mother he had frequently attended the Stundist meetings; but to see Halya he had often gone to the village church.

This evening he was sitting in the cottage, at the Stundist prayer-meeting, with one of their hymn-books in his hand. Some were singing by heart, not knowing how to read. In one corner, seated at a plain deal table, was Loukyan, facing the little congregation. He was about fifty-five years of age, with a small, pensive face, a thin grey beard, and large dreamy hazel eyes, shining with intelligence and gentleness. He was softly humming the tune, and following with his forefinger the lines of the hymn in the small book lying open before him. He had long known every word of it; but, none the less, he liked to see the printed words.

Paul had taken a seat near to Loukyan. He was a tall, slim young fellow of twenty-two, with one of those handsome and regular faces, with clear-cut features, which are sometimes met with among the Oukrainian peasantry. He was one of the finest singers in the neighbourhood, with a pure tenor voice, which rang out clearly among a chorus of voices. Loukyan gave out the hymn, and Paul joined in the singing; but he heard neither his own voice nor any other. The words of the hymn absorbed him:—

> "When I survey the wondrous cross
> 　　On which the Prince of glory died,
> My richest gain I count but loss,
> 　　And pour contempt on all my pride.
>
> See, from His hands, His head, His feet,
> 　　Sorrow and love flow mingled down:
> Did e'er such love and sorrow meet,
> 　　Or thorns compose so rich a crown?
>
> Were the whole realm of nature mine,
> 　　That were a present far too small;
> Love so amazing, so divine,
> 　　Demands my soul, my life, my all."

Paul sang these words almost unconsciously. The meaning of them was burning itself into his mind with intense conviction. He had all his life been given to long reveries, which now and then deepened into trances, and waking dreams of extraordinary vividness. He was an unlearned peasant; but his imagination had been trained and exercised by the poetic legends of his country. His mind, like those of his people, was more Oriental than Occidental; and, like the prophets of the Jewish nation, he saw visions and dreamed dreams.

Now before this inward eye of his there stood in distinct clearness "the cross on which the Prince of glory died." There had been other saviours of men, who also had suffered crucifixion. But here was the chief of all, who could say, "Was ever sorrow like my sorrow?" He saw the divine face of the Prince of glory, with His crown of thorns; and the dying eyes looked into his inmost soul out of fathomless depths of grief. He shuddered as he met that gaze. But beneath the sorrow, and greater than it, because sorrow is not infinite, shone out the

c

infinite love of the Son of God. And it
was love lavished upon him, Paul Rudenko!
The parched lips said to him, "All this I
bore for thee; what wilt thou do for Me?"
His whole soul responded; in unutterable
rapture Paul sang the last words of the
hymn :

> "Love so amazing, so divine,
> Demands my soul, my life, my all."

What was this strange joy which flooded
all his inmost being? All the gladness he
had ever felt was absolutely nothing in com-
parison with this ecstasy and rapture of
adoration. It was a new life breathed into
him, such as no words could tell. He did
not hear a word of Loukyan's prayer, which
followed the singing. But when, with a slight
stir, the little congregation settled itself to
listen to the address, Paul came back to this
lower world.

Loukyan, putting on his spectacles, and
turning over the leaves of his New Testament carefully, at last read out these verses,
with a solemn and profound tenderness in
his voice :—

"That Christ may dwell in your hearts

by faith: that ye, being rooted and grounded in love, may be able to comprehend, with all saints, what is the breadth, and length, and depth, and height, and to know the love of Christ, which passeth knowledge."

Very simply, and in peasant dialect, the old man called upon his hearers to consider what human love is, as they felt it in their own hearts. The love of fathers and mothers, of husbands and wives, of children to their parents, of lovers and friends, were all touched upon.

"All this is love," he said, "and comes from God; for love is of God; and God Himself is love. And the love of God is like them all; only in this it is different—it never changes, and it never ceases. For husbands and wives, and parents and children fall out, and quarrel, and get separated, and some even hate one another. 'But who shall separate us from the love of Christ? shall tribulation, or distress, or persecution, or famine, or nakedness, or peril, or sword? Nay, in these things we are more than conquerors, through Him that loved us.' Perhaps if we could see our Lord, our love to Him would

c 2

be earthly, like these others. But He says,
'Blessed are they that have not seen, and
yet have believed.' So we must have Him
dwelling in our hearts by faith. Dwelling in
us, you hear. Why! if He was dwelling now
in Jerusalem, say! would not our hearts be
empty of Him, but full of yearning? ay! and
discontent. For He would be so far away,
and all who love Him could not travel to
Jerusalem, and bide there in His bodily
presence. No, no! We have something better
than that. He is dwelling here," cried
Loukyan, laying his hand on his heart, "and
in yours, my sisters; and in yours, my
brothers."

"Ay! ay!" fell from the lips of most of
his hearers. They had been hanging on his
words; and it seemed only natural to respond
when he addressed them so individually.
Demyan, Loukyan's nephew, spoke the loudest.
He was a sturdy, broad-shouldered young
fellow; and his round, freckled face, with its
kindly grey eyes, revealed the deep emotion
with which he listened to every word his
uncle uttered. He had risen from his seat
in the corner, and leaned towards the preacher,

in an attitude of complete abandonment. He had felt all these earthly loves; and the heavenly one was lodged in his heart of hearts. The tears rolled down his cheeks; and he wiped them away, now and then, with his great, horny hand.

"And now how much shall we love Him?" asked Loukyan, pausing and looking round on the familiar faces confronting him, "how can poor helpless creatures like us show our love to the Lord Jesus Christ?"

"I will die for Him!" cried Demyan, falling on his knees, and resting his elbows on the table. Behind his large hands burst out sobs; and his tangled fair hair concealed his agitated face.

"Ay!" ejaculated Loukyan, "it may be that we shall have to die for Him, or deny Him. Our brethren in many places are choosing now, at this very hour, between dying and denying. But I, God helping me, will die for Jesus."

"And I!" cried Paul, with a thrilling fervour in his voice and face, as he stood up, and drew near the table. "Since I came in here, I have seen Him. I saw Him nailed to the shameful cross, with a crown of thorns upon His head. And there was in His eyes a love that no words could tell. A love passing knowledge! We shall never know its fulness, no! not through all eternity. I am ready to die for Him."

For a minute there was a dead silence in the cottage. Ooliana, his mother, was not there; but every person present knew that she had been praying ardently for Paul's conversion ever since she had herself joined the Stundists. Here was the answer to her prayers. But there was a solemn note of challenge in Paul's voice, as if he looked into the future and foresaw a conflict unto death, if he persisted in obeying his conscience. Would Ooliana rejoice if her son were called to martyrdom? The idea of martyrdom was growing familiar to the little band.

"I am ready to die for Him," repeated Paul. The sound of his voice broke the spell which bound them; and sobs and murmurs of gladness followed the silence. Louk-yan stretched out his hands and clasped Paul's between them with a gesture as if he were welcoming him into the new fellowship and brotherhood.

"Thank God! thank God!" he exclaimed. "Now, Lord, lettest thou thy servant depart in peace; for mine eyes have seen thy salvation. Thou art blessed and chosen of the Lord, Paul Rudenko. If I am taken away from this little flock—from these few sheep in ·the wilderness—thou wilt be here to be their shepherd. Let us praise God together."

Then from the lips of all present rang out the Doxology of the Greek Church, which had been familiar to each of them from their earliest childhood. It was sung with deep and solemn triumph, and echoed all down the village street in the deepening twilight. Some of the peasant women took up the well-known words and tune as they sat at their cottage doors. Old Karpo listened to it till the last note died away; but he did not guess that it sounded the knell of his Halya's prosperity and happiness.

"Well sung, cursed heretics!" he muttered to himself.

CHAPTER III.

YARINA'S GARDEN PARTY.

WHEN Paul left the cottage, it was already
dark; only in the north-west a line of prim-
rose light showed softly the spot where the
sun had sunk to rest beyond the boundless
steppe. The stars hung like lamps in the dark
blue sky; and the moon was climbing slowly
upwards, though, as yet, it gave but little
light. The cool air caressed his cheek as if
with a kiss from heaven; and the clear deep
sphere of the sky seemed to clasp the earth in
its embrace, whilst the stars looked down upon
it with a loving human gaze.

"The heavens declare thy glory," he whispered fervently, sure that he was heard by
One who loved him. His whole heart was
light and glad, with such a joy as had
never entered his imagination to conceive. All
the earth was full of the glory of God. His
road ran beside a cornfield, and the tall stalks,
with their thin heavy ears of wheat pale in
the starlight, were swaying to and fro in the

night breeze, with broad, rhythmical waves, which followed one another over the field as on the surface of the sea. The gentle rustling of the ears of wheat could be hardly said to break the silence.

Presently the road began to ascend towards a low hill covered with shrubs and small trees. Little groups of delicate silver birches shook their tremulous leaves against the moon, which was now shining more fully. A stream ran beside him just below the hill—a shallow stream—with here and there an almost motionless pool, which reflected a rippling image of the moon and the willows growing on its banks. From the wood came the scent of newly mown hay; and three hay-ricks stood out tall and black against the sky. Was the earth new-born, like himself, that he saw in it a beauty, and a glory, and a harmony, such as his most vivid fancy had never yet revealed to him?

"Blind! and thou hast given me sight! Deaf! and thou hast opened my ears! Dead! and thou hast called me to life!" he said, half aloud. There was a gracious Companion walking with him as a friend, who would never forsake him, or leave him alone and comfortless. For evermore, through all the endless ages of eternity, he had found a Brother. He had almost reached a neighbouring hamlet before he knew he was near it. Already he could hear in the distance the merry choral songs he used to love so well. The road turned sharply to the left round the low spur of the hill, and ran straight into the little street. The lights in the cottage windows twinkled like glow-worms here and there. As if a door had been suddenly opened the song rang out clear and low. He could even recognise voices; that of Yarina, the best singer in the hamlet, and another voice, which made his heart leap. Yes! Halya was there; his Halya, whom he had loved so long. Almost unconsciously to himself his feet had carried him to the spot where he could find her.

Yarina was a young widow, well-to-do, and inclined to make the most of her liberty and wealth. Her former playmates, the village girls, and still more the young men of the village, frequented her house. They hardly thought of her as having been a married woman. She lived alone, with an old grandmother, in a pleasant, roomy dwelling, with a large garden, sloping down to the stream which loitered slowly past her lands. Yarina's cottage was a favourite resort. Nowhere else did the young people of Knishi, and its neighbourhood, enjoy themselves so much. The anxieties and dull gloom of middle life were not to be met with there. The old grandmother was on the verge of a second childhood, and Yarina had not lost the gaiety of girlhood. Judging by the sound of many voices in her garden, there was a large gathering there to-night, and Halya was certainly among them. An irresistible desire to see her, and tell her the marvellous change wrought in him, seized upon Paul. This was an opportunity of talking with her, without her father's or mother's presence, which he must not lose.

Yarina's cottage was in the middle of the hamlet, distinguished from its poorer neighbours by its newly painted gates and railing. It lay far back, with a wide fold-yard before it, and its black outlines stood out plainly against the sky. There was no gleam of light on this side of the house, for the Oukrainians

invariably build their houses facing the east,
even when it involves turning their backs
to the village street. Yarina's cottage looked
deserted, and but for the sounds of music and
laughter which rang round it, one would have
thought that it was uninhabited. Paul opened
the gate, and turned round the corner of the
house. It was like a transformation scene.
The low door, and a small window on each
side of it, were all wide open, and streams of
light shone through them across a smooth,
broad grass-plot, already lit up by the rising
moon. Nearly all the guests were gathered
there; a throng of young men and girls, every
one of whom he had known from his childhood. Paul drew back into the dark shadow
of the walls. He did not want to see anyone
but Halya, or to be seen by them. By-and-
bye they would scatter in small groups about
the garden. Then he trusted to finding her
for a few minutes alone.

The merry laughter and singing had ceased.
Almost the only sound to be heard was the
scraping of a shrill home-made fiddle, played
by a fiddler blind of one eye. He was
playing the gay national dance, called the

" Casatchók." The dance had just begun, and
on the smooth level lawn a circle of young men
and girls surrounded the dancers. Of these
there were only two. Yarina herself was one,
a tall, dark, beautiful woman, with laughing
brown eyes, and a pert, slightly turned-up
nose. She stood with one of her round arms
akimbo, and the attitude showed off her pretty
figure to perfection. Her full red lips were
slightly parted with a smile, as from time to
time she glided a few paces to the left or to
the right, as easily and gracefully as the flight
of a swallow when it just skims the surface
of the ground; her little red shoes hardly
seeming to press the blades of grass under her
tread. But in the Oukrainian dances the chief
part belongs to the man.

Yarina's partner was Panass, who, from
their boyhood, had been Paul's rival in Knishi.
Next to Paul he had hitherto been the most
desirable match in the neighbourhood; and now
that Paul had joined the Stundists, he would
be far before him in the estimation of the
public. He was a tall, well-made young fellow,
with an ordinary peasant-like face; but agile
and light-footed, and the best dancer in the

country for miles round Knishi. All the
crowd stood silently watching him. Panass
was whirling round Yarina, now and then
rushing towards her, and falling back as if
disheartened by her careless indifference. Sometimes he squatted on the ground in a despair-
ing mood, and then he leaped exultantly into
the air, clashing his heels together, and making
wonderful steps, not dreamed of by any dancing
master. His swarthy face was bathed in perspiration, and it kept throughout a serious,
almost gloomy expression. By this trait one
might recognise him as a genuine Oukrainian
dancer, to whom the dance was more, far more
than a mere pastime.

Paul looked from his hiding-place round
the throng of spectators. The bright light
from the open door and windows illuminated
the faces of those near the house, and the
moonlight shone full upon those on the other
side of the circle. But Halya was not among
them. Perhaps she was in the gardens beyond?
He stole softly away, and traversed the empty
walks; but he could not find her. Nearly
all the guests were breathlessly watching
Yarina and Panass.

The dance, in the meantime, was growing more and more animated. The one-eyed fiddler quickened the time and played more briskly. Panass, striking the ground fiercely with his heels, made his circles closer and closer, each one bringing him nearer to Yarina. She no longer glided away from him, shrinking from his approach; but she stood still, her arms fallen to her side, looking as if she was about to swoon away with half-concealed emotion. The only other movement of her all but motionless figure was a slight sidling to and fro of her little red feet. The dramatic dance was coming to a close. For the last time Panass squatted on the ground before Yarina. For the last time he made his circle round her with slower and triumphant steps. He had won his love; and now both stood up, holding one another by the hand. They bowed to the spectators, and moved away in different directions, indicating in this way that they were not really lovers, but had merely performed together the lovers' dance.

The one-eyed fiddler began to strum a song; but nobody listened to him. They strolled away into the garden by twos and threes; talking here in animated tones, there with hushed voices. Some of them were lovers, though they doubted whether they could ever be husbands and wives. Love was in their own power; but marriage must be decided by the arbitrary will of fathers, who were nearly always guided exclusively by sordid considerations of property and prospects. This fact, well known and recognised as an inevitable fate, gave an underlying sadness to the love-making of the young couples.

After marriage a woman becomes the absolute property of her husband, with no freedom or rights of her own. She is his servant and drudge. Her children are his, not her own. But before marriage a girl is at liberty to see, and talk, and walk out with anyone—even to stay out until the dawn, nobody blaming or suspecting her. Often the simplest, and sincerest, and purest friendship exists between two young people whose parents will not consent to their being betrothed lovers.

All the poetry and tenderness in which the southern branch of the Russian race is so rich, are concentrated on the pure, confiding, and romantic relations cherished between a Russian youth and maiden; a friendship as high-minded and self-controlled as the devotion of a knight to his lady in the best days of chivalry.

In Yarina's garden were scattered young couples. Some of them sat down together on the grass, others strayed away under the trees. Most of them paced to and fro hand in hand, flitting across the bright streams of light, and gliding away into the moonlit walks. The girls—in their snowy-white blouses, open at the throat, and their full, light skirts with brilliant sashes round their waists, and ribbons in their hair—looked somewhat like the tall, many-coloured lilies growing in the garden borders. Even the slightly stupid Panass saw the resemblance.

"You're like a living flower," he said to Yarina. "And we poor lads in our blue coats are like the bumble bees, seeking the best honey."

"The largest quantity of honey!" answered Yarina sharply.

Panass was hesitating between Yarina and

D

Halya; or, rather, his father was diligently weighing the merits of the one against the other, before sending the matchmakers.

The soft hum of whispering voices was now and then broken in upon by the sound of a kiss or a peal of laughter. In some quiet shade might be heard a tender love-song, sung in a subdued voice, and intended jealously for the ear of one listener only. All were wrapt up in themselves, and each other; and no one noticed Paul, who went once more round the garden, seeking in vain for Halya. Below the garden ran the river, glimmering in the moonlight; and a warm hurried breeze blew across it. Paul strolled down the slope, but Halya was not there.

Suddenly, from the opposite shore, came the trill of the Oukrainian nightingale, ringing as clear as a bell, and drowning the laughter and the hum of voices, with a dominant note like that of a solo-singer, whose voice rises high above the music of the accompaniment. Paul stood listening awhile, entranced by the jubilant notes. But before long, his anxiety to see Halya drew him back towards the house.

As he approached it, still keeping in the shadows, he saw Panass go through the open doorway.

"She is there!" said Paul to himself. It seemed as if a cold breath blew across his spirit, which had been on fire so short a time ago. He stood with his eyes riveted on the doorway. Presently, the pretty face he loved so dearly, and the slim, graceful form, stood upon the threshold; and Halya seemed to be gazing timidly into the moonlit garden. She had been sitting with the old grandmother, to escape the attentions of Panass; but now he had pursued her there, she felt there would be more safety for her in the companionship of her friend Yarina. Paul was rushing towards her, when he saw she was not alone. Panass was following close upon her steps, with a bandoura in his hand, on which he lightly touched a few notes, whilst he spoke to her in low tones. She shook her head, and hesitated to pass on with him out of the light, and into the moonlit garden. She had never drawn back from Paul.

Along the walls of the house ran a seat

made of turf and soil, baked hard by the hot
sun. Halya sat down on it, and Panass took
his place on the ground, at her feet, and
rested his head against her knee, as he went
on tuning the strings of his bandoura. Paul
could bear the sight no longer.

"Halya!" he cried, coming forward out of
the shadow.

She lifted her eyes to him coldly, and did
not stir from her position.

"Good evening!" she said, in a tone of
distant reserve. But Panass sprang to his
feet with a shout.

"Why, Paul! Paul the Stundist! Paul
the saint! Paul the apostle!" he shouted.
"You here among us heathens? Come here,
boys!" he bawled, "come here! Here is Paul
the apostle! Let's try him! Let's see what
he will put up with! He has thrown himself
into our hands!"

It was an unforeseen chance, which took
them all by surprise. A cruel wish arose
among the young people, especially the men,
to amuse themselves at Paul's expense. His
lot in life was so far above the average; he
was so much richer, and more handsome; so

much more gifted than any of them, that it came natural to them to wish to see him humiliated.

The young men and girls flocked towards the house at the loud call of Panass, from all parts of the garden. Some of them had still their arms entwined round each other, with the supreme indifference of rustic lovers to the jesting remarks of their comrades. They stood gazing with dreamy eyes at the scene before them. Panass continued to jeer at Paul.

"Now, you apostle," he said, "sing us one of your songs of Zion, as you call them, and let it be a merry one."

He played a few chords upon his bandoura, and began to parody a Stundist hymn to a tune which was a favourite one with the Stundists. The crowd which surrounded them began to laugh boisterously.

"Come, come, apostle!" sneered Panass. "Sing second, or be our leader. You have a fine voice, everybody knows."

Paul looked at Halya, who sat silent and motionless on the turf seat. She had turned pale, but her face was in shadow, and he

could not see that she felt any emotion. It
seemed as if she was studiously indifferent to
his presence, and the ridicule to which Panass
was subjecting him. His heart failed him.
He felt desolately alone in this throng of
familiar and dear faces. For he had loved
these mockers; he had worked with them,
played with them; gone in their company to
many a merry festival, and to sorrowful
funerals. They were his comrades, his brothers
and sisters; they had clasped hands in true
fellowship. And now! Oh, sorrowful words of
the Lord and Master: "The brother shall
deliver up his brother to death, and the father
the child; and the children shall rise up
against their parents, and cause them to be
put to death. And ye shall be hated of all
men for my name's sake."

For a moment or two a strong temptation
assailed him to meet this insensate mockery
with reviling. A voice said within him:
" Ye fools! ye pagans! you laugh at a thing
of which you have no understanding." He
almost longed to hear their stupid laughter
change into a roar of rage. He was ready
to suffer martyrdom for the Lord whom he

had seen in a vision so short a time ago. But upon this feeling of wrath, mingled with contempt, came the remembrance of the patience of the Lord Jesus Christ, "who, when He was reviled, reviled not again." A softened mood of friendliness towards his old companions took possession of him, and he turned his beautiful face towards them, with a mournful smile upon it.

"Well," he said, "for the sake of old times, never forgotten by me, give me the bandoura. I will sing you one of your favourite songs."

Panass ceased laughing, and with an air of astonishment, passed him the bandoura. The crowd grew silent, too; only the singing of the nightingale across the river could be heard. Paul sat down on the turf seat, at a little distance from Halya, and struck some chords of simple melody on the bandoura; and after a minute or two, his pure sweet tenor voice rang out the opening words of a Kossack ballad. He felt that he could not sing a hymn to that scoffing audience.

In the meantime Panass had recovered from his surprise, and now squatted down in

front of him, prepared to accompany his
singing with ridiculous gestures, provocative
of laughter and derision from the crowd.
He had expected Paul would sing a Stundist
hymn. But at the first unsteady notes of
the mellow voice which had so often charmed
them, the temper of the listeners changed. A
solemn, sympathetic mood fell upon each one
present. Even Panass, on whose face the
jeering smile had settled into a grimace,
listened with most attentive ears. The beautiful Yarina stood leaning against the door-
post, her laughing eyes half shut and dim
with tears. The ballad was a pathetic one:
the farewell of a young Kossack warrior to
the home and the friends of his boyhood.
He was going forth to fight the Paynim,
and rescue the Christian captives, held in
bondage by the infidels. But no vision of
glory and victory beguiled him; the presenti-
ment of death on the battle-field ran through
the ballad. Never more would he cross the
threshold of his home; never more clasp
hands with the friend who was dearer than a
brother; never more kiss the lips of the
maiden who was betrothed to him. And all

was well, because his warfare was for his holy creed.

Yarina listened, and it seemed to her that she was no longer a gay young widow courted by all the marriageable men in the country. She was a light-hearted, pure-minded girl again, full of good impulses. She recalled her life with her husband, who had lived one single happy year with her in this home of hers. She felt ashamed of having forgotten him so soon. These merry-makings, with their high revelry, were a dishonour to his memory. She, too, had her warfare to engage in. A desire crossed her mind to renounce this careless life. She would shut herself up in a hermitage, or a nunnery, and give all her goods to the Church. How grand that would be! And how all the world would honour her!

The one-eyed fiddler was listening and dreaming too. With head bent down he was brooding over the old times, when Cossack knights lived in Oukrainia, redressing grievances and fighting the Turks. He fancied himself a warlike minstrel, no longer fiddling at drunken feasts for a few kopecks; but mounting a horse, and riding to the wars. It was not

Petro who had knocked out his eye in a
drunken brawl; but he had lost it in noble
combat for Christ's sake, with that very same
Turkish pasha of whom Paul was singing.

And Paul's song grew stronger and more
thrilling as he felt the sympathy it evoked
in his listeners. His voice grew more and
more pathetic, and his face glowed with emotion.
Both he and they forgot the vital difference
which separated them. They were living in
the magical world of heroic memories. All
of them had been brought up on the legends
of their famous men of olden days; legends
of renown, numerous among the poetical and
romantic people of Little Russia.

The song drew near its end; the last
full, plaintive note died away into the quiet
night, echoed by the trill of the nightingale. But no one moved, or uttered a word.
Even Panass was silenced. What more was
to follow?

When they came to themselves, as it
were, Paul had disappeared. He was
himself deeply moved, and could not bear
to see them coming back to their mood of
ridicule, or even to hear their idle applause.

Halya had kept her face turned away from him; there was nothing to be expected from her. He stole quickly and silently away, and turned sadly homeward.

His road took him through Knishi again, where all was quiet in the village street. The wooden church, with its green cupola, and the wells with their long cranes; the cottages standing at the bottom of their fold-yards; the priest's stone house—all were familiar to him, and seemed to warn him that he was setting his feet in a path of terrible estrangement and loneliness. He had already lingeringly passed Halya's home, when he heard footsteps running after him. He turned, and speechless with joy, he could not for a moment breathe a word. It was Halya herself. "Halya!" he exclaimed when he recovered from his surprise. "Halya!"

"Yes!" stammered the girl, who was out of breath with running as fast as she could, "what did you come for?"

Paul seized her hand.

"My own darling!" he exclaimed, "how glad you make me! I thought you had turned away from me, and would never look at me again. Why were you so cruel to me, my Halya?"

Halya drew away her hand, and repeated her question, almost angrily. "What did you come for?" she asked again.

"Why do you ask?" said Paul, in a faltering voice; "I came to see you. Don't you know that I hardly feel alive when I cannot see you and talk to you?"

She did not answer, but stood before him with downcast eyes, and an expectant expression, as if she was waiting for something more. Her face was pale and wistful in the moonlight.

"You are not going to marry Panass?" said Paul hesitatingly.

"How do I know?" she asked, in almost a peevish tone; "father will settle all that. He would let me marry you, if you were not an infidel. It is breaking my heart. How can you renounce Christ, and all the saints, and our holy Church?"

"We infidels! We renounce Christ!" exclaimed Paul: "that is what our enemies say. But you know better, my little bird.

You know Loukyan, and Demyan, and my
mother. And I came to tell you, Halya,
that my mind is made up. I have cast in
my lot with them. I shall never enter
the church again in order to worship
God. I never have worshipped Him truly
there."

Halya was exceedingly sorrowful. Until
quite lately Paul had attended the church
services when she was present, though his
mother had long absented herself. Old
Karpo had sworn that he would never give
his daughter to a Stundist; and Paul's decision was a death-blow to her hopes. She
loved him; she could not recollect the time
when they had not loved one another.
Panass frightened her; he looked at her
with almost savage eyes of desire. If she
became his wife, he would soon treat her
as her father treated her mother, making
her into a slave and drudge, who lived
a life of daily terror. The Stundists were
not like that. They looked upon their wives
as equals; and Paul especially was so tender,
so thoughtful for her; treated her always
with so much honour, that she felt as safe

beside him as if she had been by her mother's side. She could not give him up.

"If you care for me," she said, creeping closer to him, and laying her hand on his shoulder, "listen to me. Why cannot you wait a little; come to church, and pay your dues, to please Father Vasili and my father; and when we are safely married turn Stundist if you choose. They could not unmarry us; but now"—her low whisper broke into sobs.

It seemed so simple, so feasible, so innocent a stratagem to poor Halya; whilst to Paul it sounded stark, horrible blasphemy. He shrank from her gentle touch; and his voice sounded stern as he answered her. "You do not know what you are saying," he exclaimed: "you ask me to be a hypocrite — the deadliest sin of all! I should be lying both to God and man. You torture me, my own dearest," he added mournfully, taking her hand into his, with a sudden overflow of pity and love flooding his heart. She did not know what all this meant to him.

"When you went away," said Halya,

"Panass told me his father was going to send the matchmakers to my father this very week Father will consent, I know; for they are rich folks. Oh, Paul! save me! I could not endure him when he laid his head against my knee. Paul, think what it will be if we are separated. It is not a heathen temple I ask you to come to. It is a Christian church. What harm would it do? You say you can worship God anywhere. Why not in church, to please Father Vasili? Cannot you do this little thing to save me?"

"I could give my life to save you," he answered, "but I cannot disobey my Lord and Saviour. I cannot be a hypocrite. Oh! Halya, you are dearer to me than myself; but you are not dearer than God."

"Then you have seen the last of me!" she cried, tearing her hand away, and speaking in a very bitter tone; "you give me up to Panass!"

She turned suddenly away, and ran homeward. Paul, with a heavy heart, watched her slender form hastening out of his sight; and then he turned his steps towards the farmstead, where his mother was waiting for him.

CHAPTER IV.

TESTING THE FUTURE.

OSTROX lay about half a mile from Knishi, a little hamlet containing five or six home-steads, of which Paul's was by far the largest and best kept. The fold-yard lying in front of the house was swept and orderly; the cattle-sheds and stables were trim and weather-tight; and the barns were in good repair. The whole place bore a prosperous and cared-for appearance.

Ooliana, Paul's mother, was, as has been said, one of Loukyan's earliest disciples. Their mutual seriousness, and strict observance of Church rites, had made them friends many years before; and Ooliana was speedily convinced by the same reasons which had won Loukyan to adopt the Stundist faith—they could hardly be said to have a creed. Her most fervent prayer had been that Paul should throw off the superstitions of the Orthodox Church. But her influence was constantly counteracted by that of Halya; his love for her leading him to continue his attendance at the parish church, even after he had owned himself convinced by argument that there was no true worship of God there. Ooliana had always regarded Halya as her son's future wife; and though she loved her, there was that subtle, instinctive jealousy of her, which every woman feels of the girl who is destined to steal away her son from her. Besides, now she was herself a Stundist she felt as Rebekah felt towards the daughters of Heth. There was no girl in Knishi as worthy of Paul as Halya; but in towns where the Stundists were more numerous, there were many brethren whose daughters would be more fitting helpmates. Like Rebekah, she said, "What good will my life be to me if Paul marries Halya?"

She was still a woman in middle age, strong, and capable, and business-like. Until she became a Stundist, she was very popular in Knishi, for her heart was warm and her hand open. Her fine, handsome face, and her firm, alert step had been one of the welcome sights of the grass-grown village

E

street. There was not a house she had not
entered on some errand of friendship or
charity; and Ooliana had been the first to
be summoned when a disaster of any kind
occurred. She was a good nurse and a fair
doctor; and as no doctor lived within twenty
miles, she enjoyed a large practice, without
fees.

To-night she had not been to the prayer-
meeting at Knishi because she had been
tending a dying child at Ostron. She did
not know that her ceaseless, ardent prayers
for Paul's conversion were at last fulfilled.
The church clock, quite audible in the quiet
night, struck eight, the hour when Loukyan
finished his sermon. It was usual to linger
a little while in friendly conversation; so she
could not expect Paul quite yet. The large,
roomy house-place grew dark; and she lighted
one wick of the three-socketed lamp, and put
it on the oak table, upon which she began
to lay out the supper.

In the dim light the room was full of
shadows, but it looked comfortable and home-
like. The oak table, on which there was no
cloth, was very clean, and the oak benches

standing along the walls were polished till they reflected the twinkling lamp-light. A few pictures hung against the walls, their subjects indistinguishable in the dimness. The empty icon shrine looked like a black niche in its place. of honour.

Paul's supper was ready, being kept warm in the huge Russian stove, which seemed to fill half the room. Ooliana stood at the door watching and listening. She heard the neighing of her horses, the grunting of the pigs, and the cluck of the fowls in the various sheds surrounding the fold-yard, but Paul's footsteps she could not catch. The clock in Knishi struck nine. She put out the lamp, and sat down in the window to knit by moonlight.

"He is stopping with that girl!" she said, half angrily, half sadly, to herself. The daughters of Heth are always sources of great trouble to saintly mothers. "Save him, O Lord!" whispered Ooliana; "save my son in his hour of temptation. Save the soul of my Paul!"

A few minutes after this softly murmured prayer, she heard the welcome sound of his

well-known footsteps coming near the farm-
yard. His favourite mare whinnied, and his
dog sprang out to meet him. Before he
could reach the door, the three sockets of the
lamp were lit, and a cheerful light chased
away the darkness. She saw, as he crossed
the threshold, that something unusual had
happened. There was an indescribable expression of noble decision and of deep sorrow
on his face.

Without a word, but with great tenderness, Ooliana placed his food upon the table,
and set a chair before it. For a minute Paul
sat silently gazing across the room to the
empty icon shrine. The glory of his vision
was gone, but the conviction it had wrought
remained.

"Mother!" he said, standing up and facing
her; "mother, I have cast in my lot with
you. I am a Stundist."

"Praise God!" she cried.

"Ay," he said, "they sang 'Praise God!'
and I never heard a sound so solemn in my
life. It was as if I heard the angels singing it in heaven with their harps."

"They were singing it, my son," said

Ooliana. "Our Lord says, 'There is joy in the presence of the angels of God over one sinner that repenteth.' You fill my heart with joy, Paul."

"Mother," he resumed, after a short pause, "I was full of a peace and gladness passing all understanding, till I saw Halya——"

"You must give her up," interrupted Ooliana gently. "It will be the hardest trial of all; but if the Lord requires it——"

"All that I am and have are His," cried Paul. "I will hold nothing back. But she has given up me; she has forsaken me. She will marry Panass."

A crowd of contending emotions took possession of Ooliana: profound joy over her son's conversion; vivid sympathy with his grief at losing Halya; relief at the fact that she could never be Paul's wife, and yet an ardent desire that her son's love—so faithful and tender—should be satisfied. She stood gazing at him, with all the unfathomable love and devotion of a mother shining in her clear, dark eyes. At last she broke the throbbing silence, with a supreme effort at self-abnegation.

"She is in God's hands," she said. "I will pray day and night for her that she may be brought out of darkness into light. I will pray that you may have your heart's desire. Has not our Lord said, 'Whatsoever ye shall ask in prayer, believing, ye shall receive'? You and I will pray for Halya's conversion, Paul."

"Mother," he said, "bring me the Bible, and let me open it at a venture. It may be that God will show us what is His will concerning this"

Ooliana fetched her Bible, bought several years ago, and so faithfully and constantly read that it looked as if it might have been in her possession all her life. She laid it solemnly on the table before Paul, in the light of the lamp, and both of them, with shaded eyes, uttered a mental prayer. Ooliana, with irrepressible eagerness, looked over Paul's shoulder, as he opened the closed Bible and laid his finger on a verse. She saw at a glance what it was.

"And Ruth said, Intreat me not to leave thee, or to return from following after thee: for whither thou goest, I will go; and where thou lodgest I will lodge; thy people shall be my people, and thy God, my God."

Ooliana laid her hands upon her son's bowed head. God had given them a message, a token of His will, and she must submit to it—nay, she must embrace it. The lingering, insidious jealousy must be rooted out of her heart, and Halya must lodge there, as Paul did.

After a moment or two Paul looked up to her with shining eyes.

"What does it mean, mother?" he whispered.

"Halya will go with thee whithersoever thou goest," she answered. "Where thou lodgest, she will lodge: thy people shall be her people, and thy God her God. The message is plain, my son."

"Let us pray together," she said, after a short pause of silent gladness. She was often called upon to pray at the prayer-meetings; and now, with her son kneeling beside her, she poured forth a rhapsody of supplication and thanksgiving.

Ooliana could not sleep that night. She knew that Paul had taken his first step on

a path in which persecution might drive him
to exile or death.   So far, there had been
no serious persecution in Knishi, and the
young heresy had been treated with contempt and ridicule only.   Father Vasili was
rather above the average of village priests—
an ignorant, superstitious man, generally
good-tempered towards his parishioners; but
he was very avaricious, and made hard bar-
gains for his fees.   He had occasionally refused
to visit the dying, until the family consented to
pay double dues.   He and his wife had been
very friendly with Ooliana; and although she
could no longer conscientiously pay for the
blessing of her fields and cattle and stores,
or give the Easter offerings, she still made
them handsome presents of all her produce.
The friendly intercourse was over for ever,
but, without doubt, they would send for
Ooliana if there was any sickness in their
household.

As yet the Stundists in Knishi were
not a tenth of the population.   But Ooliana,
even more than Loukyan, was an ardent proselytiser.   She longed to make every one of
her neighbours, with whom she had such

intimate relations, partakers with her of the great blessings of the Gospel she had received. She never lost an opportunity of telling the simple story of the New Testament, especially when the hearts of her hearers were softened by sickness or sorrow. Stundism was silently, but rapidly, spreading its roots in Knishi; and many a peasant, both of men and women, who went punctiliously to church, came secretly for instruction in the new faith.

But Ooliana knew well how bitterly the storm of persecution was beating upon the brethren elsewhere. Across all the blessedness and glory of Paul's conversion fell the dark shadow of terrible days to come. She could not wish that he had not joined the ranks of the spiritual crusaders, who were waging war against the deadly superstitions of the Orthodox Church. Nay! she prayed that he might be a leader and hero in the strife. If he lived, he would live unto the Lord; if he died he would die unto the Lord; living or dying, he would be the Lord's. She saw the crown of martyrdom hanging over his head, and her spirit exulted; but her mother's-heart quailed with anguish. "If it be possible," she cried, "let this cup pass from me; nevertheless, not my will, but Thine be done."

Paul had spread a rug on the turf seat outside the door, and lay down upon it in the cool and scented night air. Far off, he could still hear the trill of the nightingale that had sung to him in Yarina's garden. Low sounds from the sheds around him fell softly on his ear; above him the moon hung in the dark-blue vault; and far away the clear, distinct horizon showed where the earth and sky met. This was his birthplace, his home, his beloved country. It seemed as if all about him was tenfold dearer than it had been in the morning of that day. He could die for his country: how much more, then, could he die for his Lord? His whole soul seemed melted in a close communion with God, who filled the earth, and air, and sky, and in whom he lived, and moved, and had his being.

CHAPTER V.

PANASS.

AFTER quitting Paul in such an angry mood, Halya ran till she was breathless, spurred by a sense of having lowered herself by speaking to him. She, the richest heiress in the whole neighbourhood, her father's only child, had run after a lover who cared little for her, and she had all but besought him to marry her. Her pulses beat and her cheeks burned at the remembrance. She would go back to Yarina's, rejoin the evening guests, and forget her mortification and disappointment. The adulation she was sure to receive there would heal her wounded self-love.

"Fool, fool that I was!" she thought, boiling with indignation. "He had only to sing a song, and I was ready to follow him to the world's end. He does not love me!—no, he does not love me!" she repeated, half aloud, while hot tears rolled down her cheeks.

She had reached a well, and, leaning against its wooden frame-work, she gave way to a passion of weeping. Suddenly a sound startled her, and she lifted up her head to listen, like a frightened bird. It was nothing save the creaking of the crane above her head, but it aroused her. In a minute or two, afraid of people passing and seeing her in the bright moonlight, she let down the bucket into the well, and drew it up sparkling and dripping with water. She bathed her eyes, and eagerly quenched the burning thirst she felt in her parched throat. Then, with slower steps, pausing now and then as if in some doubt, she went on to Yarina's.

A dance was in full swing again, and Halya went on to the grass plot where it was going on, with little expression of trouble on her pretty face. Paul should know she was not inconsolable because he preferred his stupid old Stundists to herself. She was afraid her absence might have been noticed, and she tried to mingle with the crowd of guests as if she had never left it. But all at once, a voice which made her shudder spoke close in her ear.

"Ha! ha!" said Panass, with a false-sounding laugh, "Paul the apostle did not come here for nothing."

He had noticed her absence, then! No doubt he had watched her creep across the fold-yard and follow Paul's steps. And he had been watching for her return. Halya was half-frightened, and wholly provoked and miserable, but she dared not show her trouble. She shrugged her shoulders with a little laugh of scorn.

"You know best whether he came for nothing," she said. "He sang us such a song as you could never sing, nor anybody else, in all Knishi."

The words hit him hard, and he looked so vexed that she laughed.

"You don't like that," she added.

"You ran after him!" cried Panass. "I know it. I saw you flying like a bird after her mate."

"Perhaps I did! Perhaps I ran to the well to drink some water! What is that to you?" she asked, with a glance of contempt that provoked him.

All the other girls in the village were doing

their utmost to win him, but Halya was always laughing at him. It was this which attracted him to her as much as her beauty. There were other pretty girls in Knishi, but they were all at his beck. His voice changed to a softer key, and when he spoke again it seemed as if he was continuing some conversation which had been interrupted.

"But you have not answered me about the matchmakers," he said. "May I send them to your father?"

His voice was thin and piping, strangely at variance with his strong frame, and the harsh expression of his swarthy face.

"You can send them," she said petulantly; "the door is open to anybody. Father has plenty of pumpkins in his garden; and I will roast two of them in good time; one for you, and one for Paul. You shall carry Paul's to him yourself."

Panass laughed with hearty good-humour. A roasted pumpkin offered by a girl to the matchmakers, who came with a proposal of marriage, meant absolute refusal. Of course, Halya was making fun of him; and her coupling Paul's name with his, as a candidate for a roasted pumpkin, was very encouraging.

"But Paul cannot play the bandoura as I can," he said good-temperedly; "shall I sing a new song I learned from the bishop's best singer? He taught it to me when I treated him in a public-house."

"Yes," she answered, in an indifferent tone.

Panass sang a parody of such a ballad as Paul had sung, in a high-pitched falsetto voice, accompanying it with a really clever performance on the bandoura. She felt as if he, and his voice, and bandoura were all alike hateful to her. But she would encourage him, partly to vex Paul, and partly to hoodwink her companions. Instead of jeering as usual at his song, she begged him to sing another. She consented afterwards to dance with him, and when it was over, strolled away with him into a thicket of wild roses. Suddenly Panass bent his dark face to hers and kissed her lips. Halya, in a frenzy of disgust and anger, gave him a slap in the face which almost made him stagger.

"Good Lord!" he cried, after a short pause, striving to speak playfully, though tears of pain filled his eyes, "if you have such a heavy hand after we are married, you will be the worse for it. How could this little hand deal such a stroke?"

Halya was vexed beyond the power of speech. Vexed with herself for being there; vexed with Paul, who had forsaken her; vexed above all with Panass for the offensive liberty he had taken. Oh! if she had only gone in home, when she left Paul. But Panass could not boast of the kiss he had taken. Silently they went back to the guests, who were still amusing themselves in the moonlight.

Panass bade Yarina good-night in a sulky manner, and took himself away. Halya was only too glad to stay behind, and left almost the last. Yarina kissed her at parting, and said with a smile—

"Don't be too scornful with Panass. Your father will never let you marry a Stundist; and Panass is the next most desirable match. He has four yoke of oxen, many sheep and mares, and a large house; and his father will leave him a lot of money. And besides, he is a handsome man to look at. I'm right; isn't it so?" she added, speaking to some girls who were standing round them. The girls tittered; some of them with envy of Halya's chance.

"Well, then! take him," she said, laughing, "you take him, Yarina, if you like him so much."

"Take care," answered Yarina, "I am not too old. But don't be angry afterwards."

"Oh, no! dearest," cried Halya, "I can afford to lose him, if I did not lose you as my friend."

She went home sad and downhearted. Paul had forsaken her; and she knew too well her father would never let her refuse Panass, with his oxen and herds, and his expectations from his father.

"Oh! if Yarina could really help me!" she thought, "if I could only vex Panass into seeking her for his wife!"

Like Ooliana and Paul, she lay awake a great part of the night; but at last sleep overpowered her, and when the dawn came, it shone upon her pretty girlish face, sleeping with a smile upon it.

F

CHAPTER VI.

LOUKYAN AT THE FAIR.

"PAUL," said Ooliana, the next morning, after their brief prayers were ended, and they rose from their knees, "I forgot to tell you yesterday that Valerian Petrovitch came home a day or two ago. He is going to stay for a time at the old Manor House with his father. He just looked in for a minute yesterday; just the same kind-hearted, free-spoken, friendly man he always was. They say he is very strange. He never goes to church; and when he enters the poorest huts, he takes off his hat, and salutes every one, even the children. But he does not bow to the icons, or make the sign of the cross. Is it possible he is one of us?"

Paul was fond of books, and did not confine his reading, as Ooliana did, to religious works. He knew these signs, among the upper classes, did not at all imply that they had embraced the humble sect of Stundism.

"No, mother," he answered, "I'm afraid it means that he has joined himself to the men who are opposing the Tzar; and we are warned against having anything to do with them. We are within our rights in joining the Mir, and helping to manage our own village affairs. But you know the Stundists are bound to shun all men who rebel against the powers that be."

"It is a pity," said Ooliana, "Valerian visits the sick, and will not take any pay. He called about little Ivan, who is ill with fever, and told me what more to do for the child. He is very clever and learned; and he promises me he will teach me all he knows about illness before he goes away. Do you think a man who loves his neighbour as Valerian does, is not sure to love God also?"

"It seems as if that must be so," said Paul musingly.

"If you would only talk with him!" suggested Ooliana, with the sanguine hope of a true proselytiser.

"Me! mother," he said, "me! Why! he is a very learned man; and I know almost

F 2

nothing. He has been travelling all over the world the last three years; and I have never been farther than Kovylsk. I could not argue with him."

"Ah! Paul," she answered, "but our wisdom is not of this world; it is the hidden wisdom of God, which none of the princes of this world knew, or they would not have slain the Lord of Glory. But I have known Valerian from his birth; and I will speak to him myself."

Soon afterwards, when their breakfast was eaten, Paul started off to see Loukyan, to whom he was eager to impart the events of the night before, especially the oracular message from the Bible, which seemed to assure him that Halya would certainly become his wife. But when he reached Loukyan's dwelling he found the old man had started for Kovylsk before daybreak.

Loukyan started on his journey in the exquisite coolness of a summer's night, half an hour before the dawn. It was between twenty and thirty versts to Kovylsk, and his old mare, as dear to him as a friend, could not be made to go more quickly than a slow jog-trot. Loukyan's soul was full of exceeding peace; and the stillness and silence of the sleeping land responded to it. He drove slowly along the rough roads, singing hymns, from time to time, as if he must give outer expression of his inner gladness. A fair was being held at Kovylsk, and this circumstance, and a few jars of honey stowed at the back of his rude cart, were a splendid pretext for a visit to the brethren there. It was far too hot to carry wax, and the honey was scarcely at its best; but then no one would suspect that he was going on any other errand than to sell it. It was an innocent subterfuge, which did not in the least disturb his simple conscience.

Kovylsk was the governmental town. Here was the Governor's residence. Here also were the courts of law, the police offices, the prison —all the panoply of rule and justice. Loukyan nodded, with a smile on his face, to the grim jail, where he had spent six not unhappy months. The streets were familiar to him; but, as is usual with people coming from the country, the constant passing to and fro of pedestrians, and the number of conveyances through which he had to guide his old mare, made him glad when he reached his inn.

They knew him well, as he was in the habit of putting up there two or three times a year. In fact, Mitrevna, the innkeeper's wife, was a woman from Knishi, and always had a long gossip with Loukyan. It was already late; and he went to bed, without attempting to see any of the brethren.

There were more Stundists than the authorities dreamed of in Kovylsk. They had not ventured, under the immediate shadow of the Governor, to have any stated meeting-place. But about two versts from the town, the reeds and sedges by the riverside afforded them many a safe spot for worship during fine weather. In the winter they met indoors, in small detached parties, which were too insignificant to attract attention. They were learning to be as wise as serpents; whilst their tenet of non-resistance made them as harmless as doves.

Loukyan was a great favourite among the Stundists of Kovylsk. He possessed an extraordinary gift for expounding the Scripture, with a spiritual insight which enabled him boldly to strip off the outer husk of some knotty question and elicit the inner truth. He set himself strongly against any disputation on controversial questions, often quoting Paul the Apostle's advice to Timothy: "Neither give heed to fables, and endless genealogies, which minister questions, rather than godly edifying which is in faith." Or again: "O Timothy, keep that which is committed to thy trust, avoiding profane and vain babblings and oppositions of science, falsely so called : which some professing have erred from the faith." There was great loss of time, he urged, in discussing doubtful points. It was as if soldiers, in the storm and stress of battle, began to wrangle about their colours. They were on the battlefield, fighting against sin, the world, and the devil. When they had won the victory they would settle these minor matters.

To Loukyan's great sorrow and dismay, a day or two after his arrival, his old mare was stolen from the inn stable. He loved it with a real and deep affection, and feared that it must have fallen into bad hands. But it was the sin which troubled Loukyan most. Theft is not a common crime in a small country village, where everybody knows his neighbour's property almost as well as his own; and this was the first time that the sin of stealing had been brought closely home to him. He mourned over the thief, and prayed for him as if he was a brother.

But he could not return to Knishi and take his cart with him on foot. There was nothing for it but to write to his nephew, Demyan, and bid him borrow a horse from Paul, and come over to fetch him.

Loukyan carried his jars of honey to the fair, and soon sold them at a good price, for several of the tradespeople, not themselves Stundists, had sympathised strongly with him in his imprisonment some time before. There was something so genial, so straightforward, and so wise about the old man, peasant though he was, which attracted the trust and affection of all who came into contact with him.

All the honey disposed of, Loukyan strolled about the streets, with nothing to do but to dwell on the sinfulness of sin, as exemplified in the case of the thief who had stolen his old mare. On every hand he saw stores upon stores of goods; wares brought to the fair for sale; anything that could feed the vanity of the buyer and bring a profit to the seller. There was not a want of the body that did not on these stalls, and in these shops, meet with a supply. "But what about the immortal soul?" said Loukyan to himself; "is it possible that all these crowds of men like myself are mere animals, caring for nothing but meat and drink and clothing? Do they never feel there is something more?"

Just then, in a corner of a square in front of one of the churches, he caught sight of a little stall, covered and roofed in like a tent. All across the front, hanging on an iron rod, were a number of small and cheap icons; whilst inside were a few larger and handsomer ones, worth three or four roubles apiece.

"That is to satisfy the immortal soul!" thought Loukyan, drawing slowly nearer and pausing before the entrance. The wooden panels, on which the sacred images were painted, were easily set in motion, and swung to and fro as he touched one of them gently. There were, as usual, the conventional faces of the Saviour, the Virgin, God the Father, and a few of the principal saints. A young man was sitting inside the tent—a fair-haired, dreamy-eyed man, who noticed at once that Loukyan did not cross himself or salute the icons.

"You sell icons?" said Loukyan, after the ordinary greeting had passed between them. He used the word "sell" purposely, because it is considered irreverent to *sell* icons; they are always *exchanged* for the price demanded. The young man flushed angrily.

"We don't sell the sacred images," he replied. "An old man like you ought to know that is not the way to speak about them. I can barter with you."

"Excuse me," said Loukyan mildly; "but what do you barter them for?"

"For kopecks and roubles," he answered.

"Then what is the difference?" asked Loukyan. "You don't deceive me. Do you think you deceive God?"

"Why do you play the fool?" he replied; "if you wish to barter, look round my stall, and choose what you like. If you have no wares to exchange, begone, for I have no time to lose."

Loukyan looked for a moment at him with his gentle yet penetrating gaze; and the young man's eyes fell before him. He had been rude, and he confessed it, though no word was spoken. Loukyan laid all the money he had about him on the counter—notes, roubles, and kopecks. "There is all the money I have," he said, "and if you have need of it, my brother, take as much as you want. But as for your icons, I would not have them even if you gave them away for nothing. God is not like that. 'No man hath seen God at any time; nor can see Him.' The icons are false, and teach falsehoods."

"Are you in your right mind?" exclaimed the icon-seller.

"I certainly am; there is no doubt of that," answered Loukyan. "Do I look crazy?"

"But why then do you offer me all this money?" he asked—"a heap of it; and you will take nothing for it. Suppose I take you at your word?"

"I shall be content," replied Loukyan. "I suppose you sell icons to get your living. Give up selling them, and live on this money till you have found something else to do. God gave it to me, and He can give me as much more as I want."

The young man picked up the money, weighed it in his hand awhile and then, with a smile, put it back into Loukyan's purse, and returned it to him.

"I don't want another man's property," he said, "yet I see I am welcome to it. What kind of a man are you? and where do you come from. I have lived in Moscow, and seen thousands of people; but never one like you. Come and sit down beside me, if you can spare the time, and tell me why you call the icons of the holy saints false? My name is Stepan; and I come, as I said, from Moscow."

For two or three hours Loukyan explained to him the doctrines of the Stundists as to icons, and the priesthood, and the Church. Stepan listened with eager and intelligent attention.

"This cannot be settled all at once," he said, "it is too great a thing. Lend me your Testament, and I will examine into it thoroughly. To-morrow come here, or rather come to the inn where I put up."

CHAPTER VII.

AN ICONOCLAST.

EARLY the next morning Loukyan set off to find Stepan. It was not far to his inn, and Loukyan, seeing a group of people gaping and staring at something which was going on in the inn-yard, turned to join them. It was a strange scene.

Stepan was standing in the midst, with an axe in his hand, striking with great strength and fury on an icon with a silvered frame. Splinters of coloured and gilded wood, on which the sacred pictures had been painted, lay all around him in a glittering pile. He was not heeding any of the spectators; but, with the concentrated scorn of a true iconoclast on his face, he was shivering the icons to fragments, and uttering words of contempt against himself.

"Fool that I was! a fool and blind!" he ejaculated, in short interrupted cries, "to live by idols! To make them and sell them! To call them gods, and bow down to them!"

Loukyan stood transfixed in silent astonishment and admiration at the man's courage. True the bystanders, who had just turned out of the inn, were not devout members of the Orthodox Church. The landlord, Isaacke the Jew, was looking on with secret sympathy, but in abject terror lest the police should hear the noise, and make him responsible for the sacrilege. There were severe penal laws dealing with crimes against icons. Only to speak disrespectfully against them was punishable with from eight months to three years' imprisonment; and wilfully to destroy one was visited by exile to Siberia for life.

"Oh! the poor man is mad, stark mad!" cried Isaacke, from time to time; "see! the beautiful, holy icons! Worth a pile of roubles! Only a raving madman could act like this!"

Stepan had been breaking up the last icon when Loukyan entered the yard; and now he drew himself up to his full height, facing the circle with a gaze full of resolute courage, mingled with compassion. He lifted up his face, and stretched out his arms towards the blue sky above him. "Great God in heaven!"

he cried, "forgive me; I was ignorant as a beast before thee! Forgive them! for they know no better than I did!"

Loukyan stepped forward, and laid his hand on Stepan's shoulder, gazing into his face with tears in his eyes.

"Brother!" he said, "come away with me, and let us have a quiet talk together. Landlord, have you a room where we can be alone?"

"Yes, yes," Isaacke answered eagerly. "Oh! he's mad, you know," he added to the bystanders, "and this good man is his brother. He will take care of him. Come in, all of you, and have a glass or two of vodka; my best! And let us wink at this. My house is respectable; we never have a row with the police. Come in! come in!"

He shut Loukyan and Stepan up in a private room of his own, and served out his best vodka with many a heart-pang; but then what would it cost him if the police found out that holy icons had been destroyed in his yard? He had every trace of the catastrophe removed; no splinter an inch in size was left to betray it; and as soon as

possible he must get Loukyan and Stepan off
his premises.

They were deep in conversation upon the
tenets of the Stundists, when Isaacke interrupted it with an agonised appeal to them that
they would relieve him from their dangerous
presence. He was in a terrible quandary, not
knowing whether it was the better plan to
trust to his guests to forget the occurrence, or
to report it himself to the police, which must
involve him in great trouble and expense. If
Loukyan would take Stepan away, he would
do nothing, and take the chance of nothing
coming of it.

Stepan had made a sacrifice of all his
worldly goods; and he had not more money
than would last him for a few months, until
he could fit himself to earn his living in some
other way. Loukyan took him to one of the
leading Stundists, a corn-dealer; and left him
there to return home to Knishi, with Demyan,
who had arrived with Paul's horse late the
night before.

They reached home early in the morning;
and as it was already daylight, and soon the
whole world would be astir, especially Ivan,

Demyan's little son three years of age, there was not much chance of sleep. They lay down to rest awhile on the wooden bench, which ran around the sides of the larger of the two rooms which formed the whole of their dwelling. They could hear the breathing of Ivan and his mother, as they lay sleeping in the inner room.

"Demyan!" said Loukyan, "Stepan's another man who would die, or go into exile for the Lord's sake."

"Ay! there are a few of us," he answered, somewhat sleepily.

"A godly seed!" said Loukyan, "and it will be scattered here and there, and fall upon good ground, and bring forth some fiftyfold, and some a hundredfold. Stepan will bring a good harvest to his Lord."

Demyan did not reply. He was ready to die for Christ; but he was not a man of ready tongue, and he had no learning. It had been with difficulty that he had learned to read; a duty earnestly impressed on every Stundist, that they may for themselves search the Scriptures. There were moments when Demyan was sorely tempted

G

to envy the richer gifts of men like Loukyan, Paul, and Stepan. But he was a simple soul, and he contented himself with saying in a whisper, "Lord, Thou knowest all things. Thou knowest that I love Thee." These words were the anchor of his soul.

After a short rest the men roused themselves, and Demyan went off to his work with the village blacksmith, whilst Loukyan visited his numerous bee-hives, which stood in a regular row along the top of his large garden. The open steppe lay beyond, thickly covered with flowers of all kinds; and the laborious bees were killing themselves, like city men of business, in a headlong, unintermitting chase after the wealth that lay close at hand. Loukyan was obliged to take away the fresh honey every few days. He had now been away several days, and there was an accumulation of spoil. The bees hummed and buzzed about him, and settled in dozens upon his hands, which were uncovered, though he had protected his head and face with a gauze veil; but not one stung him.

Presently Paul opened the wicket-gate,

and entered the garden, standing at a safe
distance from the hustling, hissing swarm
that from time to time almost hid Loukyan
from sight. Loukyan had slightly smoked
them with a bit of burning hemp; and
they were whirling giddily about in the
air, and humming dismally, as if complaining of being disturbed and robbed of the
wealth they had so greedily gathered. Loukyan spoke to them now and then, as if they
could understand him.

"What do you make such a trouble
about?" he asked; "your hives are too full
already. You are like the rich man who was
going to pull down his barns, and build
greater. I am doing you a service, if you
only knew it. One hive can only hold as
much as it can; the rest is lost."

He turned to watch a dense swarm that
had fled off to a wild cherry tree; and then
he perceived Paul. His withered face lit up
with a smile of love and welcome.

"Good morning!" he said; "I'm glad to
see you so soon. There is so much to tell
you. That is why I asked Demyan to send
you word we were back again."

G 2

"And I was glad to come on my own account," replied Paul; "I have wanted you so much."

"What is the matter? Has anything happened to your mother?" asked Loukyan in alarm.

"No, no! Only myself," he answered. "I want your advice."

"By-and-bye," said Loukyan; "only let me take the honeycomb out of this last hive."

He opened the hive, and with a skilful hand broke off as much comb as was desirable. He placed it with the rest, which he had collected in a large jar; and then directed his steps towards the house. A few bees followed them all the way, protesting angrily.

"Go away, you foolish beasts," said Loukyan, laughing; "go and heap up riches, and others shall gather them."

The cottage was both smaller and much poorer than Paul's homestead; and the cattle-sheds were fewer. The furniture was of plain deal, and worth little; and there were no pictures on the walls. The cooking utensils consisted of a few earthen pots, one or two of which were cracked, and rudely mended with strips of canvas, as if there was not a kopeck to spare for buying new. There was no doubt Loukyan was quite a poor man; and perhaps rather improvident, for had he not offered Stepan every kopeck he possessed? But the floor was well swept, and the table dusted, and all the furniture clean. And in the chief place, where the icons formerly filled the place of honour, there was a shelf filled with books—more even than those possessed by Father Vasili. Demyan's wife was sitting by the great Russian stove, rocking a cradle with her foot. She was a young woman, with a round face, a snub nose, and with dense black eye-brows, which met across her nose, and gave her an oddly morose expression. She rose and greeted Paul with great respect.

"Here is the fresh honey, Paraska," said Loukyan; "put it in a new jar, and bring us a morsel to taste. I will look after the child."

In low tones, and with great delight,

Loukyan told Paul the story of Stepan and the risks they had both run in Kovylsk. But he spoke very cautiously, and when they heard Paraska's step, he stopped abruptly.

" Not a word to her," he whispered.

Paraska was devoted to Loukyan with her utmost soul, just as her husband was. But being a woman of common-sense, as she said, she did not always approve of what they did. There was no need to give away everything, as they would do if she did not look after them. And as for running into mischief and danger as they did, they ought sometimes to think of her and the baby. Loukyan was a little afraid of her.

She brought in a piece of honeycomb on a wooden platter, and a cake of new bread, and laid them on the table with the demure expression of a woman who knows how to behave properly when strangers are present.

" Paraska, it is beautiful honey," said Loukyan in a conciliatory tone; " better than last year."

" Oh! the *honey* is all right," she answered with half-conscious sarcasm. She went to the cradle. The baby slept quietly, with its little arms stretched out, and its soft, toothless mouth open. She threw a cover over it, to protect it from the flies, and went away again.

"I shall have a good scolding from her," said Loukyan, "about my poor old mare. And it would be worse if she knew about Stepan. He is coming to visit us by-and-bye; and as he is a man of some learning, he will probably be made a deacon. But my successor is already here," he added, gazing affectionately on Paul.

In low tones as before Paul confided to him all that had passed between Halya and himself, and the curious result of his appeal to the Bible for direction.

Loukyan listened with profound interest.

"Do not let your heart be troubled," he said. "She will join us, and you will marry her. This love is a great mystery; it comes from God, and ought to lead us to Him."

"But the match-makers are going to Karpo this very day!" cried Paul.

"From Panass?"

Paul nodded, too miserable to speak. There was no other rival he dreaded.

"She will not marry him," said Loukyan, looking at him with his kind, keen gaze. "If God wills it, man can do nothing. To be sure, no priest would marry you; but I know a German minister in the government of Kherson, who comes sometimes to Kovylsk, and he would do it for you."

For a moment Paul looked happy; but it was only for a moment.

"Halya would never consent to it," he said.

"Then it may be there is no way out of your trouble," replied Loukyan after a pause. "This is the cross your Lord calls upon you to bear after Him. Bear it bravely. Great troubles lie before us. Remember what the Apostle says about this very point. 'I suppose, therefore, that this is good for the present distress, I say that it is good for a man so to be. Art thou bound unto a wife? seek not to be loosed. Art thou loosed from a wife? seek not a wife.' Alas! the father and the husband will have bitter sorrows in the days at hand."

But Paul was too young, and he had

loved Halya too long and too much to take any comfort from the thought that he might, at some future day, be glad that her lot was not linked with his own. There was a low, distant howl of persecution, as of a wolf; but the wolf had not come to the door as yet.

CHAPTER VIII.

FATHER VASILI.

THE busiest time of the year was come, and every man and woman was toiling incessantly over gathering in the harvest. There was a constant going to and fro, and all the population of Knishi lived out of doors. Scarcely a day passed without Paul seeing Halya; but she was never alone, and she gave him no opportunity of speaking to her. Very often Panass was at her side, and her troubled and downcast face was as much averted from him as from Paul. This was the only consolation Paul had. He could have given up Halya—he had truly the spirit of a martyr, ready to sacrifice all for his religion; but he firmly believed, since his appeal to the Scriptures, that Halya was destined to be his wife. It was not, therefore, necessary to tear her from his heart; on the contrary, he must adopt every means to win her to himself.

Once he met her in the little village shop, whither he had gone to buy salt; but Panass was there also, and walked home with her, and stayed a long time at the gate talking with her, until Paul was well on the way home.

The next time he saw her he was driving a hay-cart from a meadow he owned near Knishi, and she was at the village well with the other girls, who had brought their cattle to drink from the long wooden trough made of the hollow trunk of an oak. He went at once to water his horses, and to help Halya with the oxen.

" Good day, Halya! " he said.

It was the first time they had spoken to one another since that moonlit evening when she had run after him to beseech him to remain an orthodox Churchman until after they were married.

"Good-day to you," she answered listlessly, and scarcely looking at him. She did not seem glad to see him, nor was she offended. She seemed to be in utterly low spirits.

"Are you still angry with me?" whispered Paul.

She did not reply, but lifting up her large grey eyes, dim with tears, she looked at him in a hopeless way, as if to ask, "What good would it do to be angry? Would that mend matters?"

This childish, hopeless look on her beloved face quite upset Paul. He must see her again, and soon. He must convince her, as he was convinced himself, that it was God's will she should be his wife. But there was no chance of arranging anything there, at the well. A whole herd of calves rushed to the trough, pushing away Halya's patient and slow oxen, which were just beginning to drink. It was as much as they both could do to protect the cattle, and as soon as they had finished, Halya drove them homewards, with listless step and drooping head—never even turning her head to give a glance to Paul.

It had become absolutely necessary to see Halya alone—to tell her all that had passed in his own mind, and the assurance he had received that they were destined for each other. There could be no power in her father and Panass against the will of God. Should he tell her of Loukyan's plan of their being married by a German pastor? It would shock her at first—shock her tremendously. But for himself, the more he thought of it the more feasible the project appeared, if only Halya consented to it.

The stress of harvest at last came to an end, and the community could turn their attention to matters of less moment. Paul, somewhat weary with a long spell of the hardest labour, went to visit his wicker fish-pots, which he had sunk in the river the night before. All at once he saw a band of girls coming along the banks from the washing-place; for the washing had been neglected during the harvest. They all carried a yoke with the dripping linen hung across each end, watering the ground as they marched along. Halya was the last of the little procession, and her load seemed the heaviest. She loitered a little, and let her companions get ahead of her; but she did not stop altogether or lay down her heavily-laden yoke, as she would have done in olden days. Her face was full of gloom, amounting almost to despair Paul's heart ached for her.

"Come to the water-mill to-night," said Paul hurriedly.

Halya hesitated.

"What for?" she asked, almost inaudibly.

"I have something important to tell you," he said entreatingly. "Do come."

"Well, I will come," she said, in a reluctant tone, and hastening her steps to rejoin her companions.

Paul went on his way exulting, happier than he had been for weeks. It was nearing mid-day, and he had still some distance to go up the stream; for his fish-pots were sunk in a quiet spot, removed from the noise of the village, in a long, tranquil reach of the river which the fish loved to frequent. The rustling sedges grew thickly along the margin, and Paul pushed his way through them towards a little hillock which, even in the spring floods, was rarely covered with water. Taking off his boots, he waded cautiously across to his three fish-pots, the rims of which were just visible on the surface.

It was a good haul. Paul pulled up the fish-pots to dry in the sun till night, and

loaded his creel with the fish, which were all
alive; then, putting on his boots, he hastened
home, drops of water rolling in copious streams
down his blue linen shirt.

Ostron could be reached by pursuing the
river bank and passing through a wood; but
Paul resolved to return through Knishi, and
by a short cut running behind the church.
There was a chance of catching a passing
glimpse of Halya.

But Paul had scarcely entered the village
when he saw the fat, squat figure of Father
Vasili in a dirty cassock and a worn-out felt
hat with a broad brim. His first thought
was how to avoid him, for of late Father
Vasili had been anything but a pleasant acquaintance. He regarded Loukyan and Paul
with far less favour or forbearance than the
worst drunkard in the parish. But it was
too late to escape.

"What are you trying to run away for?"
roared Father Vasili. "Ah! you have a bad
conscience, one sees that with half an eye.
But come along here. I have wanted to have
a long talk with you all this harvest time."

It was impossible to avoid the interview,

and Paul drew nearer, with one of his most respectful salutations. Father Vasili was an old-fashioned priest; good-natured on the whole, but coarse and ignorant. He had forgotten long ago the little and useless theology he had ever learned, and had devoted himself to the more profitable craft of husbandry. But for his cassock, and his long clerical hair and beard, he would not have been distinguishable from an ordinary peasant.

"Come! come!" he cried, in a thick voice, "what are you thinking of? Now, now! you can't go on playing the rebel. Eh?"

Father Vasili paused for a reply, as if he had uttered a most convincing argument.

"I am not a rebel, father," answered Paul, with a smile.

"Not a rebel! good Lord!" ejaculated the priest; "why, why! you leave off coming to church, you do not take the sacrament, and you never come to confession. It's the worst sort of rebellion; rebelling against me, and the Holy Church, and the Tzar himself. You'll get punishment enough here, and in the world to come you'll be thrown into boiling cauldrons, and have to lick red hot frying-pans for ever and ever and ever. Think over that, you scoundrel!"

"God is very merciful," answered Paul, "and if you pray for me——"

"Pray for you!" interrupted Father Vasili scornfully. "Pray for you! Why on earth should I pray for you when you never pay me a kopeck for my prayers? Reprobates as you are! Your priest might starve to death——"

"No, no, father!" cried Paul, in his turn, who knew of the large gifts his mother continued to send to her old priest. Father Vasili collected himself a little, for he did not wish to lose these welcome presents by mistimed reproaches.

"Well, well!" he said, "but I have to answer for you. How am I to leave out your name when I send up a list of all who have been to confession to the bishop? He has noticed your name, Paul. And now you have not been to confession for a whole year."

"No; we confess our sins to God Himself, and to Him alone," replied Paul.

"Oh! what horrible blasphemy!" exclaimed the priest, "the great Almighty God, with all the angels and archangels and holy saints

H

around His throne. Will he hear a poor
ignorant peasant like you? Confess to God!"
he added with a sneer of mingled contempt
and astonishment.

Paul was silent. He had no wish to enter
into any discussion with Father Vasili, for he
wanted to get home.

"Confess yourself frequently to the priest,
say the Scriptures," pursued Father Vasili, in
a loud, domineering voice, "and bring forth
fruits meet for repentance——"

"Fruits! I'm willing enough to bring
them," said Paul, with a touch of boyish
humour. "We have some fine melons in our
garden; as soon as they are ripe, you shall
have some."

"Well, well! I know you are not close-
fisted," answered the priest, unconscious of the
slight irony of Paul's speech, "I can't complain of any of you Stundists. But I give you
warning. You must not set your heart on
Halya, Karpo's girl. She must marry a
good Christian, and Panass shall be the man.
It is all but settled. The match-makers are
going there in a day or two, now the harvest
is over."

"And what will become of poor Yarina?" asked Paul.

The priest started. Yarina—he had forgotten her. Yarina, who, next to Ooliana, had been his best parishioner; open-handed, pleasant-spoken, constantly requiring his services, for which she paid him handsomely, to bless her house and fields. If she cared for Panass, he had been guilty of a terrible blunder in promoting his marriage with Halya, who would be a most reluctant bride, as everybody knew. His perturbation was extreme; and Paul watched him with mischievous delight.

"What have you in your creel?" inquired Father Vasili, to change the conversation. Paul opened it, and showed the fish still alive.

"Ah! delicious!" said Father Vasili, "and it is just Friday to-day; and mother is so fond of new-caught fish. You heretics gobble up flesh-meat every day of the week, the devil take you! You could have done well without fish if God Almighty had not made any. But what should we do on Fridays without them?"

H 2

"I will carry some up to Matoushka," said Paul, a little sadly.

"That's right," answered the priest, "and I'll put your name down this time in the list I send up to the bishop, so he shall not miss it. I don't want any disturbance in my parish, if I only get my dues. The sexton will be calling for the tithes, and it has been a good harvest; if you and your reprobate gang would only send double measure you should be left at peace for me. There is no getting a farthing from you for my ministrations; so you owe me double dues."

"I will tell them," said Paul; "but why do you call us such bad names? 'A gang of reprobates!'"

"How touchy you are!" exclaimed Father Vasili, in surprise. "Hard words break no bones. There is no getting on without using strong language."

They soon reached the forecourt of the priest's dwelling; and the Matoushka, in a green dress, a large blue apron, with a beaming smile on her round, flat face, received Paul's offering of live fish with delight, and wanted to bring him a glass of vodka.

" No, thank you, Matoushka!" he answered ; whilst the priest's face assumed an expression of contemptuous pity.

"Their crazy heads won't stand it, the fools!" he exclaimed involuntarily; and then looking at Paul he added, "well! well! I meant no harm." He accompanied Paul back to the gate.

"Take care you don't go deeper into the mud," he said; "there's a man who would help me against all of you if I lifted up a little finger."

He pointed to the house where the starosta Savely lived; and then with his heavy, shambling gait, moved off to the kitchen, where Matoushka was already busy with the fish.

CHAPTER IX.

STRONGLY TEMPTED.

PAUL was early at his trysting-place at the water-mill, and waited anxiously for Halya. It was again a moonlight night, but the brilliance and warmth of midsummer was gone; and a touch of chill, foreboding winter by-and-by, was in the night air. The grain was gone from the fields, where it had been waving in rich abundance a short time ago; and the rough stubble shone yellow in the moonlight. There was a long stretch of river here; and the water just above the mill lay twinkling with moonlit streaks. The whole place seemed asleep; but at last soft voices broke the stillness, and two slight, dark figures came across the bare fields behind the mill. Halya was not alone!

But before she reached the shadow of the wall, which concealed him, her companion went on alone along the river bank. Paul drew Halya to him; and for a moment they stood, face to face, and mouth to mouth, in a more passionate embrace than they had ever dreamed of. Halya's round arms, beautiful and strong, strained him to her for an instant; then fell despairingly to her sides. She wrenched herself away from his grasp, and sat down under the wall in a passion of tears.

"My darling!" cried Paul, throwing himself on the ground beside her.

"Oh! you are killing me!" she sobbed, "you and my father between you. Save me, Paul, save me! They are going to make me marry Panass. It would be kinder to shoot me dead. If you would only kill me with your own hand I would die gladly. But save me from Panass!"

Paul was deeply distressed. He hardly knew what to say to the weeping girl, whose sobs came thick and fast. At last she grew more calm.

"Listen! my Halya," he said; "my mother shall go to-morrow and make a definite proposal for you to your father. We are richer than Panass, and can give more dowry. Now my mother knows that God wills you to be

my wife, and she is reconciled to it. Yes;
she loves you, my Halya. We have never
formally asked for you, and Karpo will be
surprised at what we can give. Besides, what
God wills must come to pass."

"How do you know it is God's will?"
inquired Halya, in a hushed tone of awe and
gladness.

Then Paul, in many words, with interrup-
tions of fond expressions, gave her an account
of his appeal to the Bible for some clue to
guide him in his perplexity about her and
himself. Halya listened with intense interest.

"But I do not want to be a Stundist!"
she objected, when Paul repeated: 'Thy
people shall be my people, and thy God
my God!'"

"That must come if it is God's will,"
answered Paul; and Halya was silenced. The
thread of fatalism, woven into the religious
and social belief of every Russian, was
strong in her. "What will be, must be,"
she murmured.

"But, Paul," she said, "if father says I
cannot marry you unless you are a true
Christian, couldn't you, just for a little while,

come to church. Father Vasili would make
it easy for you. If you just stood inside the
porch, it would do. And we would hasten on
our marriage, and then you could do as you
chose, and me too."

It would have been a terrible temptation
but for Paul's conviction that God had willed
Halya to be his wife, and that He would
bring it about in His own way, and at His
own time. Halya would be given to him, not
to Panass, however things might seem to work
against it. He pressed his lips tenderly on
her bowed forehead.

"My dearest," he said, "if you were in
a strange country, would you go and bow
down before a dreadful idol, and pretend to
worship it?"

"Oh, no!" she answered, with a shudder.
"God would smite me dead!"

"He might not smite me dead if I went
to church," continued Paul; "but I should
say to Him plainly: 'I know Thy laws and
Thy commandments, and I will keep them
when it is convenient to me. But I will disobey them if I am to lose anything by keeping
them.' Would that please God, my Halya?"

"Oh, no!" she replied.

"And Jesus Christ, my Lord, says to my heart: 'I died for thee; what wilt thou do for Me?' Can I say: 'Lord, I must disobey Thee this once because Halya wishes it. We do not think Thou canst make us man and wife without my becoming a hypocrite.' Would that please the Lord who was crucified for you and me?"

"No, no!" she cried, with tears.

"You will not marry Panass!" said Paul.

"No, my father shall kill me first," she interrupted.

"I meant you will marry me, not Panass," he continued; "they may fight against God, but it will be of no use. My mother shall come to-morrow, and talk with your mother, and then we shall see what happens. Who knows? We may be married very soon. We will make Father Vasili as good a present as if we were married at church."

"But where else could we be married?" asked Halya.

Paul told her of Loukyan's plan; but this was not at all to Halya's mind. She had always thought of the marriage service performed with all due ceremony at the village church, and the marriage feast afterwards in her father's house. It was a depressing idea, this plan of Paul's and Loukyan's. However, the first preliminaries were not agreed to yet; and, after a while, she bade Paul farewell, and hastened to rejoin her companion, who was motionlessly gazing at the river out of hearing. It was Yarina.

"Well!" she said, half seriously, half laughingly; "does he consent to be a good Christian for your sake? You know if you marry Paul, I am sure of Panass, and I love him if you don't. Thank God! every woman does not love the same man! I'm longing to hear what Paul said."

"I will never marry Panass!" exclaimed Halya.

"I'm glad to hear it," answered Yarina; "but now we must run home. It is nearly midnight."

The next day Ooliana went to Knishi to pay a visit to Marfa, old Karpo's wife. It was more than a year since she had been there; though in former days she and Marfa had been close friends. They had been children and girls together; and they were married about the same time. Marfa had been with Ooliana when Paul was born; and Ooliana had been the first to take Halya in her arms. They had nursed and tended the babies together, and scarcely a day passed without them seeing one another. But all that had changed since Ooliana became a Stundist. Old Karpo forbade any further intercourse. Ooliana opened her commission at once.

"Marfa," she said, "it was always in your mind and mine that our boy and girl should some day be man and wife. I know Karpo has reasons against it; but you tell him what I have to say. If he will consent to their marriage I am ready to give them every rouble I possess; and as you know, and he knows, they are a good few, thank God! Old Okhrim cannot do a quarter like that for Panass. He has another child to provide for, and I have none but Paul."

"But he must come back to church," answered Marfa, though she was astounded at the magnitude of Ooliana's offer.

"That he will never do!" she replied,

"but he will not insist upon Halya becoming one of us. She shall worship God according to her own conscience. But Paul will some day be a great man among us. Valerian Petrovitch says so. Marfa, do your best to make our young folks happy."

"If it only rested on me!" she said, with a sigh; "you Stundists always seem so content and joyful! Your homes are so clean, and you grow pretty flowers under your windows. But there! you all pull together; and the husband is as loving to his wife as on the day they were married. I should wish my Halya to have a husband to love her when she is old and ugly, like me."

"Panass wouldn't," urged Ooliana.

"No, Panass wouldn't," she assented.

Marfa, in much fear and trembling, laid Ooliana's proposal before Karpo, after she had fed him with a supper he particularly relished. But he had only one ultimatum to offer; if Paul would reconcile himself to the Church, he might marry Halya; if not she should be the wife of Panass.

"Father!" said Halya, creeping timidly to his side, and laying her pretty head on his shoulder, "why must I marry at all? Are you tired of keeping me at home? I'll be very good, and please you all I can. Only let me stay here at home with you and mother."

Her voice died away in sobs.

"No, no," answered Karpo, half sternly, half jokingly. "I'll not have my only girl live to be an old maid. Besides, I want to dandle my grandsons on my knee. A girl is only half a child. I shall look for some fine bold young urchins to make my old age glad."

CHAPTER X.

MATCH-MAKING.

GENERAL NESTEROFF lived in the old Manor House, near Ostron. Since the emancipation of the serfs in 1862 his income had dwindled year by year, through neglect and mismanagement. His mode of life was extremely secluded and simple; and he was all but a cipher in the district, where formerly his will was law. His two fashionable daughters in St. Petersburg drained him of any surplus money he might chance to have. His only son and heir, Valerian, had been travelling all over the world for the last three years, indulging the Russian passion of unrest, which took possession of the nation about the middle of the present century.

Valerian returned from his travels a Propagandist pure and simple. He had studied in Western lands the various constitutions under which the nations lived and prospered;

and his heart burned within him as he thought of the condition of his beloved Russia. He was at home again among his father's old serfs, who were in reality no more free than in the old times before the edict of Liberation. He had been mingling with them during their busy weeks of harvest, helping with his own hands and fully sharing their labours, whilst he carefully studied their various characters, in the hope of elevating them during the coming winter. Ooliana was one of his chief favourites; but he had seen less of Loukyan and Paul than of any other of the peasants.

There was one man with whom Valerian could do nothing. This was old Okhrim, the father of Panass. In his youth he had been a famous reprobate, guilty of all sorts of misconduct, and a pest to the neighbourhood; but about twenty-five years ago he had suddenly amended his ways, and married a rich widow, who died a few years afterwards, leaving him his son Panass and a daughter, whom he had lately married. He was considered one of the richest farmers in Knishi; he was trading in cattle, and rented on

lease from General Nesteroff water-melon
beds in large quantities.

Okhrim was still a strong and fine-looking
man, with bushy iron-grey hair, good features,
and a bearing that was on the whole manly
and impressive. He was a far better looking
man than his son; and he knew it. What
reason was there against his marrying Yarina,
when once Panass was settled? She was rich,
but he was richer. True, she was twenty
years younger than he; but what was that?
There was not one of her many suitors who
was a more likely man. At any rate, he
would try his chance; and Okhrim seldom
failed in anything he attempted.

The day after Halya had made her fruitless
appeal to her father, old Okhrim went home
early from his melon-beds, and ordered his
servant to prepare him some dinner instantly.
He went into the closet where he kept a
box containing all his best clothes, which
seldom saw the light; and taking from it his
almost new navy-blue coat, with bright metal
buttons, and his best boots with red tops, he
hastened to dress himself in holiday attire.
Then pulling his new Astrachan cap well over

I

his eyes, he went straight to old Karpo's on a diplomatic visit.

The dinner-table was not yet laid at Karpo's house. For Halya had been washing again in the river, and Marfa was very slow in all she did, and did not pay any heed to time, so that any other woman in Knishi would do more in one hour than she did in two. Halya was hurrying about the dinner, and looking at the potatoes in the oven, when suddenly, glancing through the window, she saw Okhrim, in his unusual holiday dress, coming through the fold-yard gate. Her heart sank within her.

"Father!" she cried, "Okhrim is coming!"

"What a nuisance!" growled Karpo. "Folks want their dinners; and he takes that moment to pay a visit."

But he went out to meet his guest with no trace of irritability on his face. On the contrary, it beamed with hospitality and politeness.

"Well met!" he exclaimed. "How do you do, Okhrim Moisevitch? Come in! come in!"

"Thank you for your kindness," Okhrim answered, bowing low.

"Thanks for yours in calling upon us," responded Karpo, bowing lower.

They entered the house, and Karpo seated his welcome guest in the seat of honour, near the icon, and placed himself on a wooden stool in front of him. His curiosity and his hopes were actively aroused. Okhrim, of course, had not come simply to make a call upon a neighbour. He would not have decked himself out for that.

"Where does God bring you from?" asked Karpo, really meaning, "What are you come for?" but so direct a question would be bad manners.

"I am going to see Father Vasili to pay him my dues; and I want to bargain a little with him," replied Okhrim, surveying his bright buttons and red boot-tops.

"That's a lie!" said Karpo to himself. "If you wanted to bargain with the priest you'd go in the evening when he is drunk; but not at mid-day, when he is as keen as you are, and as hard as a flint."

He began talking of the crops, and the price of corn in the market, all the time watching his guest with his shrewd grey

I 2

eyes. Halya opened the door, and stood timidly on the threshold.

" Mother says is she to set the dinner, or must we wait?" she asked.

" Put the dinner!" growled Karpo; "everybody else has had it long ago; and we haven't yet begun. My old woman is like a lazy horse," he said to Okhrim : "she takes one step and then rests awhile. Halya is not like that; but she has been washing all the morning."

Okhrim politely stood up, and made as if he was going away; but Karpo would not hear of it. If he would not sit down to dinner with them, he must at least wait and have some tea after dinner. Okhrim accepted the invitation, and sat down near the window, a little farther from the dinner-table. This was a sure proof that he had some purpose in coming.

The meal was almost a silent one. Only Okhrim talked of the trickery of the village mayor, with whom he was not on friendly terms, as he wished to be mayor himself. Karpo and Marfa ate slowly and solemnly, whilst Halya served at the table, fetching the dishes from the oven, and now and then making a pretence of eating. But she could eat nothing; she guessed too well why old Okhrim had come.

Karpo also was almost too excited to eat, though no one would have suspected it. He solemnly crossed the loaf with his knife every time he had to cut a slice, and solidly and sternly chewed his food with extreme deliberation. His replies to Okhrim's remarks were given in monosyllables, and were very judicious and guarded, for he had no quarrel himself with the mayor. At last the meal was ended. The women cleared the table, and placed upon it a boiling samovar, with tea and sugar, and then disappeared. They knew the old men did not wish them to be present.

"Mother, darling!" cried Halya, throwing her arms round Marfa's neck, "he is come after me! He is going to ask father for me!"

"But what are you afraid of, my little girl?" asked her mother. "It is time for you to marry. All your companions are married; and you are not going to remain an old maid surely——"

"Mother, mother! don't say that," she interrupted; "that's a hundred times better than marrying Panass! Oh! I am lost!"

She was trembling from head to foot, and pressed herself against her mother, as a lamb seeking refuge from a wolf. The mother stroked her fair head with her knotty and crooked fingers.

"God bless you, my child! God bless you!" she repeated; "it's not Okhrim himself who wants to marry you."

Halya shook her head passionately, and burst into an agony of tears.

"My poor darling!" cried her mother, in a hopeless tone, "What can I do? I can do you no good, or I'd go through fire and water to do it."

"Mother, let me go out," pleaded Halya, "and if father asks for me say you've sent me to the shop, or the river, or anywhere else——"

"Go, go! dear child," said Marfa hurriedly, "I will manage somehow. And if he gets very cross, I must bear it. Go, go! It will be nothing, and you are my only one."

Halya vehemently embraced her mother,

and slipped out through the garden into the
neighbour's yard, and so gained the street
without being seen by either of the old men,
who were discussing her fate. The poor
mother sat for a long time on the turf-seat
outside the house. Her hands lay listlessly
on her lap, and from time to time she shook
her grey head sorrowfully. She knew very
well what it was to be compelled to marry
by a father; and she disliked old Okhrim
and Panass. She knew them both to be of
a hard and cruel nature. Oh! if Paul had
only remained orthodox! How happy she
and Halya would be now! They had been
very happy until the last few months; till
the Stundists had destroyed all the peace and
happiness of the place. But she could do
absolutely nothing for her only child. She
would have no voice in the match-making.
It depended entirely on the two old men,
whose voices she heard murmuring in low
and cautious tones.

Karpo and Okhrim were slowly sipping
from their saucers some very weak tea, gently
biting off from time to time minute bits of
sugar, from the lumps provided for them.

They drank for a long time in silence. To begin to talk at once would show that they did not appreciate the treat, and the solemnity of tea-drinking was not properly understood. It was Karpo who, as host, first broke the silence.

"You have splendid water-melons this year, Okhrim Moisevitch," he said; "some hundreds of silver roubles you will add to your store."

"Don't say that," answered Okhrim, with a gratified smile, "I shall think myself lucky if I make both ends meet. But what land you have, Karpo Petrovitch! There is your meadow lying close to my melon-beds—it is simply a treasure field! Well, I thought, if that meadow could be got for my children, I should die a happy man!"

Karpo pricked his ears. He expected after this preamble Okhrim would proceed to the object of his visit. But the old fox was too sly, and shuffled away from it quickly.

"Karpo Petrovitch!" he said, "what would you think if I ask you to sell me that meadow? I can give as much for it as anybody else."

"You don't want to buy my meadow,"

thought Karpo. But he did not show any sign of discomfiture; and apparently taking the offer seriously, he looked his guest straight in the face.

"For you, Okhrim Moisevitch," he answered, "I would part with it for five hundred roubles."

The price was ridiculously high, and they both knew it. Okhrim sighed and looked away.

"I must think it over," he said; and began to talk of the hard times, the difficulty of selling, and the falling off in prices. Then he fell into a confidential tone, and complained of the neglect in his household, and the little help he received from his son, who was always running after the girls, and leaving the work to chance.

"I want to get him married," he said; "that will sober him."

"That is sensible," answered Karpo coolly, as if the question did not concern him. "From a wife one cannot run away. The girls would not look at him after he was married. They'd break his head with their distaffs, if he came pottering after them."

Karpo laughed heartily, shaking again
with laughter, but never once losing sight
of Okhrim's face.

"Let your secret out of the bag, old fox,"
was the meaning of his look.

But Okhrim feigned not to understand
anything, talking as simply as a fool about
his late wife and himself. Then he went
back to the question of buying the meadow.
Karpo grew a little puzzled. They bargained
to and fro, and at last Okhrim said—

"Two hundred roubles, if you like."

It was almost as much as the land was
worth, and Karpo felt sure now his only errand
was to buy the meadow. He began to bargain
seriously, and grew warm in the discussion.
Suddenly Okhrim said, as if the idea had
just struck him—

"Do you know what I am thinking,
neighbour? Let your Halya marry my
Panass, and my property and yours will
belong to them.

Karpo was caught quite off his guard, and
he could not hide his great pleasure. The
old fox had outwitted him, and it was useless
to prolong the business.

"Agreed! I won't object to it," he said, not looking into Okhrim's face. "But how about the dowry?"

"I won't rob you," said Okhrim. "Give Halya that meadow, and two teams of oxen, a pair of horses, and six pairs of small cattle, and three hundred roubles to build a new dwelling——"

"Stop!" cried Karpo, with genuine indignation. "A Tartar wouldn't ask for more. But I cannot afford it," he added, in an apologetic tone. "My old woman and I would have to go out to service."

"Why, you could buy up the whole village," said Okhrim with a quiet laugh.

"No," said Karpo firmly, without a thought of diplomacy. "I will not beggar myself. I shall not give Halya one-half. That is all. You may cease to bother me about it."

"As you like," answered Okhrim. He turned over his empty cup, and laid on the top of it the little lump of sugar he had been nibbling at. This meant the tea-drinking was over, as well as the bargain.

"But you must have some more tea!" exclaimed Karpo. "Here, Halya! Marfa!

Who is there? Make the samovar ready
again; and bring more sugar and a lemon;
and be quick!"

Karpo was by no means astonished or
offended by Okhrim's rapacity. It was quite
natural. When one makes a bargain, one
should strive to outwit his neighbour. They
began to smoke their pipes, and entered into
an amicable and indifferent conversation, till
the samovar appeared again. They had already drunk a dozen cups each; but they set
to again, drinking persistently and solemnly,
avoiding one another's eyes, and cautiously
abstaining from a word on the subject which
both had at heart.

But the subject had been broached, and
could not be forgotten. The one who spoke
of it first would be the one to give way.
Karpo sat panting and sighing, from time to
time wiping his face on his shirt-sleeve.

Okhrim shuffled, sipped his tea, emptying
his cup again and again; and in his character
of a trader who went much into the world,
told all sorts of stories about it, to which
Karpo listened with the deepest attention.
This might have gone on for hours if Okhrim

had not accidentally looked through the window, and saw Yarina stepping across the fold-yard, and slipping round the corner of the house. Her appearance excited him, and he lost his self-possession.

"There's Yarina!" he ejaculated. "Does she come here often?"

"Sometimes," answered Karpo stolidly; "women will gossip, you know. There'll be a fine clatter in there by-and-by."

He nodded towards the inner door.

"Well! now then!" cried Okhrim, lowering his voice to a whisper; "what will you give Halya? You've got the better of me after all, you old boar!" he added to himself. He felt vexed that he had spoken; but a word cannot be caught again as a bird may. Once flown it has flown for ever.

"I must think about it," replied Karpo, filling his pipe again, and pressing his guest to do the same. Between the puffs of smoke he spoke very deliberately.

"One frock—another one—and a third one with a blue pattern. Two jackets, five pieces of linen cloth."

He went on enumerating his daughter's

wardrobe, though both of them knew well this talk was pure nonsense. The wardrobe would be provided out of the savings of Halya and her mother, and her father had nothing to do with it.

"But how about the farm stock?" asked Okhrim.

"One yoke of oxen, a cow, and twenty-five roubles in money," said Karpo.

Okhrim sighed sorrowfully.

"People will say Panass has married a beggar," he remarked, in a sad voice.

"Well, nobody shall say that," answered Karpo proudly. "I will add the bay mare; she is a capital mare, and is going to foal in the autumn. And I will give them, moreover, two pairs of sheep; my sheep are very good."

"They are good, that is true. But what is their value?" asked Okhrim.

The bargaining began again in earnest, but when the samovar was empty, Okhrim rose to take his leave. Such an important business could not be concluded at one interview. Okhrim's heir and Karpo's heiress could not be betrothed as if they were beggars.

"Come to see me," said Okhrim.

"Thanks for your invitation," replied Karpo, "and in the meanwhile I will have a talk with my wife and daughter. We must do it all in a godly manner," he added piously.

"That is right," replied Okhrim, "and nowadays you cannot do it otherwise. In our times, what the fathers said the young ones did, and no help for it; but now the young folks choose for themselves."

"My daughter is not one of those," protested Karpo.

"A word in your ear," said Okhrim mysteriously, "don't let her go to Yarina's, she meets Paul there. I shouldn't wonder if Yarina is come for her now. You must not let young folks have too much liberty."

"Marfa!" roared Karpo, in such a tone that the old woman rushed into the room in terror, "tell Halya to come here instantly and salute her father-in-law, Okhrim Moisevitch. Where is Halya?"

"Halya!" stammered the poor mother, "she's gone—I mean I sent her to the shop, and then to the well——"

"All right," said Karpo, turning to Okhrim with a confident wave of his hand,

and a smile, as much as to say that everything was right in his house and under his eye.

The two old men bowed low to one another, and Okhrim went home very well pleased with the business, as far as it had gone.

CHAPTER XI.

ARRESTED.

In the Consistory at Kovylsk a storm was gathering against the Stundists at Knishi. The story of Stepan, and his broken icons, had filtered through the town, in spite of the care of the innkeeper Isaacke. Loukyan was involved in it, and his imprisonment for six months at the outset of his career was not forgotten by the authorities. Father Vasili was known to be culpably negligent, caring for nothing if his income did not suffer. There were vague rumours also of a spirit of discontent spreading among the peasantry of the neighbourhood. The village constable reported several suspicious and secret meetings, at which, in truth, no Stundist was present; but Savely did not feel called upon to notice that fact.

Whilst Karpo and Okhrim were obstinately bargaining over their children's future, a very different scene was taking place at Loukyan's

J

poor dwelling near Ostron. Two vehicles
drove up to the lonely house. In the first were
seated two policemen, furnished with handcuffs
and fetters; and the second was occupied by
a young clergyman, a monk, not a parish
priest. He had been sent by the Consistory,
with the powers of a Government official. The
constable, Savely, was seated beside the driver,
as he had been summoned to come to Kovylsk
in order to avoid any difficulty in driving at
once to Loukyan's house.

"This is the place," said Savely, pointing
out unwillingly Loukyan's little cottage. They
entered the house together. Paraska was
bustling about the oven, preparing their frugal
dinner, when she saw the unwelcome and ter-
rifying guests entering the yard. Loukyan
was at work in the garden, lovingly loosening
the soil round the stems of some rare flowers
which had been given to him by Valerian.

"What has happened?" he asked, alarmed
by Paraska's pale face, and thinking some harm
had befallen the baby.

"Soldiers!" she gasped. "Savely is bringing them! And there is a clergyman with
them. They are just coming across the yard."

Loukyan's face grew grave. He did not speak for a minute, but cast a farewell glance on his beloved garden, his bee-hives, and all the plants he had cultivated with so much care. He knew it was a farewell gaze; but what should he say to Paraska to cheer her timid heart?

"See!" he said; "look at these flowers. A flower is one of God's pets. He clothes them better than Solomon in all his glory. But our Lord says we are much more than flowers and birds, and God in Heaven cares for us all far more. You shall take care of my flowers for me, and my bees, and cattle. They are dumb creatures, and cannot complain when they are neglected. And tell the brethren, Paraska, that I cannot go where God is not; and all will be well with me. They must not grieve too much, or lose courage. Neither they nor I can be afraid. And now let us go."

Paraska followed him, weeping.

"If they ask you about your religion," he whispered, "say what God puts into your mouth to answer; but if they ask about the brethren do not utter a word. Tell them every one must speak only for himself."

J 2

When they entered the house the men were already searching it carefully. Father Paissy was conducting the business himself. He had been sent on purpose that no important evidence against the Stundists should be overlooked. He was also commissioned to visit Father Vasili, on account of some delay in payments due to the Consistory.

Paissy was a fair-haired young man, with a small, sharp-featured face, soft blue eyes, and insinuating voice. The Archbishop was accustomed to despatch him on the most delicate and diplomatic errands, which he, with a natural love of intrigue and craft, executed with great ability. He was a born Jesuit.

" Here you are at last !—Loukyan, the Stundist apostle," he said, with an easy smile. " We want to know something more of your new religion. You have as many books as if you were a priest. Have you any other documents ? "

" It is true I teach my brethren all I learn from God," answered Loukyan, " but it is not for me, sinner as I am, to call myself an apostle. Here are all my books. Please look at them yourself, and may God help you if you read them for a good purpose."

He spoke so quietly, and with so much dignity, that Paissy was somewhat disconcerted. A very vigorous search was made for incriminating papers. They ransacked the pantry, the cart-shed, and the yard, and looked suspiciously at the bee-hives, but they did not dare to disturb them. The honey jars were inspected, and those turned upside down were lifted one by one to see if anything was hidden beneath them. No letters or papers were discovered until they opened a table-drawer and found a thick manuscript book, in which Loukyan was in the habit of writing down the notes of his sermons. Paissy seized it eagerly.

"Here is the New Gospel!" he exclaimed, with malice.

Loukyan smiled good-naturedly.

"God help us to receive the old one," he said.

A list of the books was made, and the manuscript was taken away as "material proofs." After that Loukyan was bidden to get ready to go to the court house.

Paraska began to weep and wail aloud, and Loukyan cast upon her a look of deep sympathy and pity.

"God be with you, my daughter!" he said. "Tell Demyan to see after all my affairs; he knows them as well as I do. The brethren will hold you dear for my sake. I go willingly, Paraska! Weep not for me; for, living or dying, I am the Lord's."

Loukyan was driven to the nearest court-house, where an official report was drawn up of the search, and the "material proofs" found. But, before this was finished, the court-house and the yard in front of it were filled with people. This was what Paissy wished for. He addressed them in his most persuasive tones.

"Orthodox people!" he said, "believers in saints and icons! you know that of late years rebels have sprung up among you, who wish to change the true Russian religion for the German one. But this will never do, will it, ye Orthodox Christians?"

"It will never do!" they shouted with one voice.

"Then we must stamp them out whilst

they are few and feeble," he continued.
"We must not let vermin flourish till they
eat us out of house and home. There must
be no temptation to become a Stundist; it
must be made as great a sin as murder. We
are all agreed upon that?"

He spoke in most impressive tones, but
the orthodox people were somewhat puzzled.
Their consciences assured them that the
Stundists were by no means guilty of any
great sin. At last Kuzka—a spare, middle-
aged peasant, very fond of hearing his own
voice, and with few chances of doing so
except in the public-house—pushed himself
forward.

"To be sure, your reverence," he said,
"they must be stamped out in the bud—in
the grain—because, you see, the grain—well!
the grain buds, you see."

His ideas grew so entangled that he could
only stammer out some incoherent sentences;
and he was not sustained or cheered by his
rustic audience. The peasants held themselves
aloof from the Stundists; and the good fellowship of former days had ceased. Reformers
always find opponents; and these men disturbed

the tranquil laziness of their minds. But to suppress them, to injure and persecute them, or to hand them over to the dreaded authorities, had never come into their stolid heads.

"Tell me, who among you has heard this false teacher speak evil of our holy Orthodox Church," said Paissy insinuatingly.

Not a word from the crowd. Even they saw the foreshadow of a court of law, and the mere thought of it scared them.

"Why don't you answer?" asked Paissy gently; "speak out boldly. You will not get into trouble for it."

He meant to set them at ease; but only frightened them the more by his remarks. The orthodox people kept profoundly silent.

"Did Loukyan speak to you about his religion?" inquired Paissy from Kuzka, who gaped stupidly, and scratched behind his ear.

"How should I know, your reverence?" he stammered; "I'm a poor, ignorant man. I'm quite dark."

"Dark!" repeated Paissy maliciously; "I see that, when you cannot tell whether one speaks of religion or a donkey. So it seems

Loukyan kept his new religion to himself!
He never lent books to read, or spoke to his
neighbours."

He looked round the crowd with an ironical
smile, and his eyes unintentionally fell upon
Loukyan, who stood in a prominent place
fronting the people. The old man's grey head
was bowed down; but when Paissy ceased
speaking he lifted it up, and cast a kindly
glance on the familiar faces around him.

"I lent the New Testament to all who
wished to read it," he said, in a clear, cheerful voice; "and I read it to those who could
not read it for themselves. I had found a
great treasure hidden in it; and I wished all
my dear neighbours to share it with me. It
is a treasure that grows greater by dividing
it; for it is the Truth, God's Truth, Oh,
yes! that I taught openly; not in secret.
Everybody who wished could come to hear."

"You preached! And to whom?" inquired
Paissy.

But Loukyan, though as simple as a child
in everyday matters, was shrewd and wise in
grave questions. He made no reply, as if he
did not hear the question.

"Why are you silent?" stormed Paissy; "if you preached you knew who were your listeners."

"Nay!" said Loukyan, smiling, "the father does not give up his children to destruction; and the shepherd lays down his life for his flock. There was One who heard me, the Lord Jesus Christ, who said, 'Where two or three of you are gathered together in my name, there am I in the midst of you.' Lord Jesus, we felt Thy presence!"

He spoke as simply and sincerely as a child speaks. But Paissy made a gesture of horror.

"Blasphemy! Rank blasphemy!" he exclaimed; "we hear it for ourselves. Put him in chains, and do not allow anybody to speak to him," he said to Savely, the starosta. "And I will teach you, too, you shameless cowards!" he shouted to the lookers-on; "Father Vasili gives you too much freedom. We shall have to tighten the reins a good deal. You will see it before long. We will have no heresy and no sedition in Knishi, if we have to burn every house in it with fire."

His thin lips were white with wrath; and his mild blue eyes blazed. All his sweetness and courtesy had disappeared.

"Out of here!" he shouted, "get off with you, you hounds!"

Slowly and sulkily the peasants stole out of the house; but they lingered in the court-yard to watch the departure of Paissy and Loukyan. Paissy mounted his carriage, and ordered the coachman to drive to Father Vasili.

"Now he is gone to get the church revenue from the Batushka," said one of the men, laughing; "Father Vasili will squeeze us now."

They began to disperse; but a few still loitered about, to see what would become of Loukyan. A little band of Stundists had gathered together in the courtyard, though Savely had not allowed them to enter the house, knowing no good would come of it. Ooliana and Paul were among them. Presently the blacksmith, with Demyan, his assistant, came hurrying up; and by-and-by there was heard the clanging of a hammer upon iron.

"They are chaining him!" cried Kuzka,

peeping through the nick of the door which stood ajar.

At last Loukyan, was brought out, with his head uncovered, and with fetters on his hands and feet. At the same moment the waggon, which had brought the two armed. policemen, with their swords and revolvers, drove into the yard. Loukyan said to himself: "Are ye come out as against a thief with swords and staves. Lord! Thou art giving me to drink of the cup of which Thou didst drink!"

He had not spoken his thought aloud, but it flashed across the minds of the little throng watching him, both Orthodox and Stundists alike. "As if he was a robber or a murderer!" they murmured. Loukyan's benign, kindly gaze rested upon them, as if in blessing. The Stundists crowded round the waggon to look into his face, to touch his fettered hands, to hear his beloved voice for the last time. Ooliana's pure devout face was lifted up to his.

"Loukyan!" she cried, in a clear and fearless voice, "rejoice, and be exceeding glad, for great is your reward in heaven; for

so persecuted they the prophets that were before us. We have no fear for you, brother.
Have no fear for us! We will follow in
your steps till God calls us home."

"Get out of our way, woman!" shouted
the policeman; and Loukyan, who was anxious
to avoid any demonstration that might bring
his little flock into trouble, only answered
Ooliana by a smile, full of meaning. But he
was leaving these dear familiar faces, on
which he should look no more, and he could
not go away without one word.

"Farewell, dear neighbours!" he cried,
speaking alike to the Orthodox and Stundists;
"if I have wronged any of you, or grieved
any of you, forgive me this day."

"God forgive us all!" answered the little
crowd, whose sympathies at this moment were
all on the prisoner's side. Some among them
piously uncovered their heads, and crossed
themselves, as if in the presence of an icon.

"Christ bless you, and give you peace,"
said Loukyan.

"Silence!" roared the policeman; "drive
on quickly."

But along the rough road, full of ruts

and holes, it was impossible to drive quickly. The people accompanied the waggon through the street; most of them bareheaded, as if they were conducting some personage of high standing. They dared not speak to Loukyan, nor he to them. But he was deeply touched by such unexpected sympathy from his old neighbours, who of late had been cold and even hostile to him. At the barrier gate he lifted up his fettered hands as if in blessing, and was about to speak, when one of the policemen seized him by the collar, and thrust him violently on to the floor of the waggon.

"Drive on!" shouted the policeman, "do you belong to this dog's crew of heretics, and are afraid of offending his reverence? I will show you how to drive."

The coachman gave a start, and whipped up his horses, whilst the people stood still gazing after the swiftly disappearing conveyance. Then with slow steps and sad faces, they started homewards.

CHAPTER XII

BATUSHKA AND MATOUSHKA.

THERE was much to talk about. The philosopher Kuzka was of opinion that as Loukyan
had been arrested he must be guilty of some
crime. Savely, the village elder, as an
official, approved of this opinion as manifest-
ing faith in the infallibility of the courts of
law. Yet he wanted to know something more
of the matter. Until now he had been indifferent to the Stundists, only finding them
no trouble whatever to him. He had never
had one in custody before. Paul was walking
homewards near them; and Savely and Kuzka
applied to him for information as to what
Loukyan had done. But he was crushed with
grief, and could not answer their questions.

"If you only read the Gospel," said Ooliana,
"and act accordingly, you would know what
crime Loukyan is guilty of."

"But that is not prohibited," said Kuzka.

"Not by law," said a voice behind them.

They turned and saw Valerian, who, as soon as he had heard of Loukyan's arrest, had hastened to the village court-house, hoping to get him released. But he arrived too late, and had only time to hurry after the crowd to the barrier gate. He heard Loukyan's farewell words; and his heart felt sorrowful for the little band of Stundists, so unexpectedly deprived of their leader.

"Neither Loukyan, nor any of his followers are guilty of any crime," he said; "some people prefer a very simple religion, without priests, who so often fleece both the living and the dead. That is why the Orthodox Church is offended. Is that true?" he asked the Stundists.

"Partly," said Ooliana doubtfully, "but that is not all—that is really nothing."

"Do you belong to them, master?" Savely asked in a respectful tone, but with great curiosity.

"Oh, no! my religion is quite a different thing," said Valerian, laughing, "but I did not come to talk about religion. I want to know how Loukyan's family will get on without him. If they want any help they must come to my father and me. Loukyan was my father's serf in old times, and a thoroughly good man."

"Thank you, master," said Ooliana, "you are very kind and good. But we can take care of our Loukyan's family if they need it. We are bound to help one another."

"That is right and sensible!" said Valerian heartily; "if men only knew what wonders they could do if they stood by each other, there is nothing that could not be done! Listen to me, all of you! Whenever help is needed give it, if it is only fetching a cup of cold water for a child to drink. You will be glad you have done it."

He nodded pleasantly, and turned away, leaving the people more puzzled than before. It was plain Valerian did not think Loukyan guilty of any crime.

At Father Vasili's, meanwhile, the dinner-table was spread with unaccustomed pomp. The Matoushka was anxious to treat the un-expected and somewhat unwelcome guest to as good a dinner as possible. Paissy was closeted with Father Vasili, who was passing a very anxious hour, in a perfect fever of

K

fright and vexation. Paissy was scolding him
on two points: for not paying punctually
the usual gratuities expected by the Consistory
officials, and for not keeping his flock from
the new heresy.

" You will have to answer for their souls
before God," he declaimed. " Woe to those
through whom offences come into the Church !
Remember what is said : ' It were better for
him that a millstone were hanged about his
neck, and that he were drowned in the depth
of the sea.'   Do you   understand, Father
Vasili, what that means ? "

Father Vasili only lifted up his eyes, and
sighed heavily.

" It is a common scandal," pursued Paissy,
" that the heretics have quite the upper hand
in Knishi.   The Consistory and the Archbishop are much displeased about it.   Is it
right for a village priest to patronise the
Stundists ? How shall you answer your Judge
at the Last Day, when He asks you what
care you have taken of the souls entrusted
to you ? "

Father Vasili groaned. In this world you
have your bishop as a judge; in the next

you are answerable to God. This was very hard upon a poor village priest, who only wished to live peaceably, and receive his dues.

"Ah! Father Paissy," he said, "you don't know these people; you think it easy to manage them. But talk to them about the heretics! They say 'Leave them alone. They pay the taxes regularly, and fulfil all their duties; and if they go to hell afterwards, what then? It is no concern of yours. It is their own affair; you are not responsible for their souls.'"

"But we surely are responsible," said Father Paissy. Father Vasili thought of Loukyan, industrious, thrifty and liberal, benign and genial with all his neighbours; of Ooliana, with her saintly self-denial and unswerving truthfulness; of Paul, strong and courageous, courteous to all men, and indefatigably kind to those who were in trouble. The whole little band of Stundists passed before his mind's eye; and with an inaudible groan he said to himself they were the best people in his parish.

"Do you know," Paissy resumed, "that they teach that no Christian can be a soldier?

K 2

And that usury, and profit, and wages are all wrong? Do you know they think we are all equals, and that there is no mine or thine? If you lend money you sin; you must give it, and not take advantage of your brother's necessity. There will be no trade or commerce if the Stundists get the upper hand."

"But this is terrible!" cried Father Vasili, roused at last to indignation. "This must be put a stop to! We must tear them up, root and branch. They are dangerous people. But what can I do?"

Paissy cast upon him a glance of contemptuous pity.

"I suppose you preach to your people?" he said with a sneer. "You are their spiritual father, and you must give them line upon line, precept upon precept, here a little, and there a little. If there comes a bad harvest, or a destructive storm, is it not God's punishment against the heretics, which the Orthodox are bound to share? If there is a murrain among the cattle, do not the Orthodox and heretic cattle feed in the same pastures, and drink out of the same trough? You must make them understand such things, teaching them both in church and in private. If the men won't take heed, talk to the women. It is your duty; and the Consistory will call you to account, if you neglect it."

He then went on to speak of that other serious negligence—not paying promptly the offerings expected by the Church officials. Poor Father Vasili listened with undisguised dismay; and Paissy softened his tone a little, and even promised to intercede with the Consistory for a postponement of the tribute due, if he would undertake to watch the Stundists and send in reports of their proceedings.

"But I hope we have destroyed the sect here in the egg," said Paissy.

Both went to dinner in an amicable mood. The Matoushka, who was an excellent cook, had provided an admirable impromptu meal, in her anxiety to propitiate this pillar of the Church. It was quite a success. Only the Matoushka kept complaining of the hard times and their decreasing income.

"Folks are growing cold in their faith, I say," she moaned; "they keep away from church, you know. Only come to be married and buried. In old times, you know, every house was blessed at least three times a year, and so many kopecks or roubles for that. Now everybody tries to shun it once a year, you see."

She paused to fetch a hot dish from the oven, and to fill Paissy's plate with food from it.

"People have given up dying, I say," she resumed. "To be sure, the children die like flies; but what income does a child's burial bring in, I ask you? The mother offers you a basket of eggs, and you must thank her even for that. But it's as much trouble to bury a child as a grown-up person, I say. But real people like that don't die at all. We had only two funerals last summer, and one of them was the corpse of some vagabond the police picked up, and we had to bury it for nothing. We were out of pocket by it, I tell your reverence. The death income has sunk almost to a cipher. And yet," she said with a deep sigh, "there was Father Cyril, of the Transfiguration, to whom God sent good luck a few years ago. In one summer more than a hundred people died of diphtheria in his parish. Have you seen the beautiful house he has built in Kovylsk, opposite the public gardens?"

"To be sure," answered Paissy, "it is a fine place. He is going to let it to the officers."

"Just so," said the Matoushka, "all that was built by the dead fees, I say. So the Lord raises up one, and humbles the other. All is according to His holy will."

She spoke very piously. The Matoushka had more mother-wit than her husband, and knew what was probably the weak point of their guest. At dessert, whilst she poured out a liberal measure of liqueurs for Paissy, she asked if he would not soon be appointed the chief of the priests in the cathedral at Kovylsk.

"Father Levitoff is resigning, people say," she remarked; "and there is nobody to fill his place but you."

Paissy smiled complacently. At present this was the summit of his ambition.

"I am too young for the post," he said modestly.

"It is not age, but intellect, I say,"

answered the Matoushka, "that ought to get promotion. Intellect and holiness, you know! I remember years ago when there were bishops hardly over forty. We shall see you a bishop before we die."

Paissy, having dined well, entered into an animated conversation, telling of the intrigues going on in the Consistory, and the necessity of being very diplomatic himself. In his heart he fully agreed with the Matoushka that his intellect and zeal more than counterbalanced his youth, and ought to guide the Consistory in choosing him for a dignitary of the Church. If he could only stamp out Stundism in the province, he was sure of promotion; and his first step had been taken here, in Knishi.

He left for Kovylsk at dusk. Father Vasili, after so many unaccustomed libations, could hardly move his tongue; and certainly could not comprehend a word that was said to him. But the Matoushka was as fresh and clear-minded as during the dinner; and to her Paissy repeated his shrewd instructions about the duties of her husband as a pastor. He placed his injunctions against the Stundists

in a very plain and comprehensible form. The
Matoushka promised she would do her best
among the women. Any misfortune that
happened in Knishi should henceforth be laid
at the door of the heretics.

CHAPTER XIII.

THE PANNOTSHKA'S GRAVE.

MANY curious eyes watched Ooliana and Paul the following Sunday as they walked openly down the village street to the cottage where the Stundists were wont to meet. The autumn was treading closely on the steps of the departing summer, and a soft film lay over the wide undulating steppe surrounding the village, and tempered the heat of the sun, already half way down to his winter bed. There was in the sorrowful hearts of the mother and son a feeling like autumn, looking on into a dreary winter. Yet when their eyes met a gleam of hope and courage darted from the one soul to the other.

They were passing the house of the starosta Savely, when they saw him come quickly across his yard to intercept them. Savely's mother and Ooliana had been sisters, and he had known her and loved her as a kinswoman from his

childhood. She was two years younger than
he, and he had always looked upon himself
as her brother and protector.

"Ooliana," he said, stepping in front of
them, and speaking with the air of a man in
authority, "I warn you to go home. There
is danger where you are going; danger for
you, but above all for your son."

Ooliana looked steadily into his face with
her clear, dark eyes, and a wistful smile played
about her mouth.

"I will answer you, Savely," she said,
"in the words of our Lord, 'Fear not them
which kill the body, but are not able to kill
the soul: but rather fear him which is able
to destroy both body and soul in hell.' It
is sin we fear; and not to obey our conscience
is a sin against God."

"You will perish for it!" cried Savely,
with emotion.

"We may die, but we cannot perish,"
she answered. "Our Lord says, 'No man
can pluck you out of my Father's hand.' Yes,
we are in His hand, Savely; would to God
you were there too."

Savely turned away sorrowful and ashamed;

and the mother and son, side by side, almost
hand in hand, as they had been wont to walk
when Paul was a little child, passed on to
the humble meeting-place.

Not more than half of the small band was
there, fear having taken possession of the
hearts of the least earnest among them. Loukyan's chair was empty; and at the sight of
it the tears suddenly dimmed Ooliana's eyes.
A hymn was sung, in low voices, with many a
break in it, as one after another fell a-weeping.
Just at its close, a man who had been sitting
in a dark corner came forward, and stood
before the little congregation. They recognised
in him a pedlar, who had come to sell his
wares in Knishi the day before.

"I am Stepan," he said, "begotten of
Loukyan as my spiritual father. The church
at Kovylsk has sent by me an epistle to
the church at Knishi. Let me read it to
you, brethren."

All present had heard of Stepan and his
iconoclasm. There was a murmur of welcome
before he proceeded to read the letter.

"The church at Kovylsk sends greeting
by Stepan to the beloved brethren at Knishi.

We know the sorrow that has befallen you in the loss of your beloved leader, Loukyan. He is here, near to us; but alas! beyond our reach save by our prayers, which shall rise up before the throne of God our Father by day and by night. What can be done, without bribery and corruption, shall be done; but God forbid that we should tempt any man to sin against the laws of our land! Brethren, perilous days have come. Black clouds are gathering around us, and we see no light anywhere save from above, where the sun of righteousness is shining, with healing in its beams. Look up! Lift up your hearts—yea, lift them up unto the Lord. Pray that we all may be strengthened with strength in our souls. Be strong!—be strong, we say, in the Lord!

"Brethren, you remembered us in our affliction, and sent largely of your own goods to aid our necessities. Now, then, be not backward in letting us know your needs, and we will joyfully supply them. If any among you hunger, or are in need of clothing, send us a trusty messenger, and all we have you shall share. We hold out to you the hand of fellowship and brotherhood. You are as dear as our own flesh and blood, in the bonds of our Lord.

"Beware of breaking any law! Beware of arguing and disputing! Beware of the vodka shops! Beware, above all, of those men who go about stirring up the peasantry and sowing discontent and rebellion! We are loyal to the Tzar, whom God in His infinite wisdom has placed over us. What belongs to him we give willingly. 'Render unto Cæsar the things which are Cæsar's, and unto God the things which are God's.' There is no plainer precept than that.

"And now, beloved, both men and women, farewell! Be steadfast; be of one mind; trust in the Lord; and the peace of God, which passeth all understanding, shall remain in you."

A sorrowful conversation followed the reading of this letter. Stepan told them that he had been sent by the brethren in Volysk on a mission to strengthen the scattered churches in the province by telling them of his own marvellous conversion, when the Light of Life broke in almost instantaneously on his dark and dead soul. It was agreed that after a few days Paul should drive in his cart to Kovylsk to find out anything that could be known of Loukyan, and after a few ardent and tearful prayers the little congregation dispersed.

The village well was surrounded by groups of women as Ooliana and Paul passed it on their way homewards. Ooliana paused, as usual, to exchange greetings with her neighbours, and Paul found a chance of whispering to Halya.

"Meet me this afternoon at the Pannotshka's grave," he said.

Halya nodded, but said nothing.

The Pannotshka's grave lay in the recesses of an old forest, almost two miles from Knishi. There was no road to it but a by-path which ran along the crumbling edge of a deep ravine, which was crossed by a rude bridge made of the trunk of a huge walnut-tree, flung across the chasm. In the spring this ravine was the bed of a roaring torrent, which dried up during the summer into a channel, along which lay bleached and rounded stones, which looked like the bones of

the dead. A terrible murder of a young girl
had been committed in this ravine a century ago.
According to custom, a cross was put upon
the edge to mark the blood-stained spot; but
long ago the cross, and even the mound on
which it stood, had been washed away by the
spring floods. Still the place was regarded with
the old horror. It was known to be haunted.
Belated travellers had heard distinctly the
sounds of screaming, crying, and hellish
laughter echoing through the darkness. Herds-
men with their cattle avoided the Pannot-
shkas' grave, and the stealers of wood were
not tempted by the splendid oak and walnut-
trees which grew near it, preferring the risk
of being caught by the foresters to being
caught by the evil spirits which haunted the
ravine.

Left undisturbed by man, Nature took possession of the place, and its exuberance and
extraordinary vigour arrested the eye and excited the imagination, adding incalculable force
to the impression that some invisible and
mysterious power was brooding over the place.

It was at night, however, that the Pannotshka's grave was absolutely deserted. It

was always solitary, but during the day not altogether shunned; and though Halya would not have chosen to walk there alone, she was not afraid to go to meet Paul. It was a close, sultry day in early autumn. Not a breath of air was stirring, and all nature seemed asleep as if in the sleep of death. From the cloudless sky the fierce sun poured down its rays as if they were liquid fire, and the pale stubble-fields reflected the heat on her face, her hands, and her bare feet. Not a bird chirped. Only the grasshoppers were in high glee, leaping up from under her hurried footsteps with a shrill twitter, as if they enjoyed the torture the heat inflicted on all other living things.

"Oh! only to reach the wood!" thought Halya.

Yet she did not go straight to the Pannotshka's grave. Suppose she should reach it before Paul was there! She was afraid of it even by daylight. Besides, there were reptiles there, for the spot was swampy, and she could not bear the thought of them.

She threw herself on the ground as soon as she reached the outskirts of the forest. In the deep, dry shadow of the thick trees it

L

was cool; and she laid her burning face on the soft sward. It seemed like paradise after the broiling heat of the fields.

"He must find me!" she said; "if he loves me, he will find me easily."

By-and-by she lifted up her face, and began to watch with eager curiosity the movements of a colony of ants close beside her. She forgot herself in noticing them. Some were busy striving to move a little bit of cork which had fallen from the tree above her.

"That's a family going to build a house!" she thought. Another ant was laboriously dragging along a withered stalk of grass over the uneven ground.

"That is a tree," she said, "he has cut it down. Is it his own, or has he stolen it? Probably stolen. Here is the forester running after him. Now he will be caught and sent to Siberia."

But the second ant, instead of fighting with the first, seized the stalk at the other end, and helped to drag it along.

"Oh! I wish men were like that!" said Halya, sighing heavily; "they are all against one another. Oh! I wonder Paul does not come."

The leafy trees spread their branches over her, motionless in the torpid air. Here and there through the boughs little bits of blue sky could be seen; but farther within the forest the green roof overhead grew more dense. She crept slowly and anxiously onwards in the direction of the Pannotshka's grave, and the trees began to form a thick, unbroken wall, hemming her in on every side. She felt herself very far away from home, and the forest, with its mysterious atmosphere, was enfolding her with a terrible embrace. Her heart began to beat violently; and she stopped to listen. What confused, unfamiliar sounds there were in these green vaults!

She knew she was going in the direction of the Pannotshka's grave; but she could not resist the fascination. Her curiosity, mingled with superstitious tremors, and the desire of seeing something extraordinary, carried her onwards. At last she reached the blood-stained spot, and gazed down, with a quaking heart, into the ravine.

It was a wild, enchanted chasm of tangled

L 2

brushwood growing in unpruned luxuriance. The pale grey-green of the wild rose-trees stood out against the dark hue of the nettles. Large ferns sprang up from the damp soil; and the giant hemlock grew in unchecked abundance. Hazel-bushes were crowding up against the sturdy trunks of oaks that had lived for centuries. A strange odour rose from the mingled verdure, an overpowering exhalation, which seemed to steal away her senses. This was the very spot where the demons met at nightfall, to consult what evil they could wreak upon Christians. She remembered how Avdiushka, the crazy boy of Knishi, had been just like other people, until he had wandered hither one twilight, and did not come home till dawn quite an idiot.

Suddenly she heard a loud bleating close behind her, and something rushed past her into the ravine. The blood curdled in her veins, and she tried to flee from the accursed spot. But her limbs failed her, and she would have fallen to the ground if Paul's strong arms had not caught her at that moment. She clung to him with all her might.

"The bleating!" she gasped, pointing to

the thicket, and staring with a frightened look.

"It is nothing but a strayed sheep, my Halya," said Paul; "you will not be frightened now I am with you!"

"No!" she answered, with a sob and a smile. "Why are you so late, Paul? I thought you had forgotten."

"Forgotten!" he echoed, "forgotten! That would be impossible. Why! I never cease to think of you. And I have been waiting here an hour or more, afraid that you had been hindered. Let us sit down, my darling; I have so much to say to you."

Paul looked at her bare feet, and saw that one of them had got a scratch from some bramble. He seated her on the trunk of a fallen tree, and taking off his sheepskin cap, he put both her little feet into it, touching them tenderly.

"Poor little things!" he said, "they will be more comfortable like that. My Halya! I am afraid to say what I must say to you. I am afraid of you."

"Afraid of me!" laughed Halya; but seeing Paul's agitated face, she suddenly became grave.

"Loukyan was arrested yesterday," said Paul.

" Ah! my God!" she answered. "I heard of it; poor old Loukyan!"

"He will be exiled to Siberia!" he continued in an undertone of horror.

"To Siberia! What for? What evil has he done?" asked Halya.

"For reading the New Testament, and preaching God's salvation to those who are in darkness," he replied. He went on to talk of Loukyan's apostolic life and teaching. His own heart was full of the subject, and he spoke of his leader with great warmth.

But Halya listened carelessly. She had not come to the Pannotshka's grave to talk about old Loukyan, the bee-master. She pitied him; but there were more important things to talk about.

"Halya," said Paul, "what I must tell you is this—they all say I shall be chosen presbyter in Loukyan's stead. I am one of the youngest; but I have more learning than any of the rest. Then, my darling, the post of greatest danger will be mine."

"Danger!" she cried, looking at him in perplexity.

"Yes!" he said; "what has befallen Loukyan will befall me sooner or later. I, too, shall be arrested, and sent to Siberia."

In spite of the summer heat and sunshine, a shiver ran through them both as he uttered the dread word Siberia.

"No, no!" she cried, nestling closer to him, "don't do it, Paul! Leave them. Come back to me, and the true Church! Ah! you do not love me; or you would not speak of such things. Do you love the gaol and Siberia better than Knishi, and freedom, and me?"

"No, my Halya," he answered; "but, dearest, I love God and His truth above all things in heaven and earth. Oh! if you only knew the Saviour as I know Him you would understand."

"Then I shall have to marry Panass," sobbed Halya, interrupting him; "old Okhrim came yesterday, and he and my father are making up the match. If you loved me you would save me from Panass. I could persuade my father to give me to you, if you were only a Christian. Oh! why do you make me so unhappy?"

"I knew I must tell you," said Paul,

"because if you became my wife you would have to share my lot. We shall be poor and forsaken, persecuted and exiled; and you could not endure that."

"Yes! I could—with you," replied Halya, in a delicious whisper. She pressed her cheek against his.

"Oh! I love you, Paul!" she cried; "I never loved anyone but you! Don't leave me; don't give me up! I could go to Siberia with you a hundred times rather than marry Panass!"

She lifted up her face, and fixed a long and searching gaze upon him. He was deeply moved; but his eyes were sad and steadfast. She did not find in them a sign of yielding. Her head fell down; and she broke into a passion of weeping.

"There is no chance of happiness for us," said Paul, "or rather there is only one—that you should cast in your lot with us, and let us be married by the German pastor."

Halya shook her head.

"Then God's will be done!" he murmured, yielding to that thread of fatalism which runs through all the life of a Russian peasant, and which gives to them a strange patience with their bitter lot.

They sat together, almost in silence, until the red ball of the sun touched the western horizon; and deep shadows began to creep along the forest glades. The herdsman's horns were heard in the distance; the cattle were being gathered together for the night. Paul led Halya to the outskirts of the forest; and they parted, as lovers part who have met for the last time.

Paul flung himself under a tree and buried his face in his hands. How long he remained in his hopeless reverie he did not know; but when he lifted up his head the stars were hanging like little lamps in the dark blue of the sky. To reach Ostron he must pass through the depths of the forest behind him. He fully believed in the existence of demons; but he had no fear of them. What harm could come to him whom God protected? He strode boldly into the wood.

At some little distance within the forest stood a charcoal-burner's hut, almost fallen into ruins; for since the mischance that had happened to Avdiushka no peasant could be

found to undertake any work so near the
Pannotshka's grave. What was Paul's amazement to see a light shining through the
chinks of the roof and the walls? He crept
stealthily forward, with beating pulses and a
throbbing heart. His curiosity and courage
sustained each other; when one failed the
other prompted him. He could not go on,
and leave this mystery unsolved. At last
he reached the hut near enough to see the
interior through the half-open door. There
sat Valerian; and beside him a man with a
packet of papers in his hand. They were talking in quiet tones.

"I thought I heard a footstep," said the
stranger.

"Impossible!" answered Valerian, with a
laugh; "there is not a soul in Knishi would
venture within a mile of this at night. They
believe in the devil too firmly. The devil has
been of some use for once, my friend."

They resumed their conversation in lower
tones; and Paul stole away as silently as he
had approached the hut.

His mother was watching for his return.
He could see her sitting inside the house,

with her knitting in her hands, and the well-worn New Testament lying on the table before her. Speechless and unhappy he crept to her side, and kneeling down hid his face on her breast.

Ooliana understood what he meant, and her heart was torn with conflicting emotions. She remembered when this beloved head nestled in her bosom as its only resting-place, when no pain or grief troubled it. Her baby was a man now, with a man's passions and qualities. He was suffering grievously; and his very silence was eloquent of his grief. Her tears fell fast upon his dark hair, and she pressed her lips fondly against the bowed head.

"There is no man," she said, "that hath left house, or parents, or brethren, or wife, or children, for the kingdom of God's sake, who shall not receive manifold more in this present time; and in the world to come everlasting life."

CHAPTER XIV.

HALYA'S BETROTHAL.

It was well for Halya that her father was not in when she reached home. He had gone to Okhrim's, and would probably not be back till a late hour. Marfa told her she looked upon the marriage with Panass as quite settled, and she was looking over Halya's wardrobe and the household linen they had spun together for several winters past. The mother seemed to think that any girl must be delighted at so splendid a match, and with such a dowry as her father was willing to give to her.

"Mother!" she cried, "what good will it do me for other girls to envy me? I shall be miserable!"

"Don't say that! It is unlucky," answered her mother. "God is with you. In time you may get used to it, and you will love your husband."

"You don't love my father," said Halya;

"you are afraid of him, and you are happier when he is out of the way. He does not mind striking you, if you displease him, and Panass will treat me the same, as soon as he is tired of me."

They were silent for a little while, Marfa counting out the cloths and towels into tens, when Halya broke out passionately.

" I will not marry him ! " she exclaimed.

" How can you say so ? " asked her mother. " Did you ever know any girl who refused to marry the husband her father chose? It is unheard of. He would beat you, and lock you up, and starve you, and all the men would say he was right. You would ·be obliged to give in ; it is a woman's fate to do as she is ordered. Oh yes! I know. I was a girl once, and I was afraid of Karpo. How I knelt at my father's feet and begged and prayed! I loved someone else, too. Karpo was older than me, and he also loved a poor girl. But our families were rich and they compelled us to marry. It was a bitter sorrow for me. Yes, Halya, you are not the first, and you won't be the last, my poor child."

The poor mother was softened by the

recollection of her own girlhood, and she began
to pity and cry over her daughter. Halya
did not answer; she knew her mother could
not help her.

She wept a good part of the night, and
got up with reddened eyelids and a pale face.
Karpo, coming in to breakfast, scanned her
with an attentive and searching look. He
was fond of his only child, and it vexed him
to think he might have to force her into
marriage with Panass. He watched her closely,
seeing that she ate nothing. She cleared the
table and folded the table-cloth listlessly, not
once glancing at him. It was useless to defer
any explanation.

"Well, daughter," he said, "I believe you
know that God is sending you a good husband.
Okhrim and I are pretty well agreed about the
dowry, and next Sunday we will have the
betrothal feast."

"Father!" cried Halya, kneeling before
him, and hiding her face against his knee,
"I don't want to marry. If you loved me
you wouldn't want to get rid of me in such
a hurry."

"I don't want to marry! I don't want to

marry!" repeated Karpo, with a sneer; "every girl wants to be married, and Panass is the best match in Knishi. Any other girl would light a candle before the icon and dance for joy."

"Father, I dislike Panass; I shall not be happy with him. Don't make me miserable! I am your only child."

Old Karpo felt dissatisfied with himself when he found he could not make his heart as hard as a flint against his daughter.

"Tell me," he said, "are you still thinking of Paul Rudenko?"

"Yes!" whispered Halya, pressing closer to her father.

"But if he goes on as he is he will have all his goods and his lands confiscated," said Karpo; "I know it for certain. Savely and Father Vasili were talking about it. You cannot live upon nothing, my little Halya. You are young and foolish, and do not understand what life is. It is not all petting and befooling one another. Perhaps, though, Paul is going to give up his stupid heresy?" he added, in a softer voice. If Paul would but return to the religion of his forefathers, he would no longer oppose his marriage with Halya.

"No. Oh no!" she sobbed.

"And you would marry a Stundist!" exclaimed Karpo.

"I don't want to marry the one or the other," persisted Halya; "let me stay at home, dear father! I will work, and please you in every way. I will never go out except to church. Oh! let-me stay and live with you."

Marfa had been listening in silence.

"Why hurry her, indeed?" she said now; "let her stay at home and prolong her girlhood. It is the only happy time we women have in life. She will have plenty more chances to go under the yoke."

"Shut up, you fool!" stormed Karpo, glad to find someone to vent his vexation upon; "you see the girl is almost out of her mind and hardly knows what she says, and instead of talking reason and sense to her, you begin wailing about women not being happy. No more nonsense! She shall marry Panass, and there is an end to it. We will have the betrothal feast on Sunday."

He flung himself out of the house, leaving Halya sobbing on the floor beside his chair. Marfa could not offer her any consolation. Both of them were thinking the same thing. It would be impossible for her to marry Paul, and her father would compel her to take another husband. Why not Panass as well as anybody else?

Two days later Karpo went to see Okhrim again, and the next day Okhrim came to see Karpo. They sat together for hours, discussing the most minute details of the dowry, till at last they came to an agreement on all points and shook hands over the bargain.

The same day Karpo told his daughter all was definitely settled. The girl received the fatal news with apparent indifference.

"Thank God! she is all right now," thought Karpo. He even condescended to ask Marfa what she thought of Halya.

"She seems all right," answered the mother prudently.

Indeed, Halya appeared quite reconciled to her fate. She cried no more; but helped her mother, and busied herself about the house in preparation of the approaching feast. Once

M

when she was carrying water home from the
well she met Paul, and greeted him almost
as if he was a mere acquaintance. All was
over between them. It was wrong now even
to think of him.

Long before daylight on Sunday morning Marfa was busy at her oven. Food
enough for a whole regiment of soldiers had
to be cooked. The whole house was turned
upside down. Karpo brought from the cellar
all kinds of liquors, especially mead made
from honey, and vodka. In former days
Ooliana would have been there putting her
hand deftly to everything. Ah! if Paul had
only been the betrothed lover!

Halya took out the marriage-scarf which
she had embroidered so beautifully, weaving
into every stitch bright thoughts of her happy
life with Paul. How often she had pictured
to herself how she would tie it as a sash
round Paul, and then stoop and kiss his hand
in token that she looked upon him as her
master and husband!

Busy as they were, it was essential that
all the family should go to church. It
would not do for anyone to suppose the

preparations for the feast detained them. There was no chance of Paul being there; and Halya's heavy heart was undisturbed. On their return home Marfa and Halya hastily completed their arrangements; and as the church clock struck twelve the guests began to come.

Neither Marfa nor Halya sat down to table; they went to and fro between the oven and the dining-table, serving the guests, and pressing them to eat from one dish after another. Hour after hour they sat feasting, until at last the hungriest guest declared he had had enough. Then at a signal from her father Halya went out, and brought in her marriage scarf, with its rich embroidery. Panass met her in the middle of the room, and she fastened it round him, and, bowing low, was about to kiss his hand. But Panass lifted up her pretty face, and kissed her on the lips.

"It's only once out of hundreds of times!" he said, with a foolish laugh.

The blood rushed back from Halya's face, leaving her as cold and white as marble. It would be better to die, she said to herself.

At dusk Okhrim suggested that the whole company should go down to his house to finish up the night with drinking vodka. There were no women there, he said significantly. At last Halya was left alone, for her mother, worn out with fatigue, crept away to bed. She tore off her rich betrothal dress, unbound the ribbons from her hair, and tossed them, with a coral necklace, on to the floor. They were hateful ornaments to her.

"Oh, Lord! what will become of me! what will become of me!" she murmured in agony; "oh, Paul! you might have saved me! And I love you so! I love you so!"

In the meantime the drinking went on in Okhrim's house until everyone was more or less intoxicated. Okhrim had invited several other guests, among whom was Father Vasili; and Panass assiduously filled up every glass as soon as it was empty. He was celebrating a double triumph; he had won the girl whom he had longed for, and he had ousted his rival Paul, who had always looked upon Halya as his own. Panass drank joyously to his own betrothal.

The revels were carried on far into the

night. At one end of the room half a dozen men were trying to sing together, each one with a different tune, or a different song. In another corner Karpo was caressing the red-headed Audrey, taking him for Halya, and saying in a thick voice that Panass was worth a hundred Pauls; that Paul compared with Panass was like a pig to a horse. These words were caught up by Panass, and excited his drunken imagination.

"Paul Rudenko! who speaks of a pig like him?" he shouted. "I've got Halya; and now I'd like to pound him into powder."

"Look here, boys!" cried one of the younger men, "let us go and make Paul drink in honour of this betrothal."

"Let us go! let us go!" shouted every man who could stand on his feet; and leaving the older men to continue their drunken debauch they set off to Ostron.

The gate of Paul's courtyard was locked, but in a moment it was broken by a rush of strong men against it. Heavy fists knocked at the doors and window shutters. There was a sound of a child crying within, and very quickly Ooliana opened a window.

"What is the matter?" she cried, seeing the house beset by men.

"We want Paul! where is he? where is Paul?" they shouted.

"He is not here," answered Ooliana; "Paul is gone to Kovylsk."

She closed the window sharply, and disappeared.

"She is telling lies!" vociferated Panass; "Paul is frightened, and is hiding indoors. Let us force the door, comrades."

Several of them snatched up a beam which was lying near at hand, and they were about to attack the door, when suddenly it was opened from within, and the tall, dignified form of Ooliana stood in the doorway. The men involuntarily fell back. Ooliana made a step forward, and her whole face and figure were lit up by the moon.

"Why have you come?" she asked; "Panass, Audrey, Danilo, Petro! You are all of you the sons of respectable people: many of them my dear friends. I could not be afraid of you as if you were a band of robbers. What do you want? I have Demyan's little child in my house, very ill, and you have startled him. Tell me what you want."

"We want Paul to come out and drink the health of the bride and bridegroom," said Danilo.

"You ought to be ashamed!" replied Ooliana. "Paul is gone to see Loukyan. Probably he will get into trouble for it; but my son is no coward. He risks everything to help his old friend. He never dreamed that I should be molested by our neighbours. Demyan too is gone, and there are only we two women and a baby in the house. If you don't believe me, come in and see for yourselves."

She opened the door wide, and stood on one side, as if expecting them to enter. The young men looked sheepish, and remained motionless.

"Boys!" she said in her clear and pleasant voice, "I have known every one of you all your lives. This is Sunday night; and most of you went to church this morning, and prayed to God, saying: 'Our Father, lead us not into temptation, but deliver us from evil.' And at night you get drunk, and come

to disturb poor lonely women. I know the
devil tempts you, but you must resist him,
and he will flee from you. Ask God to help
you. You are an industrious man, Panass;
and you, Danilo, are a good son; and Petro
is always helping his neighbours. There is
good in you all. Oh, my sons, be you good
men!"

She confronted the subdued and silenced
crowd for a minute longer, and then with a
cordial "Good-night!" she turned and entered
the house.

The young men felt ashamed to look one
another in the face. They dispersed quietly,
with no more shouting and singing.

CHAPTER XV.

INQUISITORS.

On his return to Kovylsk, Father Paissy went immediately to the Archbishop with a report of what he had learned in Knishi. He stated that he found religion there in a deplorable condition; the Orthodox church almost deserted, and the Stundists flourishing, without let or hindrance either from the Mir or the priest. He feared that the heresy would spread widely; but he had arrested the leader, and he had given wholesome advice and stringent directions to Father Vasili and to the starosta of Knishi.

"And the other heretic?" mumbled the old Archbishop, who was growing childish, but who prided himself on his memory. "The man who chopped the sacred icon to fragments in the market-place. Is he arrested?"

"Alas! no," answered Paissy. "He is hiding somewhere; but we are on his track.

When he is caught, he will be tried together with the Knishi Stundist on the same indictment."

"Very good!" said the Archbishop; "we must not bear the sword of God in vain. We must root out this damnable heresy by the sword, if they will not listen to reason."

The Archbishop proceeded to institute a committee for inquiry into the matter, the members of which were chosen from the Consistory, and Paissy was appointed its secretary. He became, in fact, the heart and soul of it. Along this path promotion lay, and Paissy was profoundly ambitious. He had, moreover, a sincere hatred of all heresy and schism. To him the Orthodox Greek Church was the only way to heaven; and attendance at its services, and due payment of its many claims, were the steps by which to pursue that way. There was no possibility of salvation outside its pale; at any rate, for those who had been born in it. God's uncovenanted mercies might be extended to those nations so geographically unfortunate as to be born beyond the limits of Holy

Russia; but to Russian seceders no mercy could be shown either by God or man.

Though Father Paissy had an inward conviction that Loukyan was one of those fanatics who could not be brought to repentance and recantation, he still felt it his duty to make the attempt. He proposed to the Committee that someone should see what could be done with their prisoner by argument and persuasion, and he was unanimously elected for the task, as being a priest imbued with the most truly Christian principles.

Paissy betook himself to the prison; but his benevolent feeling towards Loukyan received at once a severe shock. He found him and a fellow-Stundist taking a walk together in the prison-yard, their two warders playing in the meantime a game of cards in a corner, where they could not overhear the conversation of their prisoners. This indulgence shown to the obstinate enemies of God and the Church made Paissy's blood boil with indignation. He summoned the superintendent of the gaol, and threatened to denounce him at once to the Governor of the province. He was only appeased by the instant dismissal of the warders and the separation of the prisoners.

After this scene the task of persuasive exhortation was no easy matter, and Paissy went away without exchanging a word with either of the imprisoned Stundists.

A few days afterwards the Committee for preliminary investigation held its first meeting in the Consistory buildings. The room in which they met was adorned with the portraits of eminent archbishops, and behind the head of a large table, covered with green cloth, hung a life-size portrait of the Tzar in a massive gilded frame. The six members of the Committee sat on each side of the table, with Paissy in the middle. Before him was laid a New Testament in gorgeous binding, and beside it was a golden cross brought from the adjoining church, to give a more sacred solemnity to the judicial proceedings.

At a sign from Paissy an official summoned the warders and their prisoners. They entered by different doors, and Loukyan's heart leaped into his mouth as he saw the other prisoner was Stepan. Stepan smiled and nodded slightly. They then bowed three times, as is the custom of the peasantry, first in direct front, and afterwards to the right and left; but neither of them crossed themselves, or bowed to the icons.

They both wore a prison dress, which very much altered their appearance, giving them a meaner and humiliated look. The warders placed them side by side at the foot of the table.

"Prisoners," said Paissy, in his softest tones, "you deserve severe punishment for numerous offences against our holy Church. Your blasphemies have been a scandal to all orthodox people. But our Archbishop, in his fatherly kindness and long-suffering towards you, seeks rather to restore you to religion than to inflict penalties upon you. He will intercede for you to the civil authorities, and get you restored to freedom and to your legal rights, if you repent and expiate your crimes. By public recantation of your errors you will set a good example to those whom you have already misled into the paths of error. Listen closely to what I am about to say."

He paused for a few moments, looking at

them with a steady and searching gaze. Then
he addressed Stepan.

"Stepan Vasiliev," he said, "yielding to
the instigation of the devil, you profaned our
holy religion by publicly cleaving into splinters
several sacred icons. A fragment of these is in
our possession, and we do not doubt that it was
the divine image of the Mother of God! We
shudder at the thought of such sacrilege.
According to law you might be adjudged
to imprisonment, or to hard labour for life
in the mines of Siberia."

"I confess it," answered Stepan; "I destroyed the icons. But I had just read in
the Bible, 'Ye shall not make to yourselves
idols.' The poor ignorant peasants worship
the icons themselves; they call them God, even.
'Here is our God!' they say, and they bow
down to them and worship them——"

He was interrupted by Loukyan, who
was calmer and more experienced than his
fellow-prisoner, and who wanted to prevent
him from ruining his cause by rash admissions.

"He did not gather a crowd, your reverence," he said. "It was in the inn-yard, and
only a few people saw him."

"Hold your tongue!" cried Paissy, raising his voice; "your turn will come soon enough. Then you shall have your say. You fool!" he continued, addressing Stepan, "do you not know that if you offend against an icon you offend against the holy being whom it represents? Do you see this portrait of the Tzar?"

Paissy pointed to the picture hanging on the wall above his head.

"What is it?" he asked. "A piece of canvas covered with colours. But try only to strike it, and what would happen to you? The soldiers would tear you limb from limb. Do you understand, you stupid and ignorant blockhead? The icon is the same as the holy being it represents. If you strike it, you strike the saint or the angel it stands for. You do not understand this, yet you set yourself to teach the people!"

"But if that is so," said Stepan, "if God approves of icons, why does He not defend them from injury? You should leave it with Him. He is all-wise and all-strong."

"He has already avenged His saints by delivering you into our hands," answered Paissy.

"Write down his fanatical and blasphemous answers," he added to his secretary—a young man, a favourite and a distant relation of the Archbishop's.

The bold answers of the iconoclast Stepan did not irritate Paissy. He seemed to him nothing more than many others among the Dissenters—a simple fanatic—not dangerous in themselves, but mere followers of their leaders. Loukyan was evidently the chief person among the heretics of Knishi. If he could be got rid of there would be an end of the heresy.

"Loukyan Petrov," said Paissy, "there are many charges against you. You are put on your trial for unlawfully converting orthodox people to your German heresy. You have privily taught damnable doctrines both to old and young, who have been seduced by you from the true service of Almighty God. At your instigation this unfortunate young man was guilty of a sacrilegious crime. What answer can you make to this?"

"Neither Stepan nor any other soul could I convert," replied Loukyan; "and how could an ignorant, unlearned man like me teach others? It was the Lord Himself who taught them and converted them. If any guilt lies at my door, it is that I read to them the New Testament, and told them what God had done for my own soul. That is the book lying before your reverence on the table. You have it in a golden binding, but we have it bound up in our hearts—a golden treasure, containing the truth from God. It teaches us how we ought to live, and what to believe, and how to worship God. Reading and studying the New Testament is our only crime. We obey the laws; we pay our taxes; we pray for the Tzar every time we meet for worship. We love God, and we live in peace with our neighbours."

"Silence!" cried Paissy; "your tongue is too long. You approved of Stepan's sacrilege?"

"It was not I who approved of it," answered Loukyan.

"That is very praiseworthy," said Paissy, with a sneer. "Write that down, brother Parpheny. Loukyan, the Stundist, did not approve of the destruction of the icons."

"Stay!" said Loukyan. "Whether I

N

approved of it or not I do not say; but God approved of it, as He did when the temple of Baal was destroyed."

Paissy reddened with anger, but he restrained himself, and only said, turning to the secretary—

"Write it down carefully. Loukyan Petrov, you have instigated the people to rebel against the authorities instituted by God and the Tzar. What do you say to that?"

"It is a false accusation," he answered firmly. "We occupy ourselves, not with earthly Governments, but with heavenly. 'My kingdom is not of this world,' says our Lord. It is His kingdom that we seek, and we trouble ourselves with no questions of worldly politics. We obey not only good rulers, but bad ones. But in the matter of religion we obey God only; and neither principalities nor powers of this world, not the Tzar himself, can compel us to obey them rather than God. They may persecute us and slay us; but we shall bear death itself gladly, as the early Christians did, the apostles and the martyrs, who have received the crown of life from our crucified Redeemer."

" Then you compare yourself with the apostles and martyrs," said Paissy sarcastically, "and our orthodox Tzar is like a heathen emperor persecuting the followers of Christ. Is he like Nero or Tiberius ? "

"I know neither Nero nor Tiberius," answered Loukyan, "but God knows and searches the hearts of all men. I say again I make supplication morning and evening for the Tzar, and for all that are in authority under him. We desire only to lead a quiet and peaceable life, in all godliness and honesty."

It was quite in vain that Paissy tried to lead Loukyan into any dangerous remarks against the Government. To him the question of politics was purely indifferent. But as soon as the investigation passed over to religious topics, Loukyan was unexpectedly candid and free-spoken. He admitted that he systematically broke the canonical laws ; that he refused to take the holy sacraments ; that he would not attend the ceremonies of the Church ; that he could not conscientiously pay the priests' dues; and that he had removed the icons from their shrine in his house. He acknowledged to having christened children, and having buried

N 2

the dead, and to conducting a simple form of the Lord's Supper.

"What do you think of the holy saints?" asked Paissy.

"They were men like ourselves," answered Loukyan; "they prayed to God as we pray; they loved Him as we love Him. True they were as strong men, and we are but like babes in Christ. But we too shall grow up into manhood. The apostles saw Christ, and talked and walked with Him; and that makes their testimony of heavenly worth to us. But they were men with like passions as ourselves."

Paissy nodded. This was enough to incriminate Loukyan.

"Write it down—write it down carefully, brother Parpheny," he said to the secretary.

"Well, apostle," he continued cheerfully, "and what do you think of our bishops, metropolitans, and the Holy Synod? In your opinion they are wolves in sheep's clothing, rather than pastors of their flocks?"

Loukyan made no answer. Paissy repeated the question in a more guarded form.

"Even in heaven there are archangels set over the angels," he remarked.

"I do not know about heaven," replied Loukyan; "and we, too, have our pastors and teachers; but we think it unlawful to pay them, except such expenses as they are put to necessarily on our behalf. If any man among us is in want, we supply him with all he needs. But we cannot give money for prayer and spiritual ministry. This comes from heaven, and is the gift of God. No man among us would take money for such an office."

"Write it down!" cried Paissy, in a voice of restrained anger.

The examination went on for hours. Paissy quoted the decrees of the Holy Synod; Loukyan replied with text after text from the New Testament. The decrees of the Holy Synod were often directly contradictory of the New Testament. Paissy grew more and more irritated.

"It is simply a German religion," he cried; "all that you say you have learned from the Germans. The fathers of our Holy Church give quite a different interpretation to the passages you quote. You are among those who wrest the Scriptures to their own destruction.

You have forsaken your mother Church for a German heresy."

"Why should we not learn from the Germans?" asked Loukyan; "but indeed we learn only from the Bible. It does not signify who first brought the light to us; but we who possess it will never plunge into darkness again."

"So you persist obstinately in your heresy," said Paissy. "For the last time I call upon you to bethink yourselves, whether you will repent of this your sin, and make a public confession of your repentance; I will plead your cause with the Archbishop. Otherwise you will fare badly indeed."

"We must first obey God," began Loukyan.

"Leave God alone!" interrupted Paissy, "it is not God whom you obey; but the devil, who is the father of lies. Warders! take them away."

Every one was weary of the discussion, which was entirely useless, and apparently endless. Loukyan and Stepan were led away; and the Committee drew up a report of the proceedings to send in to the Archbishop.

CHAPTER XVI.

IN DEEP WATERS.

LOUKYAN was confined in a solitary cell, and kept apart from the other prisoners, in order to avoid, what had been frequently the case, the spread of Stundism among them. Many of them were dangerous criminals; but they were carefully guarded from the influence of the heretics.

In the same corridor was Stepan's cell, two doors away. They could not communicate with one another, excepting when one passed the door of the other's cell; and if the warder with them was not very strict, he allowed them to exchange a few words of friendship and encouragement,

The prison at Kovylsk consisted of a large, two-storeyed square edifice, with several additional buildings for the accommodation of the staff employed. It stood in the middle of a wide yard, surrounded by a high and

thick wall, which was built half-way up the
second storey. From the cells on the ground-
floor nothing but this wall could be seen.
But from the upper cells it was practicable,
by climbing on a stool, to see over the fields
and the suburbs of the town. The solitary
cells, where the most dreaded prisoners were
confined, were in the upper floor, for the
sake of safety, it being impossible to make
a subterranean passage from them; a mode
of escape not by any means unknown in
Russian prisons.

Loukyan was lodged in one of these cells.
It was small and very dirty; but it was dry
and light. It was six feet wide by ten feet
long; against the wall was a wooden plank
instead of a bedstead, and a horribly filthy
bucket was the only other piece of furniture.
It was a most uncongenial abode for a man
of very cleanly habits, and accustomed to the
pure air of an out-of-door life. But one does
not expect a prison to be congenial; and it
was at least bearable.

Twice a day food was brought to him,
consisting of bread and sour soup at mid-day,
and some kind of prison skilly at night. He

was not allowed to go out for exercise oftener than once in five days. But he felt well, and his mind was perfectly tranquil. He astonished his warder by asking for his New Testament, which had been taken from him. The request was forwarded to the superintendent; and as the reading of religious books, approved of by the Holy Synod, was encouraged in the prisons, he was allowed to have it. Now he could spend his empty hours in reading the beloved records of his Master's life and teaching, finding constantly in them new sources of strength and consolation. Very often he forgot that he was in prison. He was walking with Jesus beside the Sea of Galilee, listening to His voice; or he was standing on the Mount of the Transfiguration, gazing at his glorified Lord; or looking on with tears as the Saviour hung upon the cross; or watching His triumphant ascension into heaven. Loukyan's soul was as free as the larks he saw wheeling up to the blue sky outside the prison walls.

The first evening of his imprisonment he began to sing an evening hymn, but the warder sternly forbade it; and Loukyan obeyed,

and for the future sang only in a whisper to
himself. The days went on monotonously; one
just like the other; until he and Stepan had
been subjected to their first examination.

The day after this interview with his persecutors, Paissy entered his cell accompanied
by the superintendent.   He looked at once
with disapproval at the window, from which
a wide expanse of sky could be seen.   The
cell was too full of pleasant light.

"What! Petr Ivanovitch," he said jest-
ingly to the inspector, "it seems you are
making your prison into an hotel for passing
travellers!"

"How   so?"   said   the   superintendent;
"on   the   contrary, all   my   lodgers   are   per-
manent."

"Furnished apartments," continued Paissy,
looking about him with a smile at the plank
bed and the bucket; "but if you keep them
in such a mansion as this they will never
want to leave."

"Oh! I can alter it, if you wish," said
the superintendent; "I have plenty of rooms
in my mansion, suitable for different guests."

They exchanged a few words in an undertone. On glancing again at Loukyan, Paissy caught sight of the corner of a book protruding from his pocket. Unceremoniously he possessed himself of it.

"What is this, Petr Ivanovitch?" he asked reproachfully.

"The Testament," he answered; "it is accorded by law. I could not refuse it to a prisoner; it is for their good."

"Good for others," said Paissy; "but not good for heretics. I confiscate the book."

"He will not want it where I shall put him," answered the superintendent, with a laugh. They went away, taking the Testament with them.

"It is written in my heart," thought Loukyan: "they cannot tear it out of that."

Hardly half an hour had passed when two warders entered his cell. One of them, a stranger to Loukyan, was a tall, muscular man, with hawk-like eyes, and thin pale lips, compressed into a hard and cruel line. His name was Arefiev; and he was the special warder of the obstinate and refractory prisoners.

"That one?" he asked his comrade,

pointing at the slight and enfeebled form of Loukyan.

"Yes, precisely!" said the other warder. Arefiev snorted contemptuously. He preferred dealing with strong and really refractory prisoners, whom it was worth while to subdue. Was it likely that this thin, quiet old man could be stubborn and obstinate?

"Come out of here, you archangel!" he ordered. Loukyan obeyed instantly. His new warder led him through long, narrow galleries; and after making several turns, took him down some dark and long flights of stairs. Neither of them spoke a word.

"Have you any money?" asked Arefiev bluntly.

"No; what I had in my purse has been taken away," answered Loukyan.

"You fool!" he said, "didn't you know how to hide it, in your hair, or under your arm-pits? But have you any friends in Kovylsk, who would be willing to help you?"

"Oh, yes! I have many, here and at Knishi," replied Loukyan.

"Look here, then! I have different cells," said Arefiev: "I will put you into one of the best."

"Thank you, brother," he answered.

"But what will you pay for it?" asked Arefiev; "I will take five roubles; and only that because you are such a simple old fellow. Will that do?"

"No, no," said Loukyan, shaking his head; "we dare not give any bribes. You must do your duty to your superiors. You must put me where the superintendent bade you. I cannot tempt you to disobedience."

"Ah! that's your tack!" exclaimed Arefiev, with cruel glee; "you're one of the new saints! Very well! you may preach and pray here as long as you like."

He opened with a large key a heavy, iron-cased door, and pushed him into a dark, fetid dungeon. The door slammed—the iron bolt clanked; and Loukyan found himself in utter darkness. His hands touched the cold walls, which were covered by some soft slime. The floor was slippery with all sorts of filth. The atmosphere was so foul and noisome that at first he felt suffocated and giddy. He stood motionless for a few minutes, with closed eyes and bowed head.

When he opened his eyes he found himself no longer in utter darkness. A little pencil of light shone through the key-hole, and faintly illuminated the cell. It fell upon a corner of his awful prison. Then he saw that what he had taken for slime upon the walls were innumerable swarms of creeping things; thousands upon thousands of soft, grey, horrible creatures, covering every inch of the walls. At that sight he shuddered with horror. With the exception of his bees he could not endure insects; and in this hole he would be eaten alive by them. It was as if he had been bound hand and foot, and thrown into their power.

The whole odious mass of vermin seemed to move towards him. Already something was creeping about his skin, and stinging him. Beside himself with loathing and abhorrence, Loukyan fell upon the door, and began to knock vehemently, calling upon Arefiev to come to his help.

Dead silence was all the answer he got. Arefiev was gone to the superintendent to report upon the change made in Loukyan's cell. At last, worn out with his fruitless attempts, Loukyan looked in vain for a clean spot on the floor where he could rest his weary limbs. But as soon as he sank down exhausted new hordes of parasites besieged him. He sprang up again, and pulling his prison-cap closely over his ears to protect at least his head from their attacks, he began to walk to and fro. It was the only way in which to defend himself a little from his greedy foes.

At mid-day Arefiev brought him a jug of water and a piece of rye-bread—the customary diet for those confined in the refractory cells.

"How do you like your new lodging?" he asked, laughing.

Loukyan said nothing.

"Would you like to change it?" he went on; "but now I shall want ten roubles. Don't ask me to take less."

Loukyan still said nothing. If that offer had been made to him an hour earlier, in the first moments of horror and disgust, he might have accepted it through physical weakness. But that awful moment was over. His nerves were somewhat blunted, and his soul had gathered strength. He felt power given to him to resist the temptation.

"What will you give me to take you

into another cell?" said Arefiev; "only you
must come in here for the superintendent to
see you when he comes."

"No," said Loukyan, "I dare not bribe
you; and I cannot practise any deceit. I
must bear whatever trial God may send me."

"Ah! that is what you are, old fool!"
exclaimed Arefiev in a tone of pleasantry;
"well! we shall see what you will say later
on."

He put the scanty meal on the noisome
floor, and went away. Loukyan could not
eat. He covered the jug of water with the
bread, and again paced his narrow cage up
and down. It was about six feet square, and
contained no kind of furniture.

Two hours later he felt the first pang of
hunger. He stooped down to pick up his
rye-bread, and his fingers crushed something
soft and slimy. He threw it with disgust on
the floor; the bread was quickly covered with
a thick layer of creeping things. That day
he neither ate nor drank. By-and-bye absolute darkness filled the dungeon. He was
obliged to walk to and fro with his hand
stretched out to avoid knocking his head

against the walls. Five short steps each way was all the limit of exercise he possessed. Later on he learned to walk easily in the darkness, turning mechanically before he touched the walls. Five steps, and no more. The evening bugles sounded at the barracks. Loukyan was still pacing to and fro in his cage. The night guards came; the prison lights were lit; but still he continued his weary march, hungry, thirsty, worn-out, hardly able to move his feet, until at last, unable to struggle any longer, he sank down on the slippery floor, and fell asleep like one who is dead.

CHAPTER XVII.

THE LOWEST DEPTHS.

THE next morning the Director, in his round of duty, came to see the prisoner. Loukyan pointed out to him the noisome filth of the floor, and the slimy, crawling, living walls. Petr Ivanovitch shrugged his shoulders.

"My orders are to keep you in the refractory cells until you renounce your damnable heresy," he said; "a refractory cell is not a parlour. Say the word, and I will report it at once to Father Paissy."

Loukyan shook his head.

As an act of mercy the Director allowed him to have a parashka, and ordered the water to be brought in a jug with a lid to it.

A few horrible days passed. The torture to which Loukyan was subject was so humiliating and irritating, with no short space of cessation in which to gather courage, that

his soul was caught in bonds as bitter as
death. He was unable to think or pray; his
memory refused to recall the comforting words
of the Gospel he had embraced. Only the
words spoken by Job in his affliction rang
again and again through his wearied brain.
" When I lie down I say, When shall I
arise and the night be gone? and I am full
of tossings to and fro unto the dawning of
the day. My flesh is clothed with worms and
clods of dust; my skin is broken, and become
loathsome." Now and then, however, a voice
within him whispered—"Ye have heard of
the patience of Job, and have seen the end
of the Lord; that the Lord is very pitiful,
and of tender mercy." This seemed like a
message from heaven breathed in the depths
of hell. But Loukyan's physical strength was
decreasing. He could not stand firmly on his
feet, as if he had passed through a severe
illness. When he paced to and fro in his
cage his steps tottered, and he soon grew
tired. Not for a single moment was he permitted to leave his cell and breathe the fresh
air. Only once a day Arefiev opened the door
for a few moments to pass in his allowance

o 2

of rye-bread and water; and Loukyan took
care to be close by the door as long as it
was open. At first he ate all his bread at
once, as the only way to keep it from being
covered with vermin; and he kept the water
in the covered jug, drinking it little by little.
But after three days his appetite failed him
in that fetid hole. He could no longer
swallow the bread.

At the end of the week he was summoned to a second examination. This time
Paissy was alone when Loukyan was brought
in. Stepan was not there, as Paissy did not
wish the prisoners to encourage one another
in their obstinacy. He could hardly recognise
Loukyan, so changed was he in appearance.
This feeble, tottering old man, unwashed and
uncombed, with shrunken limbs and palsied
head, was very different from the hale and
courageous prisoner who had confronted the
Committee a week ago. Paissy gazed at him
with a long and searching look—the look
opponents give to one another before engaging
in a deadly conflict; and his face expressed
great satisfaction. His enemy was sufficiently
weakened, and would prove an easy conquest.

"Well! have you had time to bethink yourself?" he asked.

Loukyan did not answer. He wished to prolong the examination as much as possible; only for the sake of remaining longer in that large room, and of breathing that pure air. Every breath put new life into him.

Paissy, believing that the man was reasoning with himself and wavering in his heresy, did not hurry him.

"The Church would accept a late repentance," he said softly. "It rejoices over the repentance of one sinner more than over a hundred of its faithful sons, who need no repentance. Like a loving mother she must punish her disobedient children; but it is for their good only, that they may be brought back to the path of obedience. You have been severely dealt with, I can see; but it was I who ordered you to the refractory cells. I am sincerely sorry for you, old man; but I do it for the love of your soul, which must be made to submit itself to God, and to those whom God has put over you as your spiritual pastors and masters. It is better to destroy the body, than suffer the soul to sink into the endless torments of hell."

Paissy continued a long exhortation, containing all the time-honoured arguments of inquisitors and persecutors. But he met with no response from his hearer, neither by word nor look. Loukyan was absolutely dumb and motionless.

" Why do you keep silent like a block?" asked Paissy angrily. " Can't you speak?"

" I do not wish to interrupt your reverence," answered Loukyan. " You speak wisely and gently, almost like a brother. Yet you kept me in a hole not fit for a dog or a pig. And I am a man."

" You will fare still worse if you persist in your obstinacy," retorted Paissy in a quiet yet terrible voice. " It would be better for one of you to die than to have hundreds perish in hell-fire through your teaching. You are ignorant men; but there are others still more ignorant, who will follow your foolish example, and be drowned in perdition. It is our sacred duty to protect the flock committed to us, and to cast out and miserably destroy the false teachers through whom

innocent and confiding souls may be eternally
lost. In Knishi alone you have led astray a
score or two of precious sons and daughters
of our Holy Mother Church. They have followed you to their ruin in this world and in
the world to come. Better, I say, it is to
make a sacrifice of you, the head and chief
of the religious rebellion."

Whilst Paissy was repeating these hack-
neyed phrases of inquisitors, Loukyan's white
and worn face changed rapidly in expression.
He was deeply moved by the priest's sophistry,
which was quite new to him. Stepping a
little backwards, and laying a hand on his
throbbing heart, he lifted up his eyes, and a
light shone in them, as if he saw the Being
whom he appealed to.

"My God!" he cried in a lamentable
voice, "if it was not Thy truth that I pro-
claimed, if my teaching was the ruin not the
salvation of my brothers, then I implore Thee,
by the sufferings I have borne for Thee, by
the zeal I have shown for what I believed to
be Thy service, strike me here and now with
Thy just anger. Deprive me of my sinful
tongue! Blind my eyes! Let me never

again take Thy name into my mouth! Wither away my hands that I may never again lift them up to Thee in worthless prayer!"

He finished; his flushed face grew white again. Casting down his eyes, and dropping his arms to his sides, he waited in mingled dread and faith the answer of God to his appeal.

At that moment the worn-out old man was splendid. Scores of people, had they heard and seen him, would have been converted to the new heresy. Paissy saw something of the power with which the Stundist leaders addressed their hearers. He watched Loukyan with lynx-like eyes, and with somewhat assumed indifference.

"Don't play the fool!" he said roughly. "You have no audience save me. Once more I warn you to think of yourself and your family. If you persist in your fanaticism, I will leave you to rot in your cell; or if that fails, I will get you sent to Siberia to hard labour in the mines."

"You have power over the body," answered Loukyan, "to do the worst you can. But the soul you cannot touch. The blood

of the martyrs will fill up the sufferings of
Christ for the Church. He said He had not
come to bring peace on earth, but a sword.
The sword is drawn against us now, but God
Himself will sheathe it by-and-bye."

Paissy was biting his thin lips with rage.
He could have trampled upon the insolent
and obstinate heretic, who was unmoved by
his threats. But he restrained himself. There
was one other loop-hole through which to
escape the humiliation of being vanquished
by an unlettered Stundist.

He drank a glass of water, and began to
write on a large sheet of official paper.
Loukyan, who had a long sight, watched
Paissy mechanically as he wrote, in a bold,
clear hand, "I, the undersigned Loukyan
Petrov, declare." He supposed it was the
report of the examination which would be
read over to him, and he would be required
to sign it.

Having finished his writing, Paissy looked
up with a conciliatory smile in his blue eyes
and on his thin lips.

"Look here, Loukyan, you are a sensible
man." he said; "you must not ruin yourself

for nothing. We have nothing against you and your religion at all, if only you will keep it to yourself. We don't want to interfere. If you will go to hell, to hell you must go. But it is the will of God, and the Tzar's command, that we must maintain and defend the Orthodox Church by every means in our power. It is you Stundists who have introduced heresy—the new teaching, as you call it. Before you, we had nothing of the sort. Our diocese was an exemplary one, not a Dissenter in it. When we have silenced you, it will be the same again. I am deeply grieved for you, my poor fellow. Sign this paper, by which you pledge yourself neither to preach, nor to hold services, nor to attempt to convert others to your new creed. Then we will leave you in peace, and you can go back to your home and family."

With one hand he offered Loukyan the cross to confirm his oath, and with the other the paper he was to sign.

Loukyan put aside the cross, and did not so much as look at the paper.

"Tempter!" he said, "it is a subtle temptation, but the Lord will deliver me from it. Neither your promises nor your threats will move me. Woe is me if I preach not the Gospel!"

Paissy's face was distorted, and his eyes flashed with rage. He lifted up the cross, and struck Loukyan's head with all his might. The old man tottered, but he did not fall. He wiped the blood from his forehead on his sleeve.

"A good use to put the cross to!" he exclaimed, lifting up his hands to ward off another blow.

"Arefiev! warder! whoever is there!" shouted Paissy, "come here! Take the villain away to his cell, and let him rot there. He has dared to lift up his hand against me."

Arefiev, who had been dozing in the ante-room, quickly appeared, collared Loukyan, and haled him out of the room, amid a shower of brutal blows. He did not loose him till they reached the door of the cell, but before fitting the key into the lock he gave him a rough handling, as if he could hardly bear to leave off.

He opened the cell, and there came from it such a rush of foul air that Loukyan recoiled

in horror. Was it possible that he had already
lived seven days in that fetid atmosphere?
It seemed as if he could not survive it for
one hour.

"I will not go in," he cried, putting his
hands against the door-post with the strength
of desperation. "Put me into a cell fit for
men! I demand to see the Director."

"Take that instead of seeing the Director!" said Arefiev, striking him on the head
with the key.

Loukyan caught hold of the key, and by a
sudden movement twisted it out of the
warder's hand and threw it into the corridor.
Arefiev sprang upon him, but Loukyan
struggled like a man on the verge of a preci-
pice; and such was the energy of his despair,
that in spite of his physical weakness Arefiev
could not overpower him. He whistled, and
two other warders came to his aid. They all
three attacked the old man with their keys and
their huge fists. In an instant he was on the
ground, and Arefiev, beside himself with rage,
kicked and trampled upon him as he lay prostrate. His comrades, afraid he might kill the
prisoner, dragged him away, lest they should

all get into trouble. Like a ferocious bull-dog, he struggled against them to get back to Loukyan.

"Why do you go on like this?" said one of the warders. "Have you forgotten what happened to Denisov? Do you want to go to Siberia for murdering a prisoner? Beat him if he deserves it—you are right enough—but you must not kill him. You will be the worse for it yourself."

The warders, among themselves, called Arefiev a cruel wolf—not a man. But for the protection of his superiors, he would have been sent to Siberia long ago for torturing his prisoners. The last of his victims had been Denisov, who died, but his death had been hushed up. Loukyan, they knew, had friends in Kovylsk, and some investigation was sure to be made if he died.

"Let me go! I won't touch him," said Arefiev.

The men watched him closely, but the maddened bull-dog was quieted a little. Loukyan was lying motionless and breathing heavily, like some creature hunted to death. One of the warders, getting hold of the collar of his coat, dragged him into the cell, unresisted.

"Lock him up quickly; we must get back to our posts," he said to Arefiev. The latter caught hold of the heavy iron-clad door and clapped it to with all his might. He did not notice, or, perhaps, pretended not to notice, that Loukyan's right foot lay on the door-sill, and must inevitably be crushed by the closing door. A heart-rending scream was heard from the cell, and when they opened the door again Loukyan was writhing in agony.

"So your toe was caught?" sneered Arefiev. "That's not my fault. Why didn't you keep it out of the way? Never mind!" he added, by way of consolation.

Loukyan was left alone in his horrible cell. His foot had been crushed in spite of his heavy boots. It was soon greatly swollen, and, being pressed upon by the boot, which he could not get off, it gave him excruciating pain. Leaning against the loathsome wall, he began to moan. But Arefiev was accustomed to moans and cries, and paid no attention to him. After a good thrashing, it was natural for a prisoner to moan.

Presently he brought the daily allowance of bread and water. Loukyan lay with half-closed eyes, and moaned in a feeble voice.

"Have you learned reason at last?" asked Arefiev. "You will know for the future how to rebel against me!"

Loukyan could not eat any bread. At night his foot seemed to be a little easier; the pain was less sharp, as if it was quite benumbed. True, the leg now began to ache and burn; but there was nothing pressing on it, and the pain was more bearable. Loukyan even slumbered a little. The sleep refreshed him, and when his mid-day meal came he was able to eat a little; but at night he grew feverish and delirious. All sorts of strange thoughts crowded through his brain, and he had no longer any control over himself.

When, the next day, Arefiev visited the cell as usual at noon, he found his prisoner in a high fever and wildly delirious. The warder was frightened. Here was a new unpleasantness, whilst the old one was still fresh in the minds of his superiors. He locked the cell, and was about to seek out the prison feldsher to come to see the patient, whom he would remove into a better cell, lest he should die like Denisov. But at this moment the Director appeared in the corridor. Arefiev met him with a military salute.

"What have you done with the Stundist, villain?" he demanded angrily.

"Nothing, your honour," he answered; "he was very disorderly the day before last. He struck at Father Paissy, and fought with me. We were obliged to push him into the cell. Just now he is lying down. He is quite quiet."

"I know how you make your prisoners quiet, you brute," said the Director. "Where is he? There are inquiries being made about him."

Arefiev opened the cell door wide, and the light fell in upon the prisoner. His head was stained with dry blood, and his face covered with bruises. One foot was lying in an unnatural and distorted position. Loukyan was insensible.

"You dog! you will get me into trouble again!" shouted the Director, dealing a severe box on the ear to his faithful servant. Arefiev made a jerk with his head, but did not dare to defend himself.

"He began to fight himself," he said; "we were compelled to force him into the cell."

"But his foot, scoundrel! Why have you broken his foot?" he exclaimed, lifting his hand for another blow. Arefiev took a step backward to avoid it.

"By chance, your honour!" he cried, "it caught in the door."

"Have you sent for the feldsher?" he asked.

"Yes, your honour," he replied.

The feldsher came, who was considered skilful enough to attend to the prisoners. He declared fever had set in, and Loukyan must be removed at once to the infirmary.

P

CHAPTER XVIII.

STEPAN'S OUTBREAK.

IT was thanks to Stepan that the Director had
visited Loukyan's cell.

Arefiev was hated by his fellow-warders
for his quarrelsome disposition and brutal
cruelty, which from time to time had brought
down a judicial investigation of the gaol,
disagreeable to all employed in it. The news
of his brutal treatment of Loukyan spread
all over the prison, even with exaggeration.
It was said he had bound his prisoner, and
dragged him across the threshold of the cell,
closing the door upon him in such a way as
to crush many of his bones. All this was
believed, because anything might be expected
from such a brute.

At first the rumour was confined to the
warders, but it soon reached the common
criminals. On the third morning after Loukyan's terrible accident Stepan went out for

exercise; and on passing through the corridor
he passed a band of prisoners, who were being
led back to the cells. One of them called
out to him—

"Have you heard how your Loukyan has
been torn to pieces like an old rope-end?"
he asked.

The warder ordered him to be silent, unless
he wanted to get the same treatment as
Loukyan. Stepan heard no more. But these
few words made an awful impression upon
him. He imagined that Loukyan had been
pitilessly flogged.

When he returned to his cell he watched
till nobody was about except his warder.

"Pafnutitch!" he called.

"What do you want?" asked the warder.

Stepan's relations with Pafnutitch were
tolerably good. He was an old soldier, born
in Moscow, which was Stepan's birthplace;
and during his long hours of duty, he was
in the habit of wiling away the time chatting with his prisoner about the campaigns
in which he had taken part, and asking
him questions in his turn. Stepan was
a man of great intelligence, and knew how

to secure the old soldier's good-will, though his principles did not permit him to use bribery.

"Is it true, Pafnutitch, that Loukyan has been flogged?" he asked.

"Not flogged," he answered; "it was all that wild beast Arefiev; he is a wolf, not a man. He will ruin himself and bring trouble on us all. He has beaten the poor old man almost to death; and they say he broke his legs with the door. If he were really refractory—well! But to deal like that with a quiet man like Loukyan!"

Stepan's blood ran cold.

"How! Broken his legs!" he cried; "but what were the others doing? What is the matter with him now?"

"Who with? With Arefiev?" asked Pafnutitch; "oh, he is just the same as ever. He does not care a straw."

"No, no, Loukyan!" exclaimed Stepan, "what has been done for him?"

"Oh, Loukyan! he is lying still in the refractory cell," he answered.

"But he may die there!"

"Quite possible," said the warder; "it is

not the first case, and that scoundrel gets off every time."

"To the Director! Take me to the Director!" shouted Stepan in a voice of agony.

"Are you in your senses?" asked Pafnutitch. "Do you wish to be put into a refractory cell under that brute Arefiev? He'd enjoy taming a strong young man like you."

"Take me to the Director!" shouted Stepan again and again.

"I won't take you," answered the warder, as he walked off down the corridor after locking the cell door.

Then Stepan began to revolt. He knocked and kicked at the door with all his might, shouted at the top of his voice, and smashed the panes of his little barred window. The warders came, and tried to quiet him with a few blows. They tied him hand and foot; but they dared not gag him without orders. At last the Director was sent for.

"What is the meaning of this?" demanded the Director. "Are you about to stir up a riot? I will do you prompt justice."

"I do not want to make a riot," answered Stepan, almost beside himself with indignation;

"but it is illegal to torture prisoners—to break their bones——"

"Who is torturing you?" interrupted the Director. "Who has broken your bones? You are talking sheer nonsense."

"Nobody is hurting me," he answered; "but my comrade Loukyan——"

"Well! what has that to do with you?" again interrupted the Director. "Are you an inspector of the prison? How do you know what has happened to Loukyan? I know nothing about him."

"Be so good, for Christ's sake," implored Stepan once more, in his voice of agony, "to go and see for yourself whether it is true or not! And punish me as you please. I could not get anyone to fetch you till I began to revolt."

The Director ordered Stepan to be put on a diet of bread and water as a punishment. But he followed his advice, and went to make an investigation. Areliev's habits were well known to him, and it would be well to hush up the matter before it went any further.

The same evening Pafnutitch appeared with a guilty face at the door of Stepan's cell.

"Stepan! Stepan!" he called in a gentle voice. He felt grateful to his prisoner that he had not betrayed him to the Director as being his informant of Loukyan's punishment.

"What do you want?" asked Stepan sternly.

"Don't be angry with me for what happened this morning," he said: "I mean for the blows we gave you and so on. You will understand yourself it was our duty."

"God will forgive you," said Stepan; "I am not angry with you. Christ suffered in the same way; they scourged Him and smote Him. The disciple is not greater than his Lord. If they hated Him, they will hate us also."

"You have done me a great service to-day," went on the warder; "what would have been done to me if you had said I had told you about Loukyan! When he put the question to you my heart was in my mouth for fear. 'I am lost,' I thought. But you kept quiet. You returned me good for evil."

"But I only did what I ought," said Stepan; "I could not betray you."

"Anyone else would have done so, simply

out of spite," said the old soldier; "after those
blows too! But there! you may be kind to
many a prisoner, and they turn all at once
on you and play you such a trick as you never
forget. But you Stundists are like the saints
themselves."

"And why?" answered Stepan, in a low
voice, lest they should be overheard, "because
we set the Lord Jesus Christ before us as
our pattern. We read how He bore with persecution even unto death, and we strive to
bear our affliction as He did. We believe that
He is with us, though we cannot see Him,
and so we have strength to bear all things.
We could not call ourselves Christians if we
forgot Him."

He spoke for some time earnestly, and
Pafnutitch seemed to listen intently. But it
was evident he did not understand Stepan.
His brain worked very slowly, and Stepan's
words and thoughts were not familiar to him.
One thing, however, he comprehended, that
he was addressed as a friend, not as a warder,
or a foolish old man, and this touched him
to the heart.

"As for that order to starve you on bread

and water for a whole month," he said, when
Stepan paused for a moment, wondering how
he could speak more simply to him, "you
need not trouble yourself about that. I will
bring you secretly some of my own rations.
And if you wish to send out any news to
your wife, or mother, or sweetheart, trust
me. I will take a message or a letter, and
you shall not tip me for it, because you
think it wrong."

Stepan was puzzled. He could not have
bribed the man; but was it right to accept this offer? Yet it was of great importance the friends outside should know about
Loukyan.

"I have neither wife nor sweetheart, thank
God!" he said, "nor a mother. But I want
to send news to some friends, if you have
anybody who could go over——"

"To be sure I have," interrupted Pafnutitch;
"my nephew is living with me, the son of
of my deceased sister. His name is Mitiushka.
He is the son of her first husband, because
she, Matriona, married two husbands. The
first was——"

"Well, then!" said Stepan, "send the boy

Mitiushka to my friends at Ostron, the village Loukyan came from. It is about twenty miles from here, near Knishi. Tell him to inquire for Paul Rudenko. He must tell him what has happened to Loukyan, and they will send some of the brethren to minister to his wants. You know what sort of attendance he will get in the hospital."

"To be sure," said Pafnutitch, "I will send the boy the first thing to-morrow."

Early the next morning Mitiushka, a flaxen-haired boy of fifteen, set off for Ostron. He reached it after nightfall. The little village seemed asleep; not a soul was to be seen, and the boy was afraid to knock at any of the closed doors. He walked up and down the deserted street, vainly hoping to meet with somebody to direct him to Paul Rudenko. At last he noticed a stream of light shining through one of the windows. He approached it cautiously, and leaning against a railing tried to see what was going on within the house. The fence cracked under his weight, and the window was suddenly opened. Mitiushka took to his heels and ran away, only stopping when he lost his breath. But his errand had not been done. More cautiously than before he crept back again to reconnoitre the lighted window. It was closed, and nobody could be seen through the thick, greenish glass. But at that moment a quiet, kindly voice called to him.

"What do you want, my boy?" it inquired.

At first Mitiushka was taking to flight again, but the same voice went on—

"Don't be afraid. I won't do you any harm."

Mitiushka stopped. He was very curious to know who this kind man was. The gentle voice continued speaking—

"Perhaps you are in great need. You are hungry, or almost naked; or you want wood to make a fire. Well! I will supply your needs. You have only to tell me, and I will give you what I have. But to steal about in this way is not right, my boy. You are quite young; and it is easy to fall into bad ways, and offend both God and man."

Mitiushka blushed in the darkness, and tears stood in his eyes. His voice trembled.

"I did not come to steal," he said. "I was sent—I want Paul Rudenko, the Stundist. I have a secret message for him, himself," he added, with pride.

"I am Paul Rudenko, whom you are seeking," answered Paul; "who has sent you?"

"My uncle," he replied; "he is a warder in the prison at Kovylsk. It is about a man named Loukyan."

"Come in! come in!" said Paul eagerly; "you shall tell me inside the house."

He helped the boy over the fence, and aroused his mother, who was gone to bed. Together they heard all that Mitiushka knew about Loukyan.

"I must go to-morrow," exclaimed Paul.

"Yes," said Ooliana sorrowfully; "and when you are at Kovylsk, go and see Morkovin. He knows everybody, and can help you."

Paul shook his head dubiously.

"He is so timid," he said, "like a frightened hare.. He has a good heart; but I can't reckon on much help from him."

Early in the morning Paul started in his cart, taking the boy with him to within two versts of Kovylsk. It was necessary to be very cautious for the warder's sake. Paul went to his lodging, but the old soldier could give him no further news of Loukyan, except that he had been removed from the prison infirmary to the city hospital, where access to him would be more practicable. It was at the other end of the town, near the street where Morkovin lived; and Paul at once proceeded to call upon him.

It was night, and Morkovin was not expecting anyone; so a sudden knock at his door terrified him.

"Who is there?" he asked, before unfastening his bolts and bars.

"It is Paul Rudenko: let me in," answered Paul, very softly.

The door opened, and on the threshold appeared the troubled face and trembling form of a man of about forty-five years of age. He was of small stature, with a bird-like face, and a beard like a goat. His cotton cassock was worn out at the elbows. He wore in the house his old church clothes, for he had been for five years a verger in the cathedral. He had secretly joined the Stundists, but had not courage to do so openly, the more so as being an ex-verger he would have met with more condign punishment. He was now getting his living by selling vegetables. Morkovin lighted a thin tallow candle, which gave a feeble glimmer, and led Paul into his room, seating him in the place of honour under the icons. For fear of the authorities Morkovin had not removed them, but he had drawn a curtain across them to conceal them from his Stundist brethren.

It appeared that Morkovin knew nothing about Loukyan, except that one of the Consistory clerks had told him about the preliminary investigation.

"They brought seventeen charges against Loukyan!" said Morkovin, shuddering; "seventeen! and for each one he might be sent to Siberia!"

Paul listened thoughtfully. But he was not so much alarmed at the prospect of an exile to Siberia in the future as with the present condition of Loukyan in the hospital.

CHAPTER XIX.

SAFE HOME.

LOUKYAN had been carried from the refractory
cell to the prison infirmary. When they began to undress him there, it was found
necessary to cut away the thick leather boot
from the broken foot. On seeing its state
the feldsher shook his head, and uttered a
low significant hissing. It was dark purple,
with black stripes, from internal hæmorrhage.
One of the city doctors was summoned, and
he agreed with the apothecary that amputation
was necessary. He advised the Director to
allow him to transfer the patient to the city
hospital for the operation, as there only could
he receive all the needful attention.

" Your prisoner cannot escape on one foot,"
he said grimly.

In the statement sent by the Director to
the hospital authorities, no mention was made
of the brutal handling to which the prisoner

had been subjected. The accident was laid
to his own carelessness, and to his obstinacy
in not calling attention to his sufferings.
The Director always screened Arefiev when
possible, in order to maintain discipline, and
to keep at hand this wild beast, ready to fly
at the throat of an insubordinate prisoner, at
the first signal from his superior officer. There
were some cells the Director never entered
without Arefiev at his heels. It was well to
shut one's eyes to an occasional display of
brutality for his own pleasure.

When, after long hours of unconsciousness
and delirium, Loukyan came to himself, he at
first fancied he must be in some ante-court of
heaven. The blessed light was shining all
around him, and fresh air played about his
face; he drank it in with long draughts. He
felt clean and purified. He was lying on a
bed, with white sheets and warm blankets
stretched over him. It was very quiet, but
there was no longer the dead silence of the
pit where he had lain. A murmur of voices
was in his ears. But he was too weak to
lift his head and look about him. His eyes
could see the blue sky shining through a

window near his bed. A kind hand held a cup to his lips; he drank, and fell asleep again.

When he awoke his mind and memory were perfectly clear. The nurse told him where he was, in the city hospital, and he understood all. There was no doubt in his mind that death was near—the angel who would carry his soul from his maimed and suffering body into the presence of the Lord and Master, whom he had loved and served so faithfully. An ineffable peace took possession of Loukyan's soul. Not a wave of trouble rolled across the tranquil sea on which his little bark was floating into a harbour of glory. An extraordinary sweetness and light shone on his pallid and hollow face. The nurses paused and looked at him as they passed his narrow bed, wondering to themselves what thoughts could call such a beatific expression to his face.

The morning after Paul reached Kovylsk, he presented himself in the visitors' room at the hospital. He could get no information about Loukyan at first, until one of the male attendants told him that he was lying in one

Q

of the wards; but as he was a prisoner, no one could see him without a permit from the authorities.

"He is very ill," said the man. "They dare not take off his foot, and that is his only chance."

Paul hastened to the Consistory, but Paissy was not there, and no one else could give him the necessary permission. Paul tried tipping, for this was not a bribe to make a man neglect his duty, but to fulfil it. But he was assured that neither tips nor prayers would be of any avail. He must come the next day, when very likely Paissy would be there.

But it was on the third day only that Paul succeeded in getting an audience with Paissy, through the influence of Morkovin, and the judicious expenditure of three roubles. He earnestly made known his request to Paissy.

"Ah! you are from Ostron," said Paissy. "A relation of Loukyan's?"

"No, your reverence," replied Paul; "Louk-yan is not of kin to us."

"Well! well! you are related to him

spiritually?" said Paissy. "You belong to his flock?"

"We are near neighbours, and his family have asked me to go to see him," said Paul, cautiously evading the question.

"I understand," replied Paissy with a sneer. "The flock sends a benefaction to the apostle, and look for a blessed epistle from him to strengthen their faith."

"He could not write any epistle now!" exclaimed Paul. "He is lying near to death in the hospital, after being terribly beaten in prison."

Paissy pretended not to know about it.

"In the hospital! Terribly beaten in prison!" he repeated. "I must make inquiry into this; and until I know all about it I cannot give you permission to see him. Begone!"

"Oh! your reverence," cried Paul, "he may be dying even now. He has people dependent upon him; he will want to make some provision for them. For Christ's sake, I implore you to let me see him to-day."

"When I know all the circumstances," said Paissy coldly, "I will decide whether

Q 2

I can give you permission to see him or not.
You may call the day after to-morrow. I
have no time to waste with you."

At this moment a clerk entered and
whispered something to Paissy.

"Let him come in! let him come in!"
he exclaimed hurriedly. "Do not keep him
waiting a moment. Begone!" he added to
Paul, who stood hesitating, as if he had still
some petition to urge.

Paul bowed, and went away with downcast head, and a heart full of sorrow. He
saw with what sort of man he had to deal,
and feared that he should get no indulgence
from him. At the door he met Valerian,
who gazed into his face with his kind yet
melancholy eyes.

"Take courage," he whispered. "My
errand is the same as yours, and I shall
succeed."

The few days during which Loukyan had
been in the hospital had made a great change
in him. Though he was still absolutely at
peace, he had begun to notice more what
passed around him in the common ward
where he was lying. On each side, and in

front of him, stood rows of beds. Next to him on the right-hand lay a sick man in great danger, who never ceased moaning. The patients who were well enough to leave their beds strolled up and down in long grey coats, not unlike those worn in the prison. At first Loukyan supposed himself to be in the prison infirmary. These grey figures, with their haggard faces and slow steps, did not look like free men.

"How do you feel now?" asked one of the male attendants, approaching Loukyan.

"All right!" he answered cheerfully.

"How is your leg? Do you feel any pain?" he asked again.

"No; I do not feel any pain at all," he replied.

The attendant shook his head, and touched the wound.

"Does it hurt?" he inquired.

"Not a bit," said Loukyan. "I do not feel as if there was anything there."

The doctor came to examine him, and shook his head too. All present in the ward watched and listened with anxiety. As soon as he was gone the attendant was besieged with questions.

"Will they take the foot off?" they asked.

"I believe so, my good fellows," he answered.

"Ah, how horrible it is!" cried one of them. "One can swallow nothing for a whole week after seeing a man cut about while he's alive."

There was no accommodation for carrying out any operation in privacy, so that the most serious operation was performed in sight of the other patients.

"If he were only a Christian!" said a fishmonger, who had undergone an operation a short time before; "but he is a damnable Stundist, and we must suffer on his account. They should not put him in company with Christian men like us."

"Why is he worse than we are, comrade?" asked another patient.

"Worse!" exclaimed the fishmonger; "why, he is a Stundist, so they say. He has renounced Christ, and the saints, and the Holy Virgin even! The Stundists say she was a German, and everybody knows she was a born Russian, and Holy Orthodox! That's one of their lies! You ask him about it," he said to the attendant.

But the steward had no time to take part in a theological discussion, however interesting. The doctor had just called him outside the ward. When he returned, he announced that Loukyan was not going to suffer amputation.

"But why?" they all asked eagerly.

"He is sure to die before long," was the answer, "and it is of no use taking the trouble. He could not outlive it."

There was no attempt to conceal the fact, or to carry on the conversation unheard by Loukyan. In almost all countries a peasant faces death calmly, and talks of it openly. Loukyan heard all that was said, and a smile, pathetic and glad, dawned upon his face. He had a desire to depart and be with Christ; yet he could not help mourning for those he must leave behind him in great peril and affliction.

"And my son Paul!" he murmured to himself.

At that moment it seemed as if all other figures vanished from the ward, and only Paul stood in sight, looking down on him with unspeakable love and sympathy in his eyes. Had God sent Paul to him in a vision? But at Paul's side stood Valerian, who did not look at all like a vision. Yet Loukyan gazed at them almost in bewilderment. Disturbed by his silence, Paul stooped down over his bed.

"Don't you know me?" he asked. "I am Paul, from Ostron."

"I thought it was a vision, and God had sent it," answered Loukyan in a weak voice. "Who is with you?"

"This is Valerian Petrovitch," he replied. "I could not have got permission to see you but for him."

"That is good," said Loukyan. "God will reward him! If you had been much later you would not have found me alive."

Valerian approached the dying man and examined him carefully, like a doctor. Paul watched him with profound anxiety.

"Don't grieve too much, my son," said Loukyan. "I know myself my hour is come. Paul! I have so longed to hear your voice once more, singing as I think the angels will sing when I enter heaven. Sing me, 'Safe Home.' Could you?"

Paul lifted himself up, and summoned all his courage. The patients gathered round the bed. The fishmonger stood in the front, staring. Paul's clear, melodious voice rang through the ward. He sang a hymn well known in the Greek Church, and a few voices joined with him in the refrain of each verse—

> " Safe home, safe home in port!
>   Rent cordage, shattered deck,
>   Torn sails, provisions short,
>   And only not a wreck:
>   But oh! the joy upon the shore
>   To tell our voyage-perils o'er.

> " The prize, the prize secure!
>   The athlete nearly fell;
>   Bare all he *could* endure,
>   And bare not always well:
>   But he may smile at troubles gone
>   Who sets the victor-garland on!

> " No more the foe can harm:
>   No more of leaguer'd camp,
>   And cry of night-alarm,
>   And need of ready lamp;
>   And yet how nearly he had failed—
>   How nearly had that foe prevailed!

" The lamb is in the fold,
　　In perfect safety penned :
The lion once had hold,
　　And thought to make an end ;
But One came by with wounded side,
And for the sheep the Shepherd died.

" The exile is at home !
　　Oh nights and days of tears !
Oh longings not to roam !
　　Oh sins, and doubts, and fears !
What matter now, when (so men say)
The King has wiped those tears away ? "

The doctors and their staff were by this time visiting another ward, so there was nobody to interrupt Paul's song.

"That is like heaven !" breathed Loukyan when the hymn was finished.

Paul flung himself on his knees beside the bed, and pressed his face on Loukyan's pillow, sobbing like a child. A profound silence filled the ward.

" I have fought a good fight !" said Loukyan joyously, " I have finished my course. I have kept the faith. Henceforth there is laid up for me a crown of glory, which the Judge, the righteous Lord, shall give me in that day."

Then with a sudden change of tone to one of humble simplicity, he added, "Lord, if I have said these words presumptuously, forgive thy servant."

He lay silent for a few minutes, as if to gather strength. Then he turned to Paul, and with a great effort laid his hand on the head pressed against his pillow.

"I leave you to go on with my work," he murmured; "the harvest is rich and great, but the labourers are few. I have laboured, and you will enter into my labours. Feed the hungry, clothe the naked; visit those who are sick and in prison. Remember our Lord says, "If ye do this to the least among my brethren, ye do it unto Me."

"How can I take your place?" said Paul.

"We can do all things through Christ, who strengthens us," Loukyan answered. "He will never leave you nor forsake you. Have faith in Him."

Paul raised his head, and wiped away the tears which dimmed his sight. Loukyan's peaceful face was clear to him now.

"I was afraid to take a task too heavy for me," he said.

The eyes of the dying man grew bright as they rested on Paul's young face.

"Too heavy for you; but not too heavy for you and our Lord," he said. "You will lift up that cross, and carry it for the glory of God. I can foresee your end, my son. Much tribulation and sore affliction for the flesh; but the sunshine of God for the spirit. It will be well with you to the end, even if you give your life for our faith, as I have done——"

Loukyan's voice became strong and sonorous. He raised himself on his bed, and Valerian quickly stepped to his aid, and supported him. A wonderfully solemn gladness shone in his face. He stretched out his hands with a gesture of welcome.

"Can this be death?" he cried in a tone of triumph. "Oh! it is life! It is life eternal!"

A great excitement possessed the circle of bystanders. One or two kissed Loukyan's hands; others pushed forward, if only to touch his bed. Many of them embraced Paul. All were weeping as if their dearest friend was passing away. Loukyan sank back again on his pillow, with glazing eyes, and with a grey pallor on his face.

Valerian watched the sad scene with deep emotion. He was shaken, too, but in a different way. It appeared to him as a burst of fanaticism, and an aimless wasting of spiritual energy, which might have been used for a far better cause. With a sigh he left the ward.

The next morning when Paul arrived at the hospital, he heard that Loukyan's corpse was in the mortuary. He was permitted to see it. There it lay, next to another dead man, with an air of infinite repose and everlasting peace on the worn features. It was buried the same night secretly, by order of the Consistory; because rumours about him were rife in the town, and neither the clerical nor the civil authorities wished to have the manner of his death investigated. The Stundists could not learn where his grave was.

CHAPTER XX.

VALERIAN THE AGNOSTIC.

Paul was putting his horse into his cart
for his return home, when Morkovin hurriedly
appeared, hatless, and breathless with fright, to
say that two gentlemen were inquiring for
him, one of whom looked like a Government
official. An official was an object of terror to
poor Morkovin.

He and Paul went into the house, and found
Valerian, who had brought with him the secretary of the justice of peace.

"We have some business to talk over
with you," said Valerian. "We want to take
action for the murder of Loukyan; and I am
come to ask your opinion as a representative
of the Stundists."

"Of course I approve of it," cried Paul
eagerly. "What do you think, Morkovin?"

Morkovin waved his hands deprecatingly.

"Don't ask me," he said; "nothing

will come of it. You will only get into trouble."

"Nonsense!" declared Valerian; "our laws will not allow of such barbarities. Anyhow, such a scandalous case must not be left to pass unnoticed like that."

"But what can you do against them?" Morkovin persisted. "They are all one lot and hang together. You will present your petition to the Public Prosecutor; but as the case belongs to the Ecclesiastical Department, it will be sent on to the Consistory, to this same Father Paissy himself. I tell you a raven does not pick out a raven's eyes. You will get into trouble, that is all."

"But it is the right thing to do," said Valerian; "if we are all afraid of getting into trouble every sort of wrong will prosper. I could not rest without doing something."

His opinion prevailed. Together with Paul he drew up a draft of the complaint to the Public Prosecutor. In it were related the facts of the case, as far as they knew them, and an investigation was urgently required.

The secretary willingly undertook to re-write the petition with the customary formalities,

and to send it down to Valerian for his sig-
nature.   It was decided that Paul, as a
Stundist, should be kept out of it.

Valerian had come to Kovylsk in a return
post-carriage ; so he willingly accepted Paul's
offer to drive him home in his cart.   The
afternoon had come before they started on their
long drive.   It was a clear, sunny day in
autumn, and the summer heat was gone.
From the fields rose a thin white mist, which
was driven to and fro by a slight breeze, here
and there looking as if semi-transparent sails
were gliding over the waves of a green sea.

The far-off woodlands were wrapped in dark
blue, and were already mingling indistinguish-
ably with the blue horizon.   The road stretched
before them, a long white line, altogether lost
in the distance.   Paul dropped the reins, leaving
his horse full freedom ; the beast was going
home, and knew it.   Paul was longing to have
an earnest conversation with the man whom
he had hitherto instinctively avoided.

The feeling of distrust Valerian had evoked
in him was replaced by one of deep gratitude
and sympathy.   Without his timely aid he
would never have seen Loukyan again.   Though

Valerian had never approached the subject of religion with him, Paul now felt convinced that he could not be an unbeliever. Scholars and philosophers might have their own modes of speech; but he no longer doubted that Valerian believed in his own way, and that in secret he was full of sympathy with the Stundists. His mother had always told him it was so; and now he was fully satisfied she was right.

Paul was five years younger than Valerian, and with all the eagerness of youth, he began to talk to him of Loukyan's glorious death, and of the good news he had heard in Kovylsk of the spread of Stundism. There had been many conversions lately, in spite of the growing persecution—a relentless and deadly persecution, which seemed to have its spies everywhere. It seemed only to deepen the enthusiasm among the brethren, and to awaken sympathy for them among the orthodox.

"God's truth penetrates everywhere, even into the cathedrals and the prisons," said Paul; "as it was in the days of Nero, when St. Paul was put to death, so it is now."

"Indeed?" said Valerian, in a tone of curiosity.

R

Paul told him of a prison warder and some old colleagues of Morkovin who had lately joined the Stundists. Valerian listened attentively; the spread of Stundism among the peasantry was profoundly interesting to him. He saw in it a field where his own political propagandism ought to find good soil. This confirmed Paul in his ingenuous supposition that Valerian was a believer, and it gave him courage to speak plainly.

"I want to ask you a question, Valerian Petrovitch," he began, looking away from his companion; "do not be angry with me. I speak to you from my heart."

"Pray ask me any question. Why should I be angry?" replied Valerian encouragingly.

"What, then, are your views about religion?" asked Paul, turning his honest and serious gaze upon him; "I hear people talk all sorts of nonsense about you, and I have partly believed it. But now I know you better. You are like Loukyan, always ready to help anyone who is in need of help, as if they were your brethren. Now you are willing to get yourself into trouble for Loukyan's sake. How can it be that you should care so much for the bodies of people, and have no care for their souls?"

"But I do care," replied Valerian; "when I meet with a sensible and sober man or boy I provide him with books for his improvement. Have you not seen any of them?"

"Oh yes, I have," said Paul; "books upon agriculture, and the care of cattle. About the stars, too, and the history of former times. They are good books."

"There are others which you have not seen," continued Valerian, with a penetrating glance at Paul's earnest face; "those books which you say are good, are all food for the brain—that is for the soul."

Paul looked at him with a perplexed expression.

"Is the brain the soul?" he asked; "you are a learned man, Valerian Petrovitch. Have then the animals souls as we have? But all those books, good as they are, are vanity if the man who reads them knows nothing about God. If you can teach a man how his soul can be saved from sin, he will be grateful to you."

"Of course he would! But more than

R 2

that, he would make you rich. He would pay handsomely for his soul's salvation. The priests found out that long ago," answered Valerian, rolling up a cigarette. He did not want to enter into a religious discussion, and wished to pass over the question with a joke.

"Oh! the priests!" repeated Paul gravely ; "who does not know they think chiefly of plundering and fleecing their people both alive and dead? But I was speaking of the religion of the New Testament. It says, ' Freely ye have received, freely give ! ' And again, ' And him that taketh away thy cloak, forbid not to take thy coat also.'"

"One would go very naked at times," said Valerian.

"But that is not like the priests," continued Paul.

He spoke of his religious views, not like a controversialist, but as a simple peasant, penetrated by the pure, unselfish teaching of the Gospel. The social condition of the world would be altogether changed, it appeared to him, by a religion of true brotherly love.

Paul was deeply moved. His mother, he knew, was praying fervently for Valerian's conversion, and as by an inspiration from heaven, his own soul yearned for it also. The image of Loukyan lying in Valerian's arms was before his eyes, and he sincerely believed that a portion of Loukyan's spirit had descended upon himself. If Valerian could be won to God through him at this hour, how certain would he be that he was chosen to be a leader and a teacher of the people!

Valerian listened to him with profound interest. Never before had he heard a simple peasant so eloquent. Paul attributed his attention to other motives, and proceeded to expound all the simple tenets of the Stundists; their objection to a paid priesthood, their abhorrence of icon-worship, their opposition to vodka drinking, and to war, and their doctrine of universal brotherly love.

"What you say about love and brotherhood is quite right," said Valerian; "all right-minded people desire it, and work for it. But all that has nothing to do with religion, either of the Orthodox Church, or the Stundists."

Paul looked astonished, not understanding how one thing could exist without the other.

"The priests are persecuting you in the

name of the same Christ, and quote texts from
the same Bible," said Valerian.

"But those who raise up persecutions
cannot be real Christians," he replied. "If
they obeyed Christ they would not hate and
persecute us."

Valerian listlessly nodded his head. Paul
had uttered a truism.

"But suppose for one moment," he said,
"that the Stundists were the most numerous
and the strongest, would you not pull down
the orthodox churches, and destroy the icons,
and shut up the public-houses, and try to
compel people to agree with your doctrines?
The orthodox people would get it hot from
you, and cry out that they were being persecuted and made martyrs of. Are you sure
you would not annihilate them for the glory
of God?"

Paul felt a little staggered. This side of
the question had never occurred to him. It
was true he would ruthlessly destroy the
icons, and shut up the vodka shops. But
could he be guilty of any other form of
persecution?

"No," he answered, shaking his head.

"Our Lord says: 'All they that take the sword shall perish by the sword.' Christ would not have any one persecuted; and when the people are left alone, they do not persecute us for our religion. It is the priests who stir them up against us."

"Your priests would do the same," said Valerian in an undertone, as if speaking to himself. He turned aside, looking at the mist-laden fields and the distant horizon.

"But we have no priests," persisted Paul. "Was our Loukyan a priest?"

"No, no!" replied Valerian, turning to him with vivacity; "Loukyan was an apostle. But the apostles are the forerunners of the priests. First come Peter, Paul, Luke—they sow the seed; then come Father Vasili and Father Paissy to gather in the harvest. It seems a law of nature, and nothing can be done against it."

He puffed at his cigarette energetically, sincerely anxious to end the conversation. But Paul could not be put off with his half sayings.

"But what then are your real views?" he exclaimed.

Valerian did not respond at once; he was wavering. It seemed a pity to disturb the harmonious convictions and the peace of mind of this single-hearted and enthusiastic young peasant. But he felt sorry at the same time to leave such an able man to throw himself away upon a groundless illusion. Breaking does not always imply destroying. Stones cast down from an insecure building may form a new, more solid, and better edifice. Valerian had his own convictions, and the desire to convert Paul to them overpowered him.

"In my opinion," he said, "the world would be wiser and happier if we got rid of these things altogether."

"What things?" asked Paul gravely.

"All these."

He laid his hand on a bag of books, chiefly New Testaments and hymn-books, which Paul was taking home to Ostron. Paul looked at him rather with pity than reproach.

"They are mostly God's Word," he said; "there are a few hymn-books. The earth and the heavens may pass away, but the Word of the Lord abides for ever. You may not believe it," he added, turning to Valerian and smiling radiantly, "but something happens to me in my own life, it seems a trifle, of no concern, yet I find something in the Testament that exactly meets my case. I am struck with astonishment."

Valerian smiled back again.

"What is the Word of God?" he asked.

"The Bible; above all, the New Testament," answered Paul promptly.

"But every religion has its sacred book," said Valerian; "and the priests declare that they also have the Word of God. The Jews hold to the Old Testament, and reject the New; the Mahomedans have their Koran; the Buddhists their Rig-Veda. How can you be sure you possess the true and only Word of God?"

Paul looked perplexed and disconcerted. No doubt had ever been presented to him before as to the Bible. The Orthodox Church itself accepted it as a true and only revelation.

"Give me your Testament," said Valerian. Turning over the leaves like one well acquainted with its contents, he pointed out the apparent discrepancies and contradictions in the Gospels. Paul read and listened with ever-deepening dismay.

"Look here!" said Valerian, reading the story of the dumbness of Zacharias, the father of John the Baptist, "it is said that after being struck dumb, he continued his service in the Temple. Have you got the Old Testament with you?"

Paul gave him a copy of the whole Bible.

"Good!" he said. "Now listen! In Leviticus the strict command is given by Jehovah: 'Speak unto Aaron, saying: "Whosoever he be of thy seed in their generations that hath any blemish, let him not approach to offer the bread of his God."' And again· '"No man that hath a blemish of the seed of Aaron shall come nigh to offer the offerings of the Lord made by fire: he hath a blemish; he shall not come nigh to offer the bread of his God. He shall eat the bread of his God, both of the most holy and of the holy. Only he shall not go in unto the vail, nor come nigh unto the altar, because he hath a blemish."' That is clear, Paul?"

"Yes," he answered.

They were going at a foot's pace. The

sensible horse, finding himself unchecked, felt it a suitable time for going at his own rate.

"Then if a priest with any defect could not serve in the temple," said Valerian, "this account of Zacharias must be a pure invention, written by someone who did not know the Jewish law."

"That is so," exclaimed Paul, struck with amazement, as if he had all at once seen some clever trick.

"Who do you suppose wrote the Gospels?" asked Valerian.

"Matthew, Mark, Luke, and John," replied Paul.

"Ah! but you do not know," said Valerian, "that not one of these books was written till many long years after Christ is said to have lived. He wrote nothing Himself, and as far as we can tell none of His immediate disciples wrote anything. It was all done from memory and tradition. I suppose, if we tried to find out the true story of the Pannotshka's murder, we should find it impossible to do so. So it is with the story of Christ's life. No wonder there are discrepancies and mistakes made in it. Of late years learned men have

come to the conclusion that none of these
Gospels are authentic. They are a tissue of
legends."

"Do all learned men say so?" asked
Paul in a tremulous voice.

Valerian hesitated a moment.

"No," he answered reluctantly; "but the
number that maintain the truth of the Bible
is rapidly diminishing; and they are mostly
priests, who have an interest in keeping up
its authority."

"What then is truth?" said Paul, in an
undertone.

"It maddens me," exclaimed Valerian
vehemently, "to see good, true, honest men
like you and Loukyan, and hundreds of
others, throwing away your lives in following
a phantom. You might be so happy! Why
should not you marry the girl you love, and
live comfortably in the house of your forefathers, and gather your own little ones about
your knees? It is because you imagine you
serve a Being who never lived; or who if he lived,
was a man like yourself, whose memory has
been glorified and deified by the friends who
loved him. You sacrifice all for nothing."

" But you do not go to church," stammered Paul.

" Ah! I run no risk, I shall excite no observation," continued Valerian ; " young men of my class are not expected to be church-goers. But you know you bring upon yourself all kinds of dangers and penalties by not doing as other peasants do. And all for nothing ! There is no reward in the world to come. There is no Christ! There is no God! Or if there be a God we know nothing about Him."

Valerian spoke strongly, as he had a great desire to root out of Paul's mind the super-stitions for which he was imperilling his welfare and freedom.

" Oh, my God!" cried Paul, in a voice of utter anguish; and he stretched out his hands to the pale evening sky above them. Suddenly he sprang from the cart.

" Drive home!" he said; "tell my mother I shall be there before midnight."

He rushed across the fields lying fallow in their winter barrenness, and was quickly lost to sight in the thin white mist. Valerian called after him again and again, but in vain.

CHAPTER XXI.

WHAT IS TRUE?

PAUL did not know in what direction he was wandering, but instinct carried his steps homewards. He felt like a man who has just suffered from a shock of earthquake. The solid earth seemed to tremble beneath him, and threaten to open under his hurrying feet and swallow him up alive. He could not at present command his thoughts, which were entangled in a maze of terror. By-and-bye the night closed round him, adding to the bewildering effect of the thin mist. His progress was impeded; he was compelled to attend to his steps. Recalled partly to himself, he found that he was following the border of a large forest.

All at once he felt himself in a place he knew. The moon had risen above the mist, and poured down a flood of pale light upon the spot where he stood. The air had been absolutely motionless until now; but as if some spell of silence had been broken, the wind began to wail in a low murmur, which rose every moment higher and higher until the roar of a gale rushed through the forest trees around him. It seemed as if all nature was moaning and crying, with shrieks of horror and despair. He was standing by the Pannotshka's grave.

All the old stories of demons haunting this place rushed into Paul's mind. If Valerian had tried to shake his faith in Christ, he had not attacked his belief in the devil. Paul stood gazing into the dim ravine, and listening to the roar in the forest. Alas! that he had ever met with Valerian! The words he had spoken were burned in as with fire upon his heart. "No world to come! No Christ! No God!"

Suddenly the thought flashed across him that Valerian had given himself up to Satan. The place where he stood suggested it. The interview he had witnessed in the deserted charcoal-burner's hut seemed to corroborate it. Satan could transform himself into an angel of light; and Valerian, with his kind-heartedness

and his devotion to the poor, might
prove a very successful emissary of Satan.
That must be the solution of what had just
passed.

He went listlessly homeward, almost fear-
ing to meet his mother, yet feeling as if
in her serene presence this untold misery
would pass away. He had much to tell her
about Loukyan; and yet it seemed as if
all the glory of Loukyan's death had melted
into thin mist, like this autumn vapour surrounding him.

Ooliana was watching eagerly for his arrival. Valerian had brought in the cart,
and delivered Paul's mysterious message. She
had been full of anxiety about him ever since
he had gone to Kovylsk, knowing that he
might be thrown into prison simply for being
a Stundist. But now she knew him to be on
his way homeward she was content. Valerian
simply told her Loukyan was dead, and left
Paul to give her all particulars. He did not
wish to be there when Paul arrived.

She heard his step at last in the court-
yard, and ran to meet him. He clasped her
to him in a strong embrace. How good it

was to feel his mother's arms about him! This at least was true.

They went into the house together hand in hand, and sat for a long time talking about Loukyan's death, and the loss it caused to the Stundists. At last Ooliana laid her hand fondly on her son's shoulder.

" My Paul," she said, " Halya was betrothed last Sunday to Panass."

Then she was indeed lost to him! That promise given to him when he made his appeal to the Bible was false—false as Valerian said all the rest of the book was. This confirmed his assertions. And he had lost Halya for a falsity!

" My boy!" said Ooliana, " it is God's will, and that will is best. Perilous times are coming. The shepherd has been slain, and they will not spare the flock. We must stand together firmly; and Halya could not have walked along this path with us. It is you who will have to take the lead now Loukyan is taken away from our midst. You are young, but you have more learning and more wealth than any of the others. You will have more in your power. There is no one else to replace Loukyan, and do his work."

s

There was a feeling of maternal pride stirring in her heart. Yes; there was no one like Paul among their little band. He was sure to be elected their presbyter. No doubt was in her mind as to his fitness for the post, or his willingness to accept it.

"Mother!" he cried in a passionate voice, "do not say that again. I replace Loukyan! I will not listen to you. You do not know what you are saying."

"I only say to-day what everybody else will say to-morrow," answered Ooliana. "It is too late for us to see even Demyan. But bad news one should keep under lock and key; only good news ought to fly out quickly."

Paul went to his room, but not to sleep. He lighted a small lamp which stood on an oak table, on which lay a few books as he had left them a few days ago when he started off to Kovylsk. He recollected the calm joy and strength he had gathered from them only those few days ago. He remembered quite well the chapter he had read in the Gospel of St. John— that Gospel which Valerian emphatically declared to be unreliable. He turned over the leaves and read it again—read and re-read it. It was the account of Lazarus being raised from the dead by the Lord Jesus Christ. Oh! what strong consolation and triumph did it bring for Loukyan's death!

"But if all that is not true? If it was invented years afterwards by someone who wished to glorify a friend?" whispered a low, still voice.

"God save me!" murmured Paul, in horror. He looked round; it would not have astonished him in the least if he had seen some bodily shape of evil. But there was nothing to be seen but black shadows in the corners of the room.

He read the chapter again, but the beautiful charm was gone. He could not imagine himself any more sitting with Mary in Bethany at the Saviour's feet, weeping when He wept, and rejoicing, with unutterable joy, when the grave gave up its dead at the Saviour's command The words passed through his brain, but his heart remained untouched and cold—as cold as the brave heart of Loukyan laid for ever in the grave.

"What if it is all false?" The icy-cold question chilled his inmost soul. The poison of doubt had entered there, and was mingling subtly with every thought. He pushed away his beloved Testament with a trembling hand. In his soul everything grew dim.

"My God! what will become of me?" he cried in horror.

Until to-day he had believed as simply as a child believes. Every line of the Bible had been read by him as God's own Word. To doubt their utter truthfulness would have been as impossible as to doubt the light of the sun or the solidity of the earth.

Now he felt the extreme horror of the savage who sees the disc of the sun eaten up by an eclipse, or feels the steadfast earth quaking under his feet.

Thoughts which drove him almost to madness surged through his brain. If the Bible was not true, then what was there in the world that was true? He had never before experienced the torture of doubt, and now its sharpest pains beset him. The words Valerian had spoken sounded mockingly in his ear: "There is no world to come! There is no Christ! There is no God!"

No world to come! Then indeed they, the

Stundists, were of all men the most miserable. Loukyan had given up his life in vain. His mother, Ooliana, was passing her time in a dream. His own existence was blighted in all its future, and Halya, who was lost to him, would live a fruitless life of misery. Was it too late to save himself and Halya? No Christ! Was all that beautiful story of a Saviour's sojourn on earth only a fable? Had there never been a Son of God moved with love and pity for the wretched race of men? But if man was no more than the brutes that perish, why should One come down from heaven to ransom him? He had had a lovely vision of a Redeemer and a Brother ever at his side, invisible, but not unfelt. He had fancied that this Lord of his was holding him by the hand, as a mother holds her little child along a stony path. If there was no Christ, this had been all delusion and a lie.

But when he thought of the terrible words, "There is no God!" a pang almost as of death wrung his heart. No God! no Father in heaven! no infinite, unchangeable love! This world was hell if there was no God.

He sank on his knees, and laid his bowed

head upon the table. Cold drops of perspiration gathered on his forehead. His excited imagination suggested that he was given over to the power of Satan. There was no doubt in his mind of the existence of this tormentor: he was fighting against him and his temptations.

"Lord have mercy upon me! Lord save me!" he groaned.

"What Lord?" murmured a voice, whether in his ear, or in his mind only, he could not tell.

He rose from his knees. He was suffocating; his brain was on fire; his throat was parched as after a dusty journey on a sultry day. He crept softly into the kitchen to get a draught of water. His mother heard him, and came out to see what was the matter.

"Are you ill?" she exclaimed, frightened. "You are as pale as death."

For a moment Paul thought to tell her of the fearful conflict he was undergoing. But why expose her to the horror of such doubts? This simple and pure soul, why should it be tossed on such a storm as the tempest of his doubts and fears? His tongue clove to the roof of his mouth.

Ooliana recollected that Loukyan's death and Halya's betrothal were new griefs to her son. This accounted for his silence and bewildered gaze. She gave him water to drink, and laid her cold hands on his fevered forehead.

"Go to bed, my son," she said, "and try to sleep. God give you sleep!"

CHAPTER XXII.

A FUNERAL SERVICE.

THE next day the Stundists met together—a solemn and sad knot of mourners—to honour the memory of their leader and their first martyr. All were present; both old and young. Even those who had timorously absented themselves since Loukyan's arrest were animated by his death to rejoin their comrades. When Ooliana and Paul entered the house where they assembled it was already full. Paul wished to take a place by the door, but the little congregation made way for him to the table, spread with a white cloth, on which lay the Bible and hymn-book; and bread and wine for the simple rite of the Lord's Supper, which was to be solemnly partaken of by the brotherhood before dispersing. Old Kondraty, one of the first converts in Knishi, was seated at the table, and he offered the book to Paul to conduct the service; but he shook his head in refusal. It was natural that he, who had been present at Loukyan's death, should be too much overcome to be able to take Loukyan's post. The service was accordingly led by Kondraty, who, though not an eloquent man, was intelligent and well versed in the New Testament.

A psalm was sung, and then Kondraty opened the New Testament and began to read clearly, but with a peasant's slowness, and with here and there a mispronunciation, which no one but Paul remarked.

"And the word of God increased, and the number of disciples multiplied in Jerusalem greatly; and a great company of the priests were obedient to the faith. And Stephen, full of faith and power, did great wonders and miracles among the people.

"Then there arose certain of the synagogue, disputing with Stephen. And they were not able to resist the wisdom and the spirit by which he spake. Then they suborned men, which said, We have heard him speak blasphemous words against Moses and against God.

"And they stirred up the people, and the elders, and the scribes, and came upon him,

and caught him, and brought him to the
Council, and set up false witnesses, which said,
This man ceaseth not to speak blasphemous
words against this holy place and the law;
for we have heard him say that this Jesus
of Nazareth shall destroy this place, and change
the customs which Moses delivered unto us.

"And all that sat in the Council, looking
steadfastly on him, saw his face as it had
been the face of an angel."

Dead silence reigned in the room. Under
the impression of recent events, this narration
had gained a peculiar significance. The cases
were so similar. It seemed as if the tale
was told, not of Stephen, so long since dead,
but of Loukyan, their leader, who a few weeks
ago taught them with his living voice. The
persecuting Jews, were they not the members
of the orthodox church? The elders and
the scribes were the clergy and the officials
who, unable to confute his teaching by arguments, had seized him and cast him into prison.

Both men and women began to weep.
Covering his face with his hands, Paul shed
silent tears, which relieved for a time his
throbbing brain. The bright, joyous face of

the dying Loukyan dispelled for the moment his doubts and sorrows.

Kondraty went on reading slowly, omitting nothing. The long historical speech made by Stephen somewhat relieved the agitation of the audience. The sobbings ceased; sighs were heard less often. All listened patiently and with deep attention. But the tragical catastrophe came at last.

It is not Stephen standing before his judges; it is Loukyan sternly denouncing his persecutors for being the betrayers and murderers of Christ, the just One. The persecutors are cut to the heart, and are gnashing their teeth in rage. They are Paissy and his colleagues. The place is not the Sanhedrim in Jerusalem, but a Russian Court, with a green-covered table surrounded by Russian priests and officials, before whom Loukyan is standing.

All faces grew pale. Some with trembling hands wiped the perspiration from their brows. Moans and sighs were heard again. In the closely crowded room a burning tension was felt, as if the whole drama was developing before their eyes. The reader went on :—

"But he, being full of the Holy Ghost,

looked up steadfastly into heaven and saw
the glory of God, and Jesus standing on the
right hand of God, and said, Behold, I see
the heavens opened, and the Son of Man
standing on the right hand of God.

"Then they cried out with a loud voice
and stopped their ears, and ran upon him
with one accord, and cast him out of the city
and stoned him."

Kondraty's voice failed him. It was too
real. The grief of the whole audience broke
out afresh. At last, in broken accents and
sobbing breath, he read :—

"And they stoned Stephen, calling upon
God and saying, Lord Jesus, receive my spirit.

"And he kneeled down, and cried with
a loud voice, 'Lord, lay not this sin to
their charge. And when he had said this he
fell asleep."

"They killed him! they killed our own
dear one!" cried Paraska, the wife of Demyan,
and immediately cries and lamentations filled
the room. The suppressed excitement burst
out again. Kondraty was distressed. Above
all, he wished to avoid hysterical emotion.
He stood up, waving his hands and addressing

them; but in the tumult his voice was inaudible. Paul, with a pallid face and reddened eyelids, rose from his seat, confronting the people. In an instant all was still.

In a very simple manner, as simply as the story of the Crucifixion is told in the Gospels, Paul gave to them the account of Loukyan's death and his last words. The sorrowing congregation were soothed into more tranquil grief. It was as if the benign and joyous spirit of Loukyan was among them.

"And now," said Kondraty, when Paul finished, "we must choose another teacher and presbyter; one who can go to other churches, and visit them for us, and take counsel with other presbyters and leaders. There is only one fitted for the post. You all know him. You can guess who it is. But we should like the election to be unanimous, and you shall consider of it for a week. I name Paul Rudenko."

"There is no one but Paul," exclaimed a few voices.

"Let it be well thought of, and well prayed over," said Kondraty.

But Paul rose again, and confronted the

congregation with a face as pale as death. He had foreseen this, yet had hoped that Kondraty might be chosen as presbyter, as he had been a member of their community from the first. It was impossible for him to fill this post. All looked at him anxiously. He must speak now. With a great effort he commanded his wandering thoughts.

"Brothers!" he began.

His eyes were dull and his voice thick. The congregation was puzzled. In the back seats they stood up to see and hear him better.

"Brothers!" he repeated, in a firmer voice, striving hard to subdue his agitation, "I am grateful for all your goodness. But I dare not accept this office. Kondraty ought to succeed Loukyan. It would be useless to elect me. No inducement on earth could persuade me to be your teacher."

His voice sank, and he added—

"I am not worthy to be the least among the brethren!"

The last words burst out involuntarily, as a cry of despair. They were caught only by Kondraty and Ooliana. The congregation did not hear them; but there was something in

Paul's manner which made it clear that this refusal of office was not made from modesty, real or assumed. No one dared to remonstrate with him, or urge him to retract his decision. But what could be the meaning of this refusal, so decisive, and so incomprehensible?

"What is to be done?" whispered one to another; "whom shall we elect?"

"Brethren," said Kondraty, "let us postpone this affair. God will enlighten and instruct us all. Let us in the meanwhile pray earnestly to Him that He will guide and support us through all our trials."

Nobody replied. The Lord's Supper was partaken of, according to their simple rites; and the congregation dispersed. Paul had left as soon as he finished his speech.

CHAPTER XXIII.

A DISASTROUS WINTER.

To the burden of his inward conflict was now added a load of misunderstanding of Paul's conduct. His refusal of the leadership provoked much gossip, and many fantastic conjectures. Some said Paul had committed a crime; and remorse, and the dread of being found out, made him shrink from such a post. Others insisted that he was studying so much that he fancied himself a learned man, and would perhaps found a new sect of his own. Others again said he was afraid; Loukyan's death had stricken him with dread of the same fate.

Not being able to master his unbearable doubts, and unwilling to disturb his mother with them, Paul came to the unfortunate conclusion to consult Father Vasili, who was the only man in Knishi that had had any experience in theological questions. It was possible he might know some refutation of the objections Valerian had raised in his mind. He took a handsome present in his hand, which he left in the kitchen with the Matushka, and presented himself before Father Vasili.

The Batushka was astonished to see him, but made him very welcome, and bade him sit down. He was not a proud priest, and always received his parishioners in a homely and hospitable manner. They forgave him many faults for this condescension.

" I am glad to see you, my son," he said; " what can I do for you? I cannot interfere about Karpo, and Panass, and Halya. No! no! you should have stayed among us in our Holy Mother Church; and I should have blessed your marriage with Halya before this."

" It is not that," said Paul sorrowfully; " I have given up Halya. But I came to ask you a few questions, Father. I have been talking to a man, a learned man, who seems to know everything; and he tells me the Gospels are not authentic, so the scholars say, and were not written by St. Matthew, and St. Mark, and St. Luke, and St. John.

T

And it seems to me there are things in the New Testament not true."

"How? What?" interrupted the Batushka, his face reddening with anger; "not true! Oh! this comes of leaving your Church! First a heretic, and then—you villain—an infidel. These are your thoughts——"

"But I want to know—I only came to ask you," stammered Paul.

Father Vasili would not hear another word.

"Get out of my sight! This very moment! You apostate! You castaway!" he shouted, driving him out of the room as he might have driven a wild beast. As they passed tempestuously through the kitchen the Batushka caught sight of the two well-fed geese Paul had brought as a present; and seizing them by their web-feet he flung them into the yard after his retreating parishioner. But the Matushka quickly rectified this mistake.

The rumour of this interview spread quickly through the village. Father Vasili gave an account of it at the inn to Karpo, Okhrim, and the starosta Savely, which made them roar with laughter, yet inwardly foam with

rage. The Stundists heard of it; and some
of them suspected Paul of returning to the
Orthodox Church. Others believed that he
had abjured religion altogether, and was, as
Father Vasili declared, an atheist, like Valerian, who did not conceal his free-thinking
opinions. Gradually their relations towards
Paul changed. They shunned his society, and
in a certain manner excluded him from their
community. The orthodox, though they dis-
approved of the Stundists, accepted their
judgment upon Paul, and in their turn
avoided him. From being one of the chief
and most popular persons in Knishi and
Ostron, a few short months had made him
a pariah among his own people.

Valerian heard the report, and rejoiced at it.
Such a man as Paul would be a great addition
to the ranks of the Propagandists, who were in
secret seeking to teach the peasantry its rights,
its powers, and the wrongs it suffered. Most
of his colleagues were nobles, or men of the
learned professions; but here was a peasant of
great intelligence, of uncommon eloquence, and
of enthusiastic temperament, who could do
marvels of work among the peasants, so difficult

T 2

to arouse. He sought Paul eagerly, but Paul shunned him as he would have shunned Satan in person. Valerian terrified him. Doubt was agonising, but what would conviction be?

Ooliana could not fail to hear and see what was going on, and her patient heart was sorely tried by it. She had always looked forward to Paul being Loukyan's successor, and had rejoiced at the prospect, though she knew well what a post of danger it would be; but now, instead of being the first among the little band of disciples, he was the last—even if he was counted among them at all. He continued to go to the meetings, but he sat at the door, making his escape as soon as Kondraty pronounced the last benediction. The elder men among the Stundists did not give him up. They remembered Loukyan, and the high expectations he had formed about Paul, and they stood unflinchingly in opposition to the general verdict against him. It seemed to them that the young man was passing through a period of deadly temptation and conflict, through which he would pass and come out more than conqueror. They would not allow the community to choose definitely a successor to Loukyan, and they decided to wait till Easter, Kondraty continuing to conduct the services.

Paul saw that his mother suffered profoundly, though she tried to hide it from him. He could not speak to her of his doubts, and as a rule he became very silent. The inward struggle absorbed him, and he could see no end to it. After the acute anguish and horror of the first few days he fell into a state of apathy — a dull frigidity of mind which made him indifferent to everything and everybody. Once the starosta Savely spoke in his hearing of the new house Panass was building for Halya, but he listened listlessly. The Bible had promised Halya to him, and the promise was untrue. His heart was like a stone, and seemed to have lost the capacity of throbbing either with pain or pleasure.

So the gloomy days and long nights of winter crawled slowly away. Paul worked hard during the daylight, but in the evening he sat idle and languid by the great stove, watching his mother as she sat knitting, with Testament and hymn-book open on the table before her. His own Testament lay untouched on the shelf in his room, with the other books, which no longer possessed any charm for him. If they were not true, their falsehood was the worst falsehood in life.

It was a disastrous winter in Knishi. Instead of heavy snow-storms there were torrents of rain. The river overflowed its banks, flooding the fields on each side. The undrained marshes became swamps of mud. A murrain broke out among the cattle and sheep, and the richer men who owned flocks and herds suffered losses from which the poorer peasants were almost exempt. Old Karpo lost the bay mare which was to have been part of Halya's dowry, and a score or two of sheep besides. His losses amounted to almost as much as the dowry he had promised to give to his daughter. Panass began to go more often to see Yarina.

Then typhus fever came, and entered the unventilated and often very dirty homes. One after another were stricken down by it, but chiefly the children. The Matushka had not forgotten Paissy's counsels. Everywhere she diligently traced the calamities that befell the people to the anger of God against the Stundists. When a child lay moaning on its death-bed, and at last the sobs ceased and the little eyes closed for ever, she said the saints and the Holy Mother had taken it away for fear it should become a heretic. The fever itself was the finger of God stretched out against those who were indifferent to the Orthodox religion.

Father Vasili preached the same doctrine from the pulpit. Not for years had he addressed such large congregations. The most notorious drunkards in the place flocked to hear his tirades against the damnable Stundists. The dead village was being roused to life by the underground teaching of the Propagandists and the open secession of the Stundists; and the return to life is fraught with painful throes. Knishi was not the peaceful, mouldering place it had once been.

In former times Ooliana would have been the faithful, constant nurse at every sick-bed. She was renowned for her knowledge of remedies and alleviatives; and, as there was no doctor within twenty versts, she had filled the post of one without fee. But no one sent for her now. Her cool touch and watchful gaze, and all but inexhaustible patience and loving-kindness, were wasting unclaimed, and in many cases refused, as if she had the evil eye. It was well for Knishi that Valerian was at hand. He was kept busy.

"Halya is stricken with the fever," said Ooliana one day to Paul. He did not answer.

"They will not let me see her," she went on, "but Valerian is attending her. He was here to-day to beg for a New Testament. Halya is raving for one. I sent her yours."

"Good God!" cried Paul. It was a little well-worn book, in which he had marked his favourite verses, but he had not opened it now for weeks. It seemed to tempt him into lower depths of misery.

"Mother," he said, "do you believe the Gospels are true?"

The ice was broken. The mother and son looked into one another's souls, and the winter of his doubt was over.

"Ah, my Paul!" she said, "you have listened to Valerian. He asked me the same question. But we are not called upon to believe in the Bible. It is God, it is Christ, we must believe in. There may be mistakes in the Gospels, there are spots in the sun. It is not the Gospels that save us, but our Lord Christ."

"But if it is a fable?" suggested Paul.

".It is no fable!" she exclaimed. "Who could invent such a fable as that God so loved the world that He gave His only begotten Son, that whosoever believeth in Him should not perish but have everlasting life? There are fables about God, but not like that. It could not have entered the heart of man to invent that."

She spoke with strong conviction; and her sincere, guileless face, pale with the winter's seclusion, glowed with fervour.

"Oh, if I had never heard Valerian!" cried Paul.

"Ah! I have heard him," she answered, "and I showed to him the words of our Lord: 'I thank Thee, O Father, that Thou hast hid these things from the wise and learned, and hast revealed them unto babes. Even so, Father, for so it seemed good in Thy sight.' And I read to him too the words of the apostle Paul: 'For the preaching of the cross is to them that perish fool-

ishness, but unto us which are saved it is
the power of God. For it is written, I will
destroy the wisdom of the wise, and will bring
to nothing the understanding of the prudent.
Where is the wise? where is the scribe?
where is the disputer of this world? Hath
not God made foolish the wisdom of this
world?' And again I read to him: 'Eye
hath not seen, nor ear heard, neither have
entered into the heart of man, the things which
God hath prepared for them that love Him.
But God hath revealed them unto us by His
Spirit; for the Spirit searcheth all things, even
the deep things of God. For what man
knoweth the things of a man, save the spirit
of man which is in him? Even so the things
of God knoweth no man, but the Spirit of
God. But the natural man receiveth not the
things of the Spirit of God, for they are
foolishness unto him; neither can he know
them, because they are spiritually discerned.'
These and other sayings I showed to him."

"And what did Valerian Petrovitch say?"
asked Paul.

A fine sweet smile flitted across Ooliana's
face.

"He said 'Invincible ignorance,'" she replied, "and we shook hands and parted good friends."

For a few minutes Paul remained silent. It seemed to him as if he had touched the hem of the wisdom of this world, and had been smitten almost to death by it. "The common people heard Christ gladly." Did not he belong to the common people?

"Mother," he said, "Halya has my Testament. Give me yours."

She placed it in his hands, and pressed a kiss upon his cheek. He went away to his own room, and spent the night in silent study and prayer.

CHAPTER XXIV.

A SIGN AND A DREAM.

HALYA's marriage had been delayed by the attack of fever which laid her prostrate during many weeks; and when she was finally pronounced by Valerian to be well and strong again, Lent had begun, during which double fees are demanded in the Orthodox Church for pronouncing the blessing upon a married couple. Neither Okhrim nor Karpo was willing to pay double fees.

Paul was gradually retracing his steps towards his former faith. Once more he ventured to partake of the Lord's Supper. He became again a constant attendant at the week-day meetings, as well as the Sunday services. But he took no part in them except as a silent listener.

He had been at a weekly evening prayer-meeting, and was returning home alone, his mother having gone in to see Kondraty's wife, who was ill. Reaching the border of the forest, he saw the dark figure of a woman sitting on a fallen tree. Paul did not recognise Halya, and would have passed her. He did not even recognise her when she rose and came forward to meet him, so altered was she by her illness.

"Paul!" she cried, "Paul!"

Her voice made him tremble, and he looked at her in bewilderment.

"Halya! you here!" he ejaculated.

"I was waiting for you," she said. "People tell me all sorts of things about you—different things. So I wanted to ask you."

"What about?" he asked, striving to speak calmly.

"Are you going to give up the Stundists?" she asked. "Are you coming back to us? Valerian says you will never be the same again. I expected you would come and tell us, father and me. But you kept away; and oh, Paul, I nearly died! So I thought, I will go myself." She finished in a reproachful tone.

"No," said Paul, "no. I could never drift back to your Orthodox Church. But it may be I shall leave the brethren."

Halya looked at him with wondering eyes. Why should he leave his brethren if he did not come back to the Orthodox Church? But she did not question him. The delicate feeling of a loving woman told her there was something very sad and momentous in this enigmatical answer In the twilight she saw how changed his face was. There was no boyishness left in it; it was the face of a man who was going through a great sorrow.

"Tell me everything," she exclaimed in a burst of sympathy, and clasping his hand in hers. "Perhaps I shall understand. Why are you so sad always? Is it for my sake?"

"You could not understand it, child," he answered softly.

"I shall! Try me only," she persisted.

They were standing under a wide-spreading oak, which threw its bare branches far against the evening sky. The wind was playing among the fine lace-like twigs, which were showing a little sign of breaking into buds. In a few weeks the boughs would be green with leaves.

"I have been like this tree," he said, "dead with the winter. If a worm had been gnawing at its roots it would never have lived again. And a worm has been gnawing at the root of my faith; if I cannot cast it out I shall never live again."

She did not understand him, but she saw that he suffered.

"Oh! my love!" she cried, "why should you suffer like this? But I love you the more for it now."

She suddenly flung her arms round his neck, and he felt her breath upon his cheek.

"Only tell my father you are leaving the Stundists, and Panass shall never see me again," she murmured.

"My darling, do you love me still?" he said. "I thought you had quite given me up and forgotten me."

"Don't be foolish!" replied Halya tenderly. "I told my father to-day that life is nothing to me without you; and that I would rather drown myself than marry Panass. Only you come and say you will leave the Stundists. And listen, Paul, in your ear. Panass will marry Yarina, for she is in love with him, and my dowry is all lost."

"Halya!" he said, "I could never go back

to the Church. The Orthodox priests have killed my dear Loukyan: and could I ask for their blessing? Never! That could never come to pass!"

"But father and I had nothing to do with killing him!" answered Halya.

She sank down on the ground, and tears streamed from her eyes. All she had been dreaming and hoping for, which seemed almost realised, was dispelled suddenly by Paul's words. Yes! he could never return to a Church that had killed his friend.

"Halya, my beloved!" whispered Paul, bending over her. But at that moment the sound of cart-wheels and the hoof-beats of a horse were heard coming along the road. Halya sprang to her feet at once.

"Hide yourself," she exclaimed; "we must not be seen together."

He disappeared hastily into the forest.

When the cart passed by, and the sound of wheels died away, Paul came back to the oak tree. But Halya was gone. He followed slowly along the footpath she must have taken, feeling that as long as he trod in her footsteps he had not altogether parted from her. He wished he had asked her for his Testament, which she still kept in her possession. Was it only in the delirium of fever she had wished for it? Paul felt sad; but it was a quiet and tender sadness which had nothing in common with the dull, sullen apathy which for so many weeks had possessed his soul. This had been gradually passing away; and now the unexpected meeting with Halya had quite dispelled the cloud. Her tenderness, and her decision never to marry Panass, had refreshed and quickened his arid spirit as a warm, abundant shower refreshes a field scorched by the sun. Halya loved him, and him only, for his own sake simply. God would yet give her to him.

Yes! Loukyan was right. God is love; and where there is love among men there is God. All blessings come from the heart of God. And not only by means of books did God speak to the soul of man, but by all the joy and happiness which come to it. Halya's love, his mother's love, God's love flooded his inmost spirit with unspeakable joy.

Absorbed in these thoughts, he strayed from the path, and was soon wandering amid

U

the tangled brushwood of the forest, stepping
mechanically over the spreading roots of the
trees.   A   bird, frightened   by his footsteps,
flew off its roosting-place, fluttered about in
the obscure gloom, and rising in the air over
the trees for a minute, swooped down heavily
among the bushes. This roused his attention.
Through the dark, interlacing branches overhead he could see the clear vault of the sky.
From the deeper obscurity of the forest the
stars shone more brightly than in the open
fields, and seemed to look down upon him
with loving eyes.   Paul gazed at them for
a long time.

"It is like looking into Halya's eyes," he
thought to himself.

He had already missed the way to Ostron,
and now tried to make a road for himself,
guided by the pole-star.   Suddenly he saw
before him a glade he had never seen before,
though the forest was familiar ground to him.
Much timber had been sold last autumn, and
the wood-cutters had been busy all the winter.
The glade stretched before him, every fallen
tree and every shrub, and the brown heads of
dead hemlock were glistening in a fine bead-

like frost, whilst the steady rays of the moonlight shone in silvery streams upon them.
Every shade of colour disappeared as if melted
in this silvery shining. The green grass, the
brown hemlock, the dark rough trunks of
the trees, all seemed chiselled and graven out
in pure silver, like the silver kingdom of a
fairy tale.

In the middle of the glade rose a low
hillock, on which lay two or three fallen trees.
Paul's feet carried him there, and he stood
motionless, looking round in wonder and
admiration.

He was completely surrounded by trees,
shutting out all other scenes except the glade.
There was no sign of a human habitation.
He was quite alone in the presence of that
deep, pure sky, with its loving and searching
eyes. He felt as if he was lifted up to it as
on the open palm of a giant's hand. All nature
was sleeping. Only the watchful stars scintil-
lated tranquilly, and looked down upon him
kindly from blue, unfathomable depths. A
warm, simple, child-like emotion took possession
of him. It was the first time since his conversation with Valerian that the dull chilling

U 2

feeling of doubt was replaced by an outburst of filial confidence in God. He lifted up his face to the heavens above him.

"Oh! my Father!" he ejaculated, "Thou who hast made the sky and covered it with stars, and made the earth and filled it with life, teach me how to understand Thee."

He knelt down and prayed fervently, passionately, as he had done in the first days of his conversion. Yet it was not a prayer; it was rather a candid confession, a living outpouring of his soul to a living Being. The conviction that God heard him grew as his passionate, vehement, incoherent monologue went on. Soon he was not satisfied with his outpouring. He paused and listened attentively. His impassioned soul longed for an answer. He was waiting for a sign.

The night was wonderfully calm. The frost was slight. The moon poured down its silvery rays. The motionless air stirred neither the withered hemlock nor the blades of grass.

A soft warm breeze passed for a moment over his eager, upturned face. It stirred his hair like the touch of a tender hand, and died away. He knew not whence it came, nor whither it went.

"So is every one that is born of the Spirit," said a voice within him.

Paul trembled. The sign he had prayed for, which he hardly dared to ask, had been granted to him. His eyes filled with tears; his heart melted with joy. God had spoken to him.

His whole soul was penetrated with new life and vigour. No trace of doubt was left. The true light had shone upon his darkness, and the shadows fled away. Henceforth, he would walk in the light, and be a child of the light.

No more would questions of genealogies, and strifes of words, and perverse disputings, trouble him. He knew that the Spirit of God had come to him. He could doubt it no more than he could doubt his own existence.

He felt unspeakably happy. He longed to see his mother, and to tell her and the brethren the blessing that had been granted to him. But he felt so tired he could hardly move.

He resolved to rest for a few minutes. Sitting down, and leaning against the trunk of a tree, he listened to the eerie sounds of the night, and gazed dreamily down the moon-lit glade. A branch cracked, and fell in the forest. A marmot whistled afar off. Under the brushwood a hedgehog moved cautiously, scenting the air with its sharp little snout, either for prey or danger. It pricked up its bristles, and looked sharply about it. In an instant an owl flew out of a tree, and making a half-circle in the air, swooped down upon the little animal, and catching him in her claws, flew away to her nest. Paul would have rescued the hedgehog, but his limbs felt heavy. He could not prevail upon himself to be up and stirring.

The owl, meanwhile, appeared to come close within his reach. If he stretched out his hand he could catch it. But it did not seem to care for his presence, and began to clean its wings with its beak. Presently he saw it was no owl at all, but Father Vasili, and the wings were a brown silk cassock, which the Batushka wore on grand occasions. His feet were in leather boots, trimmed with fur, and with low heels.

"I'd better get away from here as soon

as possible," thought Paul; "the Batushka looks very angry to-day."

But Father Vasili was already beckoning to him with his hand.

"Come here! come here!" he repeated; "not authentic, did you say? You thought you were an apostle yourself, so you could run down the blessed Gospels——"

Paul rose, anxious to pacify him, and to say his doubts troubled him no more. But Father Vasili floated away from him as he drew nearer, still, however, beckoning with his hand.

"Wait a bit!" cried Paul. But the Batushka did not listen, but continued to float soundlessly away through the air.

Suddenly the Batushka and the forest disappeared. Paul found himself in a deep dark cavern, with a low, rocky vault. He was shivering from the penetrating dampness, which seemed to pierce through to his bones. The thick, heavy air, was motionless. Not a sound, not the faintest murmur was audible. All was mute and darksome. A voice said to him, 'Death reigns here!' He wandered to and fro, but everywhere he felt only the narrow confines of a tomb. At last he sat down exhausted on the floor of the grave. All at once a voice said in his ear—

"Arise! let us go hence."

It was Halya's voice. Paul rose quickly. She stood before him in a pilgrim's garb, with a staff in her one hand, and a chaplet in the other. Her face was grave and stern. She did not even look at him, but glided forward, and Paul followed unquestioningly. But though they walked a long time the cavern remained the same; it seemed to move with them. The same thick walls and rocky vault surrounded them like a circle of stone.

"What is this?" cried Paul. "We are tramping along always in the same place. We shall never get out of this grave."

"How can you say so?" asked Halya reprovingly; "do you not see we are already there?"

He lifted up his head, and saw that the path through the kingdom of Death had led him to a church porch, with a steeple surmounted by a cross, which glittered in the moonlight.

"Why!" exclaimed Paul; "but it is a church!"

"Yes! a church," said Halya, "our own church. Did I not tell you I wanted you to go there?"

"Leave me alone," he cried, "I would sooner return to the grave."

"Come in," urged Halya; "it is the house of God."

"No," he said; "they have made the house of prayer a den of thieves. I will not go in."

He broke away from her with vehemence.

Laughter and discordant songs rang through the stillness of the night, and woke Paul from his slumber. It was a party of half-drunken peasants going home from a public-house where they had been keeping the eve of their patron saint's day.

Paul rose and rubbed his eyes. His clothes were wet through, and his limbs benumbed. He waited to let the merry band of boon-companions pass by, and then he hastened home, deeply impressed by his vivid dream.

314

CHAPTER XXV.

THE PATRON SAINT'S DAY.

DURING the preceding week Father Paissy had been making arrangements with Father Vasili for himself preaching a sermon against the Stundists on the patron saint's day. The starosta Savely had been summoned to Kovylsk to receive important instructions.

"The Consistory expects that every Stundist in Knishi shall be present on this occasion," said Father Paissy. "Mind! everybody," he added sternly. "I will show no indulgence to anyone who connives at the heresy."

Savely scratched his head behind his ear.

"How is it to be done, your reverence?" he remonstrated. "If they won't go I cannot force them, with none but lame Ermoshka to help me."

"Call a private meeting of the Mir," said Father Paissy, "and make what arrangements you choose; but come they must."

The meeting of the Mir was held in the District Court House, not in the open air as usual, when any of the villagers could be present. On Savely explaining the object of the meeting, nobody said a word. The peasants sullenly kept silence.

"What a nuisance they are!" said Karpo at last. "They give quiet peaceable folks no rest.

"That is true," agreed Savely. "They hang round my neck like a stone."

"But why should we humour them?" asked old Sheelo. "Let us drag them to church by force, or drive them in with sticks, like a set of troublesome beasts, as they are."

"Why should we be so considerate for these vagabonds?" said Okhrim. "They have given us trouble enough."

It was settled that early the next morning the starosta Savely, with the members of the Mir and some younger men who would be summoned privately to their aid, should visit the houses of the Stundists, and, driving them to church, lock them in there until the hour of the morning service. Soon after daybreak, therefore, the villagers divided into two bands:

one to go to Ostron, to collect Paul,
Ooliana, and other heretics who lived between
that hamlet and the church; and the second
to proceed to the opposite end of the parish
for the same purpose. The younger men
greatly enjoyed the prospect of a resistance
and disturbance.

"Come, boys—all and everybody!" cried
Panass. "Let us flog the Stundists to church
like naughty children. I'll go for Paul
Rudenko."

The crowd divided as it had been arranged.
Many more joined them as they passed along
the village street. The secret had been so well
kept that this order from the Consistory caused
universal astonishment. A few months ago it
would have excited their anger and indignation,
but the sermons of Father Vasili and the
insinuations of the Matushka had borne
fruit. The Stundists had brought down
calamities and vengeance from Heaven on the
whole community.

At sight of Paul's homestead the crowd
stepped out more quickly, as soldiers rushing
to an assault. It was a prosperous and peace-
ful-looking dwelling. The barns and sheds

around it were better kept than any other farm in Knishi. The fold-yard was orderly, and a garden—a rare thing among them—lay on one side of the house. The fold-gate was open, for the cattle had just gone out to the well, and the crowd rushed in boisterously.

Paul was sitting with his mother in his own little room, which looked out into the garden. He had found her, when he returned from the forest, lying asleep on the bench in the kitchen. She was sitting up for him, and had fallen asleep out of sheer fatigue. He woke her up and told her briefly about his prayer, and the sign given to him in the forest. "Thank God!" she exclaimed. "Now at last I know that you will never forsake our Lord Christ."

She had gone to bed in profound happiness, such as she had never experienced in her life. Her son was now indeed hers through all eternity. "For if we suffer with Christ, we shall also reign with Him!" she murmured, as she fell asleep.

Paul was now telling her his story in all its details, whilst she listened with glistening eyes and fervid face. He had just finished his curious dream, and they were conjecturing what its meaning could be, or if it had any meaning at all.

Their quiet conversation was interrupted by the sound of loud rough voices, coming nearer and nearer.

"What can it be?" said Ooliana. "A noise in the street—a fire, perhaps."

Paul went into the outer room, looking into the fold-yard.

"Here are a throng of people rushing into our yard," he called out. "What can be the matter?"

A loud, heavy knock at the door answered him. He threw it open, and found himself in front of an unruly crowd ready to break into his house.

"What do you want, neighbours?" he asked.

"We want you, and your old witch-mother, and all of your brood!" shouted Panass, seizing him by the shoulder. Paul freed himself by a sharp, unexpected movement, and Panass staggered back upon the nearest in the crowd.

"Strike him down, boys!" he shouted

again. "Don't let his evil eye fall on you. Strike him before your arms wither."

Several men rushed upon Paul.

"But what do you want? What has happened?" asked Paul, in a quiet, untroubled voice.

"You are to come to church," answered the starosta Savely, who had forced his way to the threshold, on which Paul stood. "The Consistory have given orders. Father Paissy comes to-day to exorcise the Stundists—to cast out the devils that have taken possession of you."

"To the church!" exclaimed Paul, with such a joyful, yet surprised, expression on his face that the bystanders were struck by it. "That is what my dream meant," he thought to himself, and his heart exulted at this indubitable sign of the will of God.

"Brothers!" he said, "I will go with you to the church; I, and my mother, and all the rest of us."

"How cunning he is!" cried Panass, as the crowd fell back a little at this unexpected acquiescence.

Paul did not hear him. He turned away

to speak to Ooliana, who was just come to
the door.

"Mother!" he whispered in excitement,
"now it is quite clear what was meant by
my dream."

"What is it?" she inquired.

"They are come to compel us to go into
the church," he answered. "The Consistory
orders it. You know we must not resist.
We will not make them take us by force."

"No, no!" she replied.

Those few words were exchanged in an
undertone. Then they faced the crowd hand
in hand.

"You may go, friends," said Ooliana, after
bowing thrice to the crowd. "We will follow
you to the church, and bring all the brethren
with us. Only give us time to collect them
together."

She spoke in the kindly, cheerful voice so
familiar to them all, for there was not a
household which she had not entered as a
helper or consoler; and the fighting disposition, even of the young men, was dispelled by
her tranquil courage. They looked at one
another, and from Paul to his mother, with

great curiosity. This conduct on their part was a riddle which needed a solution.

"Are you coming back to the Christian religion?" asked Koozka in a hesitating tone. "We thought we could hardly drive you in with whips and scourges. Now all of a sudden you seem glad to go."

"We never have forsaken the Christian religion," answered Paul. "And we obey the laws, when they are not opposed to God's commandments. If you will leave us in peace we will gather the brethren together in Kondraty's cottage, and come without fail in good time to church."

"Savely," said Ooliana, "you have known me all my life. Did I ever tell you a lie? Trust Paul and me, and not one of the Stundists shall fail to be there. If they refuse, I will send you word in time to compel them to obey the order."

"I will trust you, Ooliana," replied Savely.

Ooliana locked the house, and again bowing to the crowd in three different directions passed through the midst of them with Paul beside her. The people straggled after them, in warm discussion of their extraordinary

v

conduct. They watched them go from one house to another, and soon the Stundists, by twos and threes, made their way to Kondraty's cottage.

When all were assembled, Paul stood up, and with simple eloquence told them of the great deliverance wrought for his soul by God. He did not disturb them by telling what doubts had assailed him. But he spoke with full assurance of the revelation of God to his inmost spirit.

"And now," he cried, "who will come with me to testify to God's truth before Father Paissy and our Batushka?"

"Every one of us," they answered.

"But only half of us are here," said Ooliana.

At that moment a great noise was heard again in the village street. The second band of men, commanded by old Karpo, which had been gathering the Stundists from the other end of the parish, were returning from their search. The little congregation in Kondraty's cottage hurried into the street. In front of the approaching crowd marched Karpo with Demyan beside him, whose face was covered with bruises, and whose caftan was torn in several places. He had no hat on, and his hands were tied behind his back with a rope, the ends of which were held firmly by two peasants, as if he had been a mad bull. He resisted all the way, and was driven on with blows and pushes. Behind him came a little cluster of men and women, frightened and lamenting, but not resisting as Demyan did. Ooliana stepped forward.

"Karpo," she said, "there is no need for this violence. Let me speak to Demyan, and he will resist no longer."

"It's you and your son we want," growled Karpo. "Without the ringleaders the rebels are nothing. Get hold of them, boys."

"Bethink yourself," said Ooliana; "your church is not a police-station, where people are dragged by force. My brothers and sisters," she added, addressing the Stundists, "we have decided to go quietly to church. There is no sin in that. God is there as He is every-where, and our fathers and mothers wor-shipped Him there. We can go there with-out disobeying Him. Nay! we are bound to go if the Mir commands us; only we cannot

v 2

bow to the icons, or pray to the saints. Let
us then go peaceably, and listen to the sermon
Father Paissy is going to preach. We may
learn something from it. At any rate we
shall not sin against God, or cause any of
our fellow-men to sin against Him."

"But why didn't you say all that before?"
said Karpo.

"If you had come and told us what the
Mir commanded," answered Ooliana, "no one
would have resisted."

"That's true," cried Demyan. "Loukyan
always said 'Obey the Mir, if it does not
order you to disobey God.' But I did not
understand. They caught me and tied my
hands, and drove me before them to worship
the icons. I will submit myself, now I know
it is the Mir."

The band of persecutors stood still, confused and ashamed. They were unwilling to
confess their own stupidity in not making it
clear what was demanded of the Stundists.

"Oo lew! oo lew!" was suddenly heard in
a wild wail. It was the crazy imbecile of the
village, Avdiushka, who was running down the
street, waving his hands. "Oo lew! oo lew!

Knock them down! kill them! burn, burn, burn them!" he muttered, shaking his tangled head, and disappearing as suddenly as he had come upon the scene.

"The young devil!" cried Karpo, "to frighten us just now!"

The crowd began to laugh, and gradually dispersed, while Demyan and the rest of the Stundists went into Kondraty's cottage to get ready for the enforced attendance at church.

CHAPTER XXVI.

EXORCISING THE STUNDISTS.

THE church was crowded. Everyone antici-
pated something extraordinary; and none but
childish old people and helpless invalids remained at home. When Halya came, accompanied by her parents, the place was almost
full. She did not want to occupy a con-
spicuous position, and she pushed through the
crowd to a corner where few could see her.
Yarina followed her closely.

"They say," whispered Yarina, "the
Stundists will be made to kneel in the middle
of the church, and to confess their sins before
all the people. Then Father Paissy will cast
out the devils that possess them. It will be
awful! They'll writhe about, and foam at
their mouths; and they will be like dead
men and women when the devils leave them."

"Is it possible?" cried Halya in the
utmost alarm.

"The diatchok* says so," continued Yarina; "they will be forced upon their knees, and ordered to say all sorts of things against themselves. And if they won't the clergy will burn them with candles."

"In the church? How can you talk such nonsense?" said Halya indignantly.

"It is quite true," Yarina persisted; "the diatchok told me; and he is the man to know. As to your Paul, he has already got a good thrashing. He would not come to church. 'You may kill me, but I will not worship your idols,' he said. You know he calls the icons idols."

Halya's heart sank. Yes, Paul had called them idols to her.

"What else?" she asked: "go on, go on!"

Yarina was silent because she had just seen Panass enter the church, and was trying to attract his notice.

"Well, then! he said, 'I will never worship your idols.' They dragged at him, but he stood like a rock. They set upon him, and beat him, and he fared so badly at their hands that he is now lying at death's door

---

* The chanter of the Psalms in the Russian church.

—one eye knocked out, and a leg and two ribs broken——"

"What do you say? It is impossible," murmured Halya, horror-stricken.

"It is true," said Yarina: "godfather Terenty told me so. He himself set his leg, and put a compress on his eye."

At this moment the sound of triumphant and harmonious singing was heard above the murmur of voices in the church. All were silent. It was the mingled voices of men and women singing a solemn yet exultant hymn.

The Stundists were marching in an orderly procession to the church, through the village street; and every voice chimed in as they moved slowly along, Paul leading with his clear, pure tenor. Savely, the starosta, who was in the church, went out instantly, with his lame assistant. The Stundists were coming on, with exultant faces, as though some scene of triumph lay before them.

"Silence! you fools! you madmen!" roared Savely; "do you think I will stand this nonsense? What do you mean by this howling?"

"Do you ask as a friend, or as the starosta?" said Ooliana.

"As your friend," he replied; "Ooliana, I have always been your friend. Listen to me. Do not enrage Father Paissy, and our Batushka."

"We wish to show we are not afraid, or ashamed," answered Paul.

"Then I forbid you as your starosta," said Savely; "and you boast that you keep the laws. I forbid all singing and uproar."

"Then we must obey," replied Paul, reluctantly; "we are bound to obey you as our starosta."

"If you would only obey me altogether," said Savely mournfully, "all these troubles would come to an end. But you heretics are as obstinate as pigs and mules. Come along quietly now."

Just before the singing ended an old-fashioned carriage had driven up, and old General Nesteroff, in his military uniform and badges, with his son Valerian, descended from it. Valerian had come for once to church, being deeply interested in this movement against the Stundists. He caught sight of Paul's handsome, enthusiastic face.

"Good heavens!" he muttered, "he is lost

to our cause! And what a loss!" **A way**
was made for the General and Valerian to the
only seat in the church — a long black oak
bench near the rood-screen, which shut off the
high altar, and within which none but the
priests may enter. On the rood-screen hung
some dark, discoloured icons, so bedimmed by
the fumes of the incense that scarcely a feature
was distinguishable. The old General bowed
devoutly before them; but Valerian made no
more sign of reverence than did the Stundists,
who had entered the church immediately behind
them. He took up his post in a corner from
which he could have a good view of the
congregation. There the peasants stood, closely
packed together. He saw their shaggy heads,
and stolid, patient faces, their bent shoulders,
as if they were always bearing a yoke. It
was nearly mid-Lent. The women, who fasted
more scrupulously than the men, were sallow
and haggard-looking. The Stundists, who
stood in a group about the middle of the
church, were fresher and cleaner. They were
in their workaday clothes, for this was one
of the feasts so frequent in the Russian Church
which they did not keep, as the rest of the

villagers usually kept it, by idleness and
drunkenness. Ooliana, who stood foremost
among the women, wore a black silk handker-
chief on her head, which framed her placid
face something like a nun's hood. Demyan's
wife was close behind her, with her boy in
her arms — a little fellow of fifteen months,
who could hardly be kept quiet. Several
other of the Stundist women had been obliged
to bring their children, having no one with
whom to leave them. Valerian's heart ached
at the sight of the crowd before him. They
were the sons and daughters of his own mother-
country, Holy Russia; poverty-stricken, ignorant,
superstitious; not knowing their rights as
men, but living lives and dying deaths but
little above the dumb brutes they dwelt amongst.

"Here they come!" cried Yarina to Halya,
as the Stundists entered, "and there is Paul
himself! Heavenly Tzaritza! How beautiful
he is!"

Halya opened her eyes, which she had
closed with a half-fainting sensation. Yes!
Paul's face was to her beautiful beyond words.
The dark locks of hair fell over his broad
forehead, and under them gleamed eyes full

of the fire of courage and high emotion. There was no face like it amid all the faces that surrounded him. Paul looked round the church: and for an instant Halya fancied his eyes met hers. But she was not sure, and her heart sank within her.

"He is not thinking of me!" she said to herself.

She felt unhappy again. She pitied him so that she longed to let him know it. But he did not look her way again.

Now the General had arrived, the service began at once, Father Paissy and Father Vasili celebrating it together. Father Vasili was so much excited that he made several mistakes. He had never seen his church so crowded, and his head felt giddy. For the same reason the diatchok chanted the Psalms out of tune. It was a long monotonous service, but very few prayed. Even among the Stundists none prayed save Ooliana.

Her thoughts went back to the old days, when her father and mother had brought her here to worship God and the saints. The prayers to the saints were lodged in her memory. Then she recalled the times when

she had come hither with her husband; and
her little son Paul clung to her skirts and
bowed when she bowed. Those were precious
days; but they were the days of her ignorance. She had been afraid of death then, and
terrified at the thought of the Day of Judgment. Now all that fear was gone. Love had
cast out fear. The Lord God Almighty called
her His daughter; and she, looking trustingly
into His unseen face, cried, " Father ! " She
prayed silently, with tremulous lips and closed
eyes, as she had never prayed before.

The service was ended; the curtain drawn;
and the priests went into the sacristy to divest
themselves of their gold and embroidered vestments. The diatchok brought a lectern and
placed it in front of the rood-screen. There
was a stir of expectation through the closely
packed congregation. In a few minutes
Father Paissy appeared in a cassock and bowed
slightly to the crowd. Father Vasili, with
a humble mien, ventured to seat himself on
the same bench as the General. Both of the
priests felt flattered by the presence of gentle-
folks; and Father Paissy intended to dis-
tinguish himself before them.

" In the name of the Father, and of the Son, and of the Holy Ghost ! "

The congregation stirred again and pressed forward. Some of them coughed nervously, as if they were going to speak. Father Paissy read his text emphatically.

" ' Do not I hate them, O Lord, that hate Thee ? and am not I grieved with those that rise up against Thee ?

" ' I hate them with perfect hatred : I count them my enemies.'

" So said David, the man after God's own heart. Let us see, then, how David treated his enemies."

Father Paissy read solemnly and slowly the passages in the historical books of the Old Testament which describe the torturing and the slaughter of the Amalekites and Moabites, and the inhabitants of the other cities conquered by David.

" Who now are the Amalekites, the Moabites, the enemies of God ? Where do they dwell ? I will show them to you."

He pointed to the band of Stundists standing in the midst of the congregation ; and for a few seconds an intense stillness pervaded the church.

"Now listen to the command of God," continued Paissy. "'Go and smite Amalek, and utterly destroy all that they have, and spare them not; but slay both man and woman, infant and suckling, ox and sheep, camel and ass.' When King Saul disobeyed the Word of God he was set aside from being king. Will our Tzar risk the vengeance of Almighty God? Will you bring upon yourselves untold calamities for the sake of these enemies of His? Let me explain to you how they are the enemies of God."

He gave an explanation of the Stundists' faith, strangely travestied; and he proceeded to accuse them of great immorality. Here was an opportunity for him to display his learning before the General and Valerian; and he made long quotations from the Fathers, with Greek and Latin phrases thrown in. The peasants stared at him. Was this the conjuration addressed to the devils which had taken possession of the Stundists?

"You see, my brethren," said Paissy, smoothing down his long beard, and rubbing his white hands, "you see what damning

errors are taught by these false prophets. It
is the darkness of ignorant heresy."

The orthodox congregation felt great
darkness in their own minds; and were quite
ready to believe in his words.

"And what are they doing? The holy
icons, which have been the protection of you
and your forefathers, they break into pieces,
casting them into the fire, or using them for
covers for pots. The holy wafers they throw
away——"

A murmur of horror ran through the
audience. The orthodox understood this.

Paissy excited himself so much that he
forgot the educated men who were listening to
him, and began to abuse the Stundists soundly.
At first indeed he called them by Biblical names
—"Jezebel's seed," and "Sons of Baal"; but
passing to a simpler phraseology, he denounced
them in a very primitive manner as ruffians,
scoundrels, blackguards, hell-hounds. In the
midst of this tirade his eyes fell upon the
indignant and disgusted faces of the General
and Valerian, who were evidently shocked by
his coarseness.

Paissy was confused, and stumbled in the

middle of a sentence. He valued very highly the opinion of educated people; and the General was well known in Kovylsk, where he might spread an unfavourable report of his sermon. It concluded, therefore, rather weakly, as he tried to please both classes of his audience. Only Father Vasili was satisfied, even boundlessly delighted with all that was said. His owl-like face and little round eyes were not for a moment turned from the preacher; and he munched with his lips as if he rolled some delicate morsel in his mouth at each well-chosen text or quotation, whispering to himself, "Clever! it serves them right, the infidels!"

"Amen!" at last said Paissy; and with another bow he disappeared into the sacristy.

Shutting the door he fell into a chair, and sighed heavily. He was not satisfied with his sermon. Now it was over, and the opportunity lost, he thought of many excellent ideas and phrases that would have made it really eloquent. Surely the devil had bewildered him, and clouded his memory! It was the presence of those damnable Stundists; especially of that old witch, whose

w

face, full of intelligence, had often caught his eye.

Paissy was so absorbed in angry reflections that he did not notice that neither Father Vasili nor the diatchok had followed him into the sacristy. He sat alone gnawing his under-lip, and mourning over his lost opportunity.

CHAPTER XXVII.

PAUL'S DEFENCE.

THE congregation did not disperse from
the church. Something quite unforeseen had
happened.

When Paissy disappeared the assembled
peasants lingered in perplexity. Was this
all? Why had he not abjured the Stundists,
and exorcised them? They had no clear ideas
as to what the exorcism would be; but they
had expected something extraordinary. All
they had got was an ordinary service and
a sermon!

Halya looked across the church at Paul.
His face was at one moment deadly pale, at
the next flushed with crimson as from some
inward struggle. There was a strange light
in his eyes. Halya grew excited as if by
some psychical or spiritual communication between them. She felt bewildered, yet not
miserable. It seemed as if she was impelled
to do something she shrank from, which made

w 2.

her shy and tremulous. Paul took a step or two forward, and cried out with an incredible effort : "Orthodox Christians! I ask your permission to speak to you."

Halya sobbed. The congregation gave a start. All eyes were fixed upon Paul Rudenko.

"Ah! you Anathema Maranatha!" exclaimed Father Vasili angrily; "how could your accursed tongue speak in the temple of God?"

Valerian stepped out of his corner, and approached the Batushka.

"Let him speak," he said persuasively; "I have a great curiosity to hear him. And you can easily refute all he says. Besides, people will say you are afraid of being beaten in discussion with a Stundist," he added in an undertone.

"What! what!" exclaimed Father Vasili; "I afraid of being beaten by that ignorant peasant! But I would rather——"

He was about to say he would rather see him have a good thrashing, but he recollected in time to whom he was speaking, and said with unexpected indulgence—

"Very well, Paul Rudenko, you may speak,

and we will hearken. But it seems to me you are rather young for a preacher or a teacher."

No abuses could have damaged Paul with his audience so much as an allusion to his youthfulness. It was but a few years since he was a boy, and everybody knew it. His emotion was so great that for a few moments he could not utter a word. The circle of old familiar faces around him made him dumb.

"Don't be afraid," whispered Ooliana; "our Lord says, 'Take no thought how or what ye shall speak; for it shall be given you in that same hour what ye shall speak. For it is not ye that speak, but the Spirit of your Father which speaketh in you.'"

Paul's face grew pale and calm.

"Lord! Thou who didst give speech to the dumb, teach me what to say that I may not dishonour Thy holy name!"

He thought he was speaking the words in his heart; but unconsciously he had pronounced them aloud.

A wave of sympathy rushed through the audience in his behalf, and the familiar faces grew more friendly. His timidity vanished. He raised his head and spoke fluently and courageously, as if he was addressing an ordinary Stundist gathering.

"Brothers!" he said, "it is not for an ignorant man like me to think of teaching you. I only wish to say a few words about our faith, which has been attacked in your hearing to-day. God, who is present everywhere, will hear me, and He will judge whether I speak the truth."

He paused for a moment to take breath. The crowd made room for him, and now he stood on the lowest step of the rood screen, in full view of the whole congregation. Halya pushed her way nearer to him, pressing forward Yarina at the same time. She could not lose a word he would say, or a movement he might make. This Paul was not a shy, timid lover, whom she could make miserable or happy by a word. He was a leader of men, a prophet; one who could guide her steps on earth towards the heavenly goal. His Testament was hidden in her bosom, and she pressed her hands upon it as she crept nearer to him.

"It is true," he went on, "that we do not reverence the icons, for God's commandment is plain—'Thou shalt not make to thyself any graven image, or the likeness of anything that is in heaven above, or on the earth beneath, or in the waters under the earth. Thou shalt not bow down to them, nor worship them.' We must obey God rather than men.

"It is true we do not pay dues to the priest, because we have one priest, the Lord Jesus Christ, who is ever at the right hand of God, making intercession for us.

"It is true we do not pray to the saints. We pray only to God, who alone can hear us from all places, and at all times. The saints were men like ourselves, and they are not present everywhere, as God is.

"It is true we do not keep the saints' days as days of idleness or drunkenness. God says we must hallow one day in seven, fifty-two days in the year. But besides these Sabbaths, the Church says we must keep more than a hundred feasts.

"It is true we do not drink vodka, because it steals away the brains of men, and brings poverty and vice into the country.

"Let me tell you very simply what we believe. We believe that Jesus Christ, the

Son of God, the Prince of Glory, King of Kings, and Lord of Lords, did, in very truth, come down from His heavenly palaces and live as we live on the earth. He became a servant, a working man, dwelling with common working people. Why? What for? Not to save us from toil, or hunger, or thirst. No! He was an hungered, and athirst, and weary often, like us. Not to save us from sorrow and death. No! He wept, and was grieved, and was troubled in spirit, and died a shameful death. He came to save us from our sins, to make the drunken man sober, the thief honest. All sin flies from His presence. Envy, hatred and malice cannot dwell where He is. Pride, and covetousness, and selfishness wither away and perish where He reigns. Oh! what a Paradise this earth would be if every man would let the Lord take away his sins!"

The profound emotion, and the evident sincerity, with which the young Stundist spoke, riveted the attention of all his hearers. Even Father Vasili listened with a grave face.

"Our Lord came," Paul continued, "to found a kingdom of love upon earth; a new brotherhood in which all men, from the Tzar upon the throne to the miserable prisoner in the lowest dungeon, should be brothers. God is the Father of all, and in His sight there is no respect of persons. We are His sons, and brethren one of another. God is love, and he that dwelleth in love dwelleth in God, and God in him. The rich man will share his goods with the poor, and the poor man will work heartily for the rich. The strong will protect the weak. Those who are happy will visit the sorrowful. The young will care for the old, and the old will counsel the young. That is the kingdom of heaven on earth, and its two laws are given by Jesus Christ our King, 'As ye would that men should do to you, do ye also to them likewise;' and the second is like unto it: 'A new commandment I give unto you, that ye love one another, as I have loved you, that ye also love one another.' Oh! what a Paradise this earth would be if all men kept those laws!"

"Ah! if that could only be!" exclaimed a wondering and sympathetic voice amid the listening crowd.

"It will be!" cried Paul. "Shall Christ have lived in vain? Shall He have been forsaken by His disciples, and given up to His enemies, and judged unrighteously, and crucified on the shameful cross, and all for nothing? No! This kingdom of His shall surely come. The will of God shall be done on earth as it is done in heaven. Nay, the kingdom of God is come. You may enter into it this day, this hour! Christ is waiting to take away your sins, the sins of every one of us. Stretch out your hand only, and He will lead you into His kingdom. You will know Him in your hearts, and you will love Him as He loves you. Heaven will come down into your souls, and you will hear the voice of God speaking to you there. Even on earth you will taste of heavenly joys."

A murmur of gladness ran through the assembly. Never had their priests spoken to them as Paul spoke. Every one amongst them understood his simple words, and their hearts vibrated to their meaning. What a Paradise earth would be! Ah! how true that was! The women sighed, and tears ran down their cheeks, and the men listened with eager attention.

"Oh! my brothers! Would God I could

die for you!" cried Paul, stretching out his
hands to them. Then, with a strong shudder,
which made him visibly tremble before them,
and with a solemn but faltering voice, he exclaimed, " Yes! I could almost wish that myself
were accursed from Christ for my brethren,
my kinsmen according to the flesh!"

A profound silence fell upon the crowd at
these words: so awful were these words on
Paul's lips, and so deep an impression they
made on the hearts of those who heard him.
Yarina was weeping on Halya's shoulder; but
Halya shed no tears. She was absorbed, fas-
cinated. She felt that she was passing through
a great crisis in her soul. Her past life was
falling from her, and it would be impossible
for her to take it up again. Paul was revealing
her to herself, and at the same time was un-
folding himself to her, and revealing a new
world, and a new and living God whom she
had not known till now. To pray again to the
saints, and to the official Deity of yesterday,
would be impossible to her.

She stood transfixed, and with her the whole
congregation, with eyes fastened upon Paul, as
if awaiting something more from him. It

would hardly have startled them if some
strange sign had followed his words. A
voice from behind the rood-screen broke upon
the silence harshly—

"What is this? Is this an orthodox church
or a Stundist meeting-house?"

It was Paissy, who had just come out of
the sacristy, and heard the last sentence of
Paul's speech.

The sound of the stern, hard voice broke the
spell which bound them. The starosta Savely
made his way to the porch and disappeared;
several of the older men followed him. Father
Vasili began to excuse himself awkwardly,
explaining that he had expected Paul to incriminate himself, and that all the people had
been very eager to hear him. Paissy did not
even look at him, but turned with a frowning
and threatening face to the congregation. He
was so enraged that he did not notice the
General approaching him, with an evident in-
tention of speaking to him.

He paced down the aisle towards Paul, the
crowd making way for him as he passed by.
The Stundists stood in a close cluster, Paul in
the front of them. Paissy paused within a few

feet of him, and for a few seconds pierced him through with a stern look of hatred and malignancy. In his pale blue eyes there flamed an evil light.

"Accursed from Christ!" he said, in a low, hissing voice. "You never said a truer word! Accursed on earth and in heaven! In the temple of God Himself you flaunt your heresies! Do you know the penalty?"

"I know it," answered Paul tranquilly; "I know it, and am ready to pay it. You cannot treat me worse than Loukyan, and he prayed for you as he lay dying."

Paissy's rage almost conquered him. He could hardly speak, but with a great effort he commanded his voice.

"Where is the starosta?" he inquired.

Panass pushed himself forward. "He has left the church, your reverence, but I will fetch him back," he said eagerly.

It was but a minute or two before he returned, and with him Savely. The village constables were still in the church.

"Keep this man under arrest until he is ordered before the Consistory," said Father Paissy. Savely nodded to the constables, who

approached Paul at once, taking off their belts
mechanically. Paul held out his hands to
them.

"Tie them behind his back!" cried Father
Paissy.

"What! In the church!" exclaimed Valerian, coming forward. "Father Paissy, this
is an outrage—a desecration. Even murderers
used to find sanctuary in a church." ·

"Take him to the porch, you fools!" said
Father Paissy, scowling at the unlooked-for
interference.

But at this moment the congregation suddenly and simultaneously rushed to the entrance, carrying with them Valerian, Father
Paissy, and a number of the Stundists. Paul,
who had no wish to resist, or to appear as if he
were running away, retreated to the wall, and
was pushed by the surging crowd into a
corner. He saw Halya struggling to get
near him, and her face wore the resolute—
almost stern—expression he had seen on it in
his dream.

"Paul," she murmured to him, when they
stood together, "let me go with you wher-
ever you may go. I will believe in your

God and join your people. My place is beside you."

Paul could not answer. He clasped her hand in his, and, lifting up his eyes to heaven, whispered with his lips a thanksgiving to God.

CHAPTER XXVIII.

A MIRACLE.

THE sudden stampede which had emptied the church was occasioned by the sight of a thin column of smoke arising from the thatched roof of old Sheelo's hut. If it had been early in the morning, everyone would have known it was only the smoke from the wood fire in his oven; but at this hour, especially during service, no smoke would come from the oven chimney.

The verger at the door had first perceived it, and he had been greatly astonished at seeing first the blue soft vapour, and then the gradually increasing volume of smoke over Sheelo's house. He was waiting in the porch to show proper respect to the General and Valerian as they left the church, and to help them into the carriage, standing in readiness for them. He glanced hesitatingly into the church, wishing the General would make haste. Still the smoke gathered and spread. He ran out a few yards. Oh! there was no mistake. The smoke was not coming out of the chimney, but from the roof of the sheds behind the house.

But, as a man used to reverent conduct in the church, the verger did not give the alarm, but cautiously sought out Sheelo in the closely packed congregation, and whispered to him his house was on fire. The old man shrieked and ran out. A few followed him out of curiosity. Then alarming shouts and cries were heard in the porch. A fire in a village of wooden buildings and thatched roofs is seldom limited to one dwelling. The congregation rushed out of the church like a torrent.

The village street formed an obtuse angle, at the apex of which stood the church. It followed the course of the river which flowed near it, but in a rounder curve. Some of the straggling cottages were nearer, others a little further from the water. They were all detached, each one surrounded by its granary, wood-barn, and cattle-sheds, larger or smaller, according to the circumstances of the occupier. For the wealth of Knishi consisted of the primitive wealth of herds and grain. All the dwellings were built of wood, with roofs of thatch or dried

x

reeds. For the last three or four weeks an arid east wind had been blowing off the illimitable steppes, drying up the moisture of the wintry rains and snows. Everything was almost as parched as in the drought of summer.

The fire started in Sheelo's cattle-shed, only a few yards from the dwelling, which was the ninth house from the church. Nearest the church-gate stood the little hut of two rooms occupied by the verger and his old father, Spiridon. The old man stood at the door shaking with palsy, and leaning on a staff. He kept muttering in his old husky voice that he had seen the imbecile Avidiushka coming out of Sheelo's cattle-shed, and crying "Burn, burn, burn them!" But no one took any notice of him: he was childish and his memory was gone. The indubitable fact was more pressing. The place had been set on fire, and no one wondered at it, as Sheelo had many enemies.

As the crowd ran down the street they saw thick puffs of smoke rising from the dry thatch in a gigantic column. Then it suddenly cleared away, as if the fire was about to burn itself out; the roof fell in, and a low yellow glow brooded for an instant over the shed. A cry of terror broke from the throats of the approaching throng. For suddenly a huge pillar of flame, which seemed to reach the skies, blazed up, tossing hither and thither flakes of fire. In the adjacent sheds were heard the screams of the horses and the bellowing of the cattle.

Old Sheelo rushed to the door, trying to unbolt it, but his hands trembled so much he could do nothing, and the bolt did not move. Valerian came to his help with a strong shaft in his hands, and with one blow pushed back the bolt and flung open the door. The maddened animals rushed out encircled with smoke, knocking down Valerian and their master in their flight. A horse was left inside tied up to the manger. Paul, who by this time had followed the crowd, covered his head with his jacket, and rushed under the already burning roof to rescue it. He came back dragging the horse by its halter.

"They want leaders!" cried Valerian to him. "You take command of one band of men, and I will order the others."

"Yes, yes!" said Paul.

x 2

He turned to Panass, who was looking on
with a stupefied face, and holding with a slack
hand a pair of horses, which escaped from him
and began to gallop madly about the yard.

"Drive them all away into the fields," he
cried; "they will trample down the people."

Panass obeyed reluctantly and listlessly,
and drove them away to a place of safety.
Valerian and a few peasants meanwhile climbed
on to the roof of the dwelling-house, hoping
to save it. They worked away with pitchforks and axes to remove the thatch, piling it
up in a safe direction, behind a wall protected
from the fire. Sheelo and some other helpers
removed the goods from his house, and brought
out first the icons in their silver frames as his
most valuable property.

"The icons! the icons!" shouted several
voices. "Let the icons see what is the
matter."

Two peasants, standing in the middle of
the yard, and facing the flames, lifted up the
largest icon. The yellow light shone upon
their swarthy faces, and flashed on the silver
frames, and on the dark image of the saint.
It was their patron-saint whose feast they

were celebrating. Surely he would save his votary!

But Valerian on the roof found it impossible to save the dwelling. The shed had turned into a huge pile of burning wood, and flakes of fire were falling in all directions: on the heads of the people, on the rafters which they were laying bare, on the dry thatch they were trying to carry away. Chains of men had been formed by Paul, and every pail and bucket in Knishi was being passed from hand to hand full of water from the river, and sent back again empty by chains of women. But Sheelo's house was already on fire.

At this instant the old General came up. He had sent his coachman post-haste to a village a few miles away, which possessed a fire-engine. He came at a critical moment. Unseen, the pile of thatch laid behind the wall had been smouldering, and before Valerian and his helpers on the roof perceived it, a black cloud of smoke filled the air.

"Come down! all of you!" shouted the General in a loud strong voice of command, rising above every other sound. They obeyed instinctively; and as the last man, Valerian himself, touched the ground, a broad flame rushed over the roof, burning away the last remnant of thatch. Valerian's hair was scorched, and his cloth coat was singeing.

"Are you hurt?" asked his father in alarm.

"Not a bit," he answered. "But what are we to do next?"

The wind was blowing in a strong and steady breeze from the east, bearing on its wings the blazing tufts of straw and thatch, which were detached from the burning house. They looked from the unextinguished fire to the poor little adjacent cottages with their high-pitched roofs and deep eaves, under which were piled up their fuel of dried reeds. The next house was already caught. It belonged to Koozka. But beyond it lay a small space free of buildings, and here the fire might be stayed. The chains formed by the men and women moved on under Valerian's direction to stop the progress of the conflagration by deluging this house with water. Koozka saw his place doomed to destruction, and stood looking on, wringing his hands and lamenting in a loud voice.

Suddenly, from the cattle-shed, which was already in flames, came an awful heart-rending scream, whether of a human being or an animal none could tell. It was the death-cry of a horse which had been forgotten—old Koozka's favourite horse.

"Save him! save him!" cried Koozka, rushing to the shed. Part of the wooden wall had burnt down, and through the opening could be seen the poor animal, standing in a paralysis of fear, among burning rafters and stalls and beams. No one among the crowd dared move. Old Koozka alone rushed forward to save his favourite.

"Come back, old man!" shouted the peasants behind him, "you will perish without time for repentance! Come back!"

But he did not listen to them. He pressed on as if he were beside himself. Paul could not bear to see him recklessly throw his life away. He rushed forward and pushed him back, flinging himself into the burning shed. As he brought the terrified horse through the flames by its burning halter, the beam over the door gave way and knocked him down.

Ooliana screamed and ran to her son, who

was lying almost unconscious on the ground.
She dragged him out of danger, and Valerian
hurried to him and examined him with great
anxiety. Fortunately, his thick sheepskin hat
had preserved him; and when Valerian touched
the place upon his forehead on which the beam
had fallen he only winced a little.

"Does it hurt?" he asked.

"Not much," answered Paul. He was still
too much afraid of Valerian to accept his care
with pleasure. He attempted to get up, but
his head felt giddy and he fell back again.

"You must take him home," said Valerian
to Ooliana; "there may be more mischief done
than we can see at once. Here is our carriage.
You shall drive home in it."

The fire pursued its relentless course.
Though the next house was soaked and
drenched with water, it retarded the flames
only for a short time. The scorching heat
dried up the artificial moisture, though hundreds
of pails of water had been poured upon the
roof, trickling down the walls and washing
off the plaster. When the flames caught it,
after smouldering sulkily a few minutes it
rose in a fiery pillar, at first as straight as an

arrow into the air, and then wavering a little. The people stood, with their hearts throbbing heavily, watching the direction it would take. On that depended the fate of the village.

The wind blew a little towards the river. On that side was safety. All at once the fiery column fell to pieces, as if struck by some powerful blow, and broke downwards in a cloud of smoke, and ashes, and sparks. But, as if reasserting itself, it rose up straight again, wavered, and beat against the air. Then with the spring of a wild beast seizing its prey it flung itself on the next building.

There was no escape, no help. The village was given up to the mercy of the flames. The house stood like a doomed man, lonely, abandoned by all, groaning at its fate. Valerian resumed his efforts further on. But smoke and cinders from the burning houses assailed him and his helpers on the roof, suffocating their breathing and blinding their sight. Their clothes began to smoulder, and they poured water over themselves to keep them from burning. But this only helped for a moment. The soaked clothes became hot, and their bodies were steamed as in a vapour bath.

The desperate conflict continued It was necessary to retreat again and again in the direction of the church. Fortunately, the wide cemetery was on that side. Still, it was surrounded by a wooden fence, rotten with age; and at the gate stood old Spiridon's hut. The church was built of timber, though it had a tiled roof; and its three cupolas were of wood painted green. The rotten fence and the thatched hut were dangerous neighbours; if either of them caught fire the church also was doomed.

Valerian, who was the leader in this tenacious struggle, bade the peasants to destroy the hut and fence; and they, understanding the gravity of the situation, set actively to work. It was partially done when the church doors were opened, and Father Paissy and Father Vasili appeared in their full vestments. The diatchok carried after them the silver bason containing holy water and the brush for sprinkling it. The choir followed, bearing crosses, and banners, and icons in a solemn procession.

Coming down the steps leading to the porch, Father Paissy took the sprinkler in

his hand, dipped it in the holy water, and
shook off the drops in the direction of the
fire. He, the diatchok, and the choir started
off in a solemn chant of one of the metrical
prose hymns of the Russian Church.

The people bared their heads, and humbly
and piously crossed themselves. The conflict
was stopped. Now that God's power was
invoked, human efforts seemed to them pre-
posterous and even irreverent.

Paissy apparently was of the same mind
with the peasants. At the head of the procession he paced on towards the conflagration,
pausing at the broken fence, sprinkling it,
and singing with redoubled zeal. The crowd
pressed round the clergy like a frightened
flock. Some joined in the hymn, lifting their
eyes towards heaven. Others cried aloud to
the icons. They all ceased to take measures
against the fire except the Stundists, who,
under the direction of Demyan, went on
demolishing the little hut at the gate.

"Father Paissy!" cried Valerian, "that
hut and the fence must come down. If it
sets on fire nothing can save the church."

"Thou art our refuge! We place our

trust in Thee," sang Paissy, not deigning to reply to Valerian.

" Boys!" shouted Valerian, "come and help to pull down the hut."

Not one of the orthodox moved. But Demyan and the Stundists worked with redoubled ardour, no one interfering with them. Demyan's strong muscular force was of the greatest service. It seemed almost supernatural. He brought down whole beams with a rattle, which mingled its noise with the chanting of the clergy. The hut disappeared. In its place was nothing but a heap of rubbish that would not burn.

But the fire was not abating. The unbearable heat and smoke compelled the priests and the choir to retreat. By degrees they were driven back to the church porch, and stood there with their banners and icons like a garrison defending its last fortress.

The voices of the choir grew husky and hoarse. The holy water was exhausted in the bason; but Paissy went on waving his dry sprinkler to keep his party in heart. The paint on the cupolas began to shrivel, and was covered with bubbles like a scalded skin.

In several places the plaster cracked and fell down.

"Father Vasili," whispered Valerian, "let us bring ladders, and pour water on the cupolas. The wood is as dry as a match-box, and may catch fire any moment."

The Batushka cast a glance at the cupolas with the experienced eye of an old village settler, and shook his head in alarm. The church would certainly be soon in flames, and his own house stood just behind it. But he dared not do anything on his own authority. He drew closer to Paissy, and told him what Valerian had advised.

"And you too are tempted!" exclaimed Paissy. "God is our refuge. In the midst of the flames He will preserve His temple."

It was a brave answer. His face was begrimed with smoke; his throat was parched; his vestments were tarnished. The flames were darting a thousand threatening tongues towards the already heated walls. Yet Paissy stood firm in the forefront of the terrified band of priests and choristers.

Precisely at this moment the wind veered a point northwards. The fiery tongues slanted

away from the consecrated edifice. The suffocating smoke grew lighter, and the heat more
bearable.

"He has stretched out His arm. The
Lord God stands up for His temple," cried
the orthodox peasants.

Paissy was exultant.

But all at once a sight was seen which
filled the peasants with horror again. The
breeze was now blowing directly down the
other side of the angle formed by the straggling
street, and the first thatched roof had caught
fire. The buildings here stood closer together,
and under the broad eaves of most of them
were stores of dried reeds. The people hurried
down towards their threatened dwellings, and
looked on helplessly, as if benumbed by this
new catastrophe. A broad stream of smoke
and fire rolled down the street. The new
current of air was steady and unrelenting.

Karpo's house stood in the midst of the
threatening stream; and Marfa, in a paroxysm
of terror, rushed in and out. Now she appeared bearing some treasure in her hands
now she stood wringing her hands and tearing
her hair. Karpo and a few neighbours were

helping listlessly. There was no escape, and everyone had lost heart.

"Halya! Halya!" shouted Marfa, "why have you run away? where are you, you hussy?"

But Halya was nowhere to be seen. She had disappeared immediately after Ooliana had taken Paul home.

"Wait a moment! I know where you are gone, shameless wretch!" she cried in an ungovernable fury.

Seizing hold of a wooden rolling-pin she was about to rush to Ostron. But as she ran into the street her progress was arrested by the sight of the clergy and choristers standing in the church porch, and chanting a hymn of thanksgiving. This gave her distracted mind a fresh turn. She stopped, and turned to the people, waving her hands passionately.

"Look there!" she exclaimed; "look what those idlers are doing. They have saved their own property, the church, and the Batushka's house; and they are overjoyed, and sing praises to God. But the village may burn to ashes before they stir."

A circle of women, joined by a few men, gathered round Marfa, amazed at her passion, and the boldness with which she attacked the clergy.

"Ah! go on with your howling!" she resumed; "when you want the priest's due you are always at hand. But when the people want help you are no good. Don't you see the village is catching fire every-where? And you stay there idling, afraid to singe your vestments, sluggards and cowards as you are!"

"Shut up, you fool!" growled Karpo. But her shrill reproaches had caught the ear of Father Paissy, and he gave a sign for the chanting to cease.

"The woman is right," he said; "in our joy for the church being saved we have for-gotten our duty to the village. Let us go forth to arrest the progress of the flames!"

In a few minutes an imposing procession was formed. Father Paissy headed it, and Father Vasili walked close behind him. Then came the diatchok and the choir. Last of all the icons, crosses, and banners, which were thus placed in greater safety. The orthodox peasants surrounded them, and joined in vigorously with the hoarse chanting of the choristers, whose throats were rough with smoke, and exhausted by their prolonged efforts. Burning fragments fell upon their vestments, and one banner was set on fire. But Father Paissy stood his ground bravely. He swung his sprinkler dipped in holy water like a magician controlling the elements with his magic wand.

The priest had a powerful though invisible ally. The sun was going down, and the cooler air blowing from the river and the great forest beyond it once more caused the wind to change and to veer northwards. This blew the flames of the house next to Karpo's across the open land at the back. By the time the procession had gone the whole length of the village, and retraced its steps, the danger was over. The people, worked up to the highest pitch of excitement, watched the tongues of flame slanting away from the houses harmlessly. Marfa fell on her knees before Paissy, and kissed his hands.

"A miracle! a miracle!" shouted the crowd. All crossed themselves; many wept, and knelt down in the dust before the icons.

Y

A fourth part of the village had been destroyed, but the rest was out of danger. The icons, the procession, and the chanting had saved it.

At this moment a cloud of dust was seen coming along the road, and a small fire-engine, drawn by two exhausted horses, and driven by a disabled soldier, drove up at a jog-trot.

" Where shall we play the engine, friends?" he called to the crowd. A sudden gust of laughter answered him. All around were smouldering heaps of ruins, which must be extinguished for fear of any fresh outbreak of the fire. There was work enough for half a dozen engines such as his. But the peril was past, and the people were full of the strange hilarity which succeeds the sense of impending danger. Valerian and his father, as they walked homeward with slow and tired steps, heard behind them repeated roars of laughter.

CHAPTER XXIX.

ANOTHER MARTYR.

TWENTY houses had been burned down, and nearly a hundred persons were left roofless. They were mostly of the poorest class, and their huts were not of much worth. But they were their homes, and the inmates had lost all their few possessions.

But the terrible day was not over. A new and a worse calamity was brooding. The bad seed so diligently sown by the Batushka and Matushka was about to bear fruit.

Paissy dismissed the choristers with the banners and icons. But he, calling Father Vasili to his side, took up a position on the steps of the church porch. A crowd gathered round him. Father Paissy could do what he pleased with such an audience. He had not forgotten the scene in the church only a few hours before, when the leader of the Stundists had boldly preached a sermon in defence of

Y 2

their heresy. A man like that was too dangerous to be left in peace, to work his wicked will unopposed.

"Orthodox people!" he cried, lifting up his voice to be heard to the confines of the crowd, "you have seen the hand of God to-day. He has given you a miracle as a sign to confirm your faith. You have sinned against Him in suffering heretics to dwell in peace among you, teaching their damnable doctrines, and leading their immoral lives. God has punished you for this sin. Who set the village on fire?"

"The Stundists! the Stundists!" shouted the people.

"No, neighbours, no!" exclaimed the starosta Savely, who had been chosen for his office because of his integrity and justice. "Old Spiridon saw the idiot Avdiushka come out of Sheelo's cattle-shed just before it set on fire."

"But no doubt God permitted it on account of the Stundists," continued Paissy, "if they did not do it themselves. The people of Knishi have allowed God's holy name to be blasphemed, and the saints to be dishonoured, and the icons to be destroyed. Is there any wonder that this judgment has befallen them? Think to yourself—if any man reviled your father and spoke evil and untrue things of him, would you stand quietly by and listen to him? And if through fear and cowardice you held your tongue, how do you suppose your father would judge you, when he came to hear of it? Would he praise you, and thank you for your love to him? God has seen, He has heard, He has known all that these reprobates have done; how they denounce His temples, and the icons, and even the cross, the holy cross on which His Son, our Lord Jesus Christ, was crucified. And you, in whose presence these things have been done, you not only did not stop these miscreants, but you bore with them and even encouraged them."

"We will bear with them no longer! We will defend our God and the orthodox faith!" cried many voices.

"That is right!" Paissy went on. "Bethink yourselves before it is too late. The Divine will has been revealed to you this day. You are ignorant people; so God would not

annihilate you as He did in old times, when
the earth opened and swallowed up those who
rebelled against Him. You have been punished slightly. Shall I tell you why? Because this morning you suffered that heretic
to utter his blasphemies here, in this temple
of God. And no man stopped him. If it had
not been so, if as soon as he opened his mouth
you had dragged him out, there would have
been no fire. You would have left the church
in time to see the idiot—if it was the idiot—and
the fire would have been at once extinguished."

This was a conclusive argument. Everybody saw and felt its force.

"Ah, my Lord, that is really true!" exclaimed old Sheelo.

"Oh, the accursed!" joined in the crowd.

There were no more doubts, no hesitation.
The Stundists were the authors of all their
calamities.

"Who says it was the idiot?" asked
Panass. "As likely as not it was one of the
heretics themselves. The idiot never set the
village on fire before."

The accusation, false as it was, and in
direct contradiction to the fact—for every

Stundist had been in the church—was received with acclamation by the crowd.

"Of course they did it," said the philosopher Koozka. "They are always glad to do mischief to the orthodox. They have been at it all the winter."

"Who was in the village at the time? Who saw anyone?" shouted Sheelo.

Old Spiridon was pushed to the front, and mumbled out his story; how he had seen somebody slip out of Sheelo's shed and run off towards the river.

"Who was it?" asked Paissy.

"He was running and howling. I thought it was Avdiushka," muttered the old man.

"Oh, nonsense! you are blind! You mistook somebody else for him," said Panass.

"How is it only the houses of the orthodox are burned, and none of theirs?" asked Okhrim, who stood beside his son.

It was true. It happened that the Stundists' houses were scattered at the two ends of the village street farthest from the fire. The crowd suddenly grew exasperated.

Some voice shouted:—"Neighbours! let us give the heretics a lesson."

The nearest house belonged to Kondraty. They rushed in, bursting open the door; but it was empty. In a few minutes everything was broken to pieces, the windows smashed, the boxes ransacked, and all their contents—clothes, books, utensils—torn into shreds, and scattered within and without the dwelling.

They went to the next house. There, too, was nobody, except two or three little children trying to hide under the benches. The people left that also in ruins.

Meanwhile, the Stundists were gone to their usual evening prayer-meeting at Loukyan's bee-farm, where they had often assembled since his death. But no one remembered that.

"Ah! they have hidden themselves. They know they are guilty, the miscreants!" cried the peasants, growing more and more excited.

There were six houses in Knishi belonging to the Stundists, which all shared the same fate as Kondraty's. The maddened mob thirsted for more vengeance.

"Let us go to Paul Rudenko's!" cried Panass; "he is the cause of all. He's sure to be at home with his broken head."

"Come! come!" roared the mob. "We ought to have begun with him. He is the cause of all."

With clubs and pitchforks in their hands, the infuriated crowd hurried through the fields to Ostron.

Father Paissy grew somewhat alarmed. He wished to teach the heretics a lesson, but he did not want the thing to run to any great excess of unlawful outbreak. Bidding Father Vasili to restrain the people in the village, he hastened after the throng that were crushing down the spring wheat in their furious progress.

Shortly after Ooliana and Paul had reached home, Halya had crept in timidly, hardly knowing how they would receive her. Paul was lying down on his bed, and Ooliana had already bandaged his grievous bruise. He was deadly pale, and his eyes looked sunken and dim; but they brightened as he caught sight of her, and he tried to stretch out his arms to her. Ooliana caressed her, and bade her sit down and watch Paul whilst she went to prepare him some food, of which he was sorely in need.

Halya sat beside him, holding her hand

in his, and telling him again and again that she loved him, and only him. She wished for nothing but to share his life, whatever its sorrows and sufferings might be. To be with him even unto death, never again to be parted from him—that was all she asked of God. She had read his Testament daily, and she believed all he said out of it was true. If it was true for him, it was true for her.

Paul listened as if he were in a dream—a dream of rapture. His head was giddy and his thoughts bewildered, and he could not say many words; but he was profoundly happy. The promise given to him months ago was at last fulfilled. His people would be Halya's people, his God her God.

Ooliana left them very much alone, only looking in now and then with a smile like a benediction on her face. She, too, was deeply agitated. The imperative summons to church —the church dear to her from a thousand associations, yet a profaned temple where she could no longer worship; Paul's noble and brave confession of faith in it; the strong impression made by it on his listeners; the fire; and now Halya's presence—all stirred her

tranquil soul into unwonted tumult. She
passed in and out of her cattle-sheds, feeding
the patient creatures dependent on her care;
flung handfuls of corn to her fowls, busied herself a little while in the fold-yard; and then,
wearied out, sat down to rest on the bank of
earth under her kitchen window.

She could see the clouds of smoke rolling
over Knishi—now almost black, now with red
reflections on them. By-and-bye, when Halya
was ready to go, she would accompany her,
if Paul was well enough to be left, and see
what help she could give. At any rate, she
could shelter a family or two under her roof.
Presently she would put on a large cauldron
for soup, that there might be supper for her
guests. Perhaps this crisis would reconcile
her to her neighbours again, the beloved
playfellows of her childhood, who had stood
aloof from her all the winter. What else
could it do?

When the sun was setting, Ooliana prepared supper, and called Paul and Halya to it.
He had recovered a little, and sat down at
the table, but he could not eat. This evening
was the happiest evening of his life—unique,

unparalleled. He wanted to celebrate it in a peculiar way.

"Mother, will you get us some wine?" he said. "We three will take the Lord's Supper together."

Ooliana rose silently, with a joy inexpressible, and took from the cupboard an earthenware jug into which she poured some wine, and brought it and a plateful of black bread, which she placed before Paul.

"Give me my Testament, Halya," he said.

Opening it, he read these words—

"For I have received of the Lord that which I also delivered unto you. That the Lord Jesus the same night in which He was betrayed took bread: and when He had given thanks, He broke it, and said, Take, eat: this is my body, which is broken for you: this do in remembrance of me. After the same manner also He took the cup, when He had supped, saying, This cup is the new testament in my blood: this do ye as oft as ye drink it, in remembrance of me. For as often as ye eat this bread, and drink this cup, ye do show forth the Lord's death till He come."

"In remembrance of Christ!" said Paul, breaking off a morsel of bread and passing it to his mother. Then, with radiant joy upon his face, he gave Halya another morsel and ate one himself. It was a sign to them all that Halya had definitely thrown in her lot with theirs.

But what was this sound breaking in upon the stillness of the evening? Ooliana heard the murmur of many voices in the distance. Could her old friends be coming to seek her ready help? She hastened to the door to meet them. The tread of many feet came nearer. But those angry shouts, those furious cries? It was a maddened mob rushing across the corn-fields lying between Knishi and Ostron.

Paul and Halya listened within doors; but the sound to them was more like the hum of insects. They smiled at one another, partly amused and partly wondering at Ooliana's impetuous movements. She came quickly back to them.

"Halya! Go away! Fly!" she exclaimed. "Let nobody find you here! Some great calamity is in store for us."

Paul threw open the window and looked out. The forerunners of the mob were already in sight.

"Halya! For God's sake go away!" he implored.

She shook her head.

"Do not I belong to you now?" she whispered. "My place is where you are. I will not be parted from you."

"Then God help us!" he said solemnly.

All three sat down to the table again, and Paul poured some wine into a wooden cup and passed it to his mother.

"We show forth the Lord's death till He come," he repeated.

Already the shouts and threats of the crowd about to make a cowardly attack upon them rang noisily in the evening air. The road was packed with the people. Ferocious faces caught the last gleam of the sun. Fists were shaken at the house. Stones were flung against the windows.

The yard-gate was unlocked as usual, and the crowd rushed furiously towards the open door. Marfa was the first to enter. She knew Halya was there, and the only way to save her from the fury of her father and Panass was to be the first to attack her herself.

"Ah! You wretch! Here you are!" she cried savagely. "Leave her to me, you men!" and getting hold of her by her hair she dragged her violently out of the onslaught of the mob. This motherly violence saved the girl.

Ooliana stood on the nearer side of the table, Paul behind it. The open Book, the plate of bread, and the wooden cup containing wine irritated the ignorant peasantry most of all.

"It is witchcraft! They are weaving a spell to do us mischief!" shouted Koozka. "We've caught them at it! They've bewitched Halya, too, and she going to be married to Panass!"

"Kill them! the heretics!" cried Karpo, "they are the cause of all our trouble. Whoso kills a heretic, seventy sins will be forgiven him in the Day of Judgment."

Paul stepped forward from behind the table, with a pale but resolute face. He was ready to meet his fate.

But Ooliana threw herself before him. The mother stood between the murderous crew

384

THE HIGHWAY OF SORROW.

and her son. With outstretched arms she sought to protect him.

"Go back!" she cried. "I call God to witness this day we have done harm to no one! Let the starosta take us if we are to be taken!"

For a few seconds there was a pause.

"Savely would favour the witch!" shouted Okhrim angrily; "strike her down now while her evil eye is off you!"

Ooliana had turned, and was gazing with deep agitation on Paul's pallid face.

"If we suffer with Christ we shall also reign with Him," she said.

The next moment she was felled to the ground by Koozka's club, and violently thrown aside into the corner beneath the empty icon shrine. Just then Paissy appeared in the crowd, pushing his way among them.

"Stop! stop!" he exclaimed, "you are not far from killing her. You might give her some blows to teach her a lesson, but you must stop short of murder. That is forbidden by God's Commandments."

He ordered them to lay Ooliana on the bench. She breathed heavily, but did not open her eyes. Paul thrust aside his persecutors and flung himself on his knees beside her.

"Speak to me, mother!" he cried, "let me hear your voice again."

He fancied a smile flickered about her mouth; but half a dozen violent hands seized him and dragged him away into the fold-yard.

"Knock him down! Beat him! Kick him!" shouted a multitude of voices.

"No!" shouted Panass, louder than any-one else, "let us bind him and throw him into the river. If he floats that shows he is a sorcerer; if he sinks he is only a heretic."

Paissy attempted to interfere.

"Orthodox Christians!" he said, "you must let him confess if he will. You must not hurry a human soul to endless perdition."

It was too late. No one listened to him.

The mob was hurrying Paul down to the river, binding his arms as they went. When Paissy overtook them they had dragged him to the little wooden pier on which the women did their washing, and were about to push him from the end of it into the river, flushed with the spring floods. Paissy called out peremptorily—

z

"Stop! Fasten a rope under his arms!" he shouted.

As soon as this was done Panass and Karpo flung him into the stream.

Paul sank.

"He is drowning!" cried the peasants; "it's clear he did not know how to save himself this time by his witchcraft."

"Drag him out!" ordered Paissy.

Several men pulled at the rope, and Paul was brought to the surface of the water and dragged on to the end of the pier.

"The Stundist is baptised now!" laughed Panass; and all who heard him echoed his words and his laughter.

"Do you renounce the Devil and all his works?" asked Paissy: the question that is put in actual baptism.

Paul was half unconscious. His brain was bewildered; but the words which were most clearly in his mind rose to his lips.

"Lord! lay not this sin to their charge!" he prayed.

The exasperated rabble yelled with rage.

"Throw him in again! Keep him in

longer! He does not feel it yet!" screamed several voices.

Paul was flung into the river again. When he was dragged out, Paissy again asked him—

"Do you renounce the Devil, and all his angels?"

Paul again murmured with a sobbing breath—

"Lord, lay not this sin to their charge!"

"Down into the water again!" shouted Paissy himself this time.

At this moment Valerian came running with full speed down the slope towards the river. He saw Paul's white face sink beneath the surface of the troubled waters.

"Drag him out again instantly!" he exclaimed; "what are you doing? Do you indeed believe in a God? And you, Father Paissy!"

Paul lay before them unconscious, if not dead. Valerian gazed down at him with inexpressible pity in his face.

"We were seeking to wash the heretic from his sins, by submerging him thrice in the water. There is nothing wrong in it," said Paissy, measuring Valerian from head to foot with a sinister and scrutinising look.

z 2

"Perhaps not according to clerical notions," answered Valerian, beside himself with indignation and pity; "but according to the civil law such torture may send you to Siberia."

He looked round at the peasants, whose faces were suddenly clouded with dread.

"To Siberia!" sneered Paissy; "this miscreant, who profaned the church, is likely to go to Siberia; but none of those who wanted to save his soul, and bring him back to the orthodox faith."

He wrapped himself in his cassock, and with a dignified step marched slowly and solemnly away. Valerian turned to the peasants.

"How could you do this thing?" he said; "don't you see the man is quite ill? He was almost killed in protecting your property, Sheelo. How could you repay him in this manner?"

"But the fire was caused by his enchantments," answered Sheelo.

"How can you talk such nonsense?" asked Valerian; "there is no enchantment such as you think of. Here, Demyan and Kondraty, help me to carry Paul Rudenko home."

A small group of Stundists had approached, strolling homewards by the river from their evening meeting at Loukyan's old home. They helped to carry the benumbed and drenched body of Paul to his own house.

Reaching it, they found Ooliana still lying on the bench, and Marfa trying to bring back Halya from a faint. The girl was lying on the floor at Ooliana's feet. Valerian went to them, and laid his hand on the ice-cold wrist of Ooliana.

"She is dead!" he cried, in a voice of the deepest commiseration; "good God! what crimes are committed in Thy name!"

He could do nothing for her; but for Paul and Halya there was much to be done. He left Paul at last under the care of Demyan. Marfa met him as he came out of Paul's room.

"Oh! Valerian Petrovitch!" she cried, "save my child! Karpo will kill her if he catches hold of her. Take her away! Hide her! Keep her till Paul recovers, and marries her. I have nobody to help me but you. I shall lose her. But oh! if Karpo should kill her!"

Halya crept to his side, and, kneeling down, kissed his hand.

"Take care of me for Paul," she said; "my father will certainly kill me. And oh! I am afraid of Okhrim and Panass. Hide me somewhere, for Paul's sake."

Valerian promised to come back for her during the night, and drive her to Kovylsk, where she could be concealed by the Stundists until Paul recovered.

Through the village the rumour had already flown that Ooliana was dead. There was shame and sorrow in many a heart in Knishi that night. There was no one who had not received some kindness from her. The homeless families knew she would have been their best benefactress; and they bewailed her loss greatly. Even the Batushka and Matushka were mournful.

"Until she became a heretic," said Father Vasili, "she was the best Christian in my parish."

CHAPTER XXX.

1892 O.S.   1893 N.S.

NEARLY three years have passed. In other countries New Year's Day has been welcomed in with merry greetings and cheerful peals of bells. But here the sad old year still lingers on its death-bed. It is December 20th. The Autocrat of All the Russias could bring his people on this point, as well as other more important ones, abreast with other civilised nations with a stroke of his pen.

A severe Siberian December is regnant. A gale is blowing from the north-east over the boundless Siberian plains, bearing on its measureless current a fine snow-dust, which is hurled in clouds and columns on the wind, burying the low forests under its drifts, filling up ravines, and blinding the eyes of men and animals. There are no obstacles to the free elements of Nature. Finding nothing in its way, the irresistible gale flies onward like a bird for days without reaching a town, or any human habitation, except the hut of some savage. We are very far away from Oukrainia here. The skies are austere; Nature poor; and helpless and pitiful is man

The cold sun is past mid-day, but it cannot be seen in the grey sky, thinly veiled by a shroud of clouds. Still duller and sadder the monotonous plain appears in this gloomy, depressing light. Here and there the tops of the stunted pine-trees stand up amid a snow-drift. But this is the only feature in the wide expanse of billowy snow.

Tramping heavily through the snow in their wide, flat boots, moved a long line of prisoners. They were weary and frozen. The coarse prison dress and the short, worn-out fur coats protected them very badly from the biting wind. Their chains, though skilfully fastened up, caught the snow at every step, impeding the march and burning the skin with frost.

At the end of this slowly moving column came a few prisoners without chains, though they were evidently considered of the most importance, as their escort of soldiers was more numerous than that of the rest of the file.

They were political prisoners, exiled without trial by administrative order, and in consequence they had not lost all their privileges.

There were only five—a young girl, exiled for distributing some pamphlets, and four men, one of whom was a boy of fifteen with blue eyes and round child-like face, not quite of a Russian type. His name was Vania, and, as a Jew by birth, he was banished to the farthest Yakutsk settlements, beyond the Arctic Circle, for some revolutionary papers found in his possession. Two others were middle-aged men, one of whom had been guilty of giving shelter to his own children, whose fate was much more severe than his own, having been sentenced to penal servitude for life.

The fourth man of the little band, who had been elected their starosta or head man, walked on dreamily a little in advance of his comrades, and presently reached the file of common criminals tramping, with the ceaseless clangour of chains, across the plain of snow.

This was Valerian. He was haggard and emaciated; but every man and woman in the long procession was haggard and emaciated too. But for the human misery of their faces, they

might have been a chain of ghosts, marching
hollow-eyed and with sunken faces in the dim
wintry light.   His banishment followed quite
naturally the events described in the last chapter.   He could not disobey his conscience, and
had begun a lawsuit to inquire into Ooliana's
murder and the ill-usage of Paul.

Paissy had proved a subtle and dangerous
opponent.   Seeing that Valerian meant to push
the inquiry to the utmost, he resolved to have
recourse to an easy and well-tried means of
getting rid of him.   He denounced him secretly
to the authorities in St. Petersburg as a revolutionary propagandist.   He had no proofs to bring
forward in support of his accusation ; but the
suspicion alone was sufficient for the authorities.   An unexpected domiciliary visit was
made to the old General's house, and in
Valerian's rooms was found a parcel of prohibited books, many of them translations of
English political writers, which he had just
received from St. Petersburg.

His fate was sealed.   Valerian was carried
off to St. Petersburg and thrown into the
fortress-prison there, where he was kept in solitary confinement for two years.   At last his lot

was changed, thanks to his father's connections, into exile to Siberia.

The greater part of the long journey had been made. They were reaching Irkutsk, where most of the prisoners would remain— some in prison, others free to get their own living as they could.

Valerian had endured the journey fairly well, but traces of extreme exhaustion were evident on his comrades and most of the exiles, who formed altogether a very large party. Shivering in their worn-out furs, they crawled despondently along, furrowing the deep snow with their numerous feet. The column length- ened out more and more. Lieutenant Mironov, the captain of the escort, lost patience.

"Get along! Look alive!" he shouted, standing on one side of the procession so that all might see him.

He was a man about fifty, with grey hair and a red face, from which the skin was peel- ing off from the frost. He had advanced in the service. During the Bulgarian war he had been under General Nesteroff, Valerian's father, who had helped him to get promo- tion.

"Close up the ranks, you beasts!" he stormed.

Swearing was a great art with him, and he enjoyed showing it off on occasions; but the presence of the political prisoners checked him to-day. They were educated men, and he restrained himself lest they should detect in him the coarseness of a peasant. Valerian, he knew, was a noble, the son of his old General.

Roused by the shouts of their stern captain, the prisoners quickened their pace, if only to prove their zeal in obeying him. They almost ran as they passed Mironov, but again they fell back into crawling more slowly than before.

Before Mironov's keen eyes passed a long line of grey-coated figures covered with white frost — young and old, men, women, and children. They had ceased talking. No hum of voices accompanied the clanking of the chains. A waggon with baggage rolled by, and a few rude carts, without springs, in which lay those too ill to walk.

A small group of exiles, somewhat detached from the rest, quickened their pace when ordered, but did not make a show of running as the others had done. This roused Mironov's anger.

"I'll teach you how to dawdle!" he shouted, raising his hand to strike a fair-haired young man of about thirty, with a handsome, thoughtful face. But at that moment he caught Valerian's eye, and his hand fell down. He gave the man nearest to him a push, and showered upon them a torrent of swearing. But oaths break no bones.

Neither the fair-haired man nor his comrade—who, by the colour of his hair and the type of his face, was plainly from the South—made any reply to the captain's insults.

The younger man carried in his arms a bundle of clothes, within which moved a living little creature. Behind him crawled a young woman, evidently his wife.

"What a fine lady! cannot carry her own baby!" exclaimed Mironov with a sneer.

The woman shivered and pressed closer to her husband, as if trying to hide herself from him. She was a pretty young creature, though her dress was in rags, and her face thin and sorrowful.

But Mironov left her alone. He strode

along with the column, gradually slackening his pace until Valerian overtook him. Valerian marched on, paying no attention to his chief, who walked beside him. Mironov coughed; Valerian took no notice.

"These common people," said Mironov in an apologetic tone, "you can do nothing with them without oaths and kicks."

Valerian smiled, and turned to him his handsome pale face.

"But do you try?" he asked.

"It is no use trying," was the answer. "They are brutes, not human beings. About you others, I say nothing," he added quickly; "you are educated men."

"And those whom you were about to strike just now, are they brutes too in your opinion?" said Valerian, indicating the little group of prisoners marching behind the baggage-waggon.

"The Stundists? Oh, no! Why they are exiled, I cannot understand. They are peaceable folk. But they were loitering, nearly a hundred yards behind the others."

"It was not on purpose," said Valerian. "See! the woman is so tired she may drop any moment. Instead of insulting her, you should give her a lift in the waggon."

"What! Ought I to order conveyances for them all?" exclaimed the lieutenant. "Waggons for four hundred prisoners! You want too much, Valerian Petrovitch."

The three prisoners who were following the waggon were Paul, Demyan, and Stepan. Stepan was sentenced to hard labour, Paul and Demyan to exile. After his mother's death Paul had found it impossible to live any longer in the house polluted by her murder. He had sold all his possessions, and gone to live in Kovylsk, where he married Halya. For nearly two years he had gone about visiting the scattered churches of the Stundists, and encouraging them amid the fury of the persecution raging against them. But his career was quickly cut short, and a sentence of banishment passed upon him. Halya chose to accompany him, and she had been allowed to take her baby, then three months old.

Demyan's wife had decided to remain with her children, of whom there were now three, and Demyan had gone to exile alone. But

the little ones were soon taken away from
the broken-hearted mother, to be brought up
in the orthodox religion. Demyan rarely
spoke or looked up. He had made his long
march with bowed down head, and eyes fixed
on the ground. His mind seemed bewildered.
But one thought was clear to him, the thought
of God. Now and then he murmured His
name in a pathetic voice, which brought the
tears to Paul's eyes. If they asked him what
he was thinking of, he always answered God.

For some time Valerian and Mironov walked
on in silence.

"When shall we reach an étape?" inquired
Valerian. "Even I am nearly tired to death."

"Very soon," said Mironov, hurrying on
to reach the head of the column.

Halya heard his shouts and curses drawing
nearer, and getting frightened started to run
on, stumbling in the heavy snow. Paul tried
to hold her back and soothe her.

"Look here, young woman!" cried Mironov,
"you are tired. Would you like to get up
into the waggon?"

Paul and Halya looked at him in astonishment, wondering if he was jeering at them,

or was in earnest. The irritable lieutenant flew into a passion.

"Ah, you hussy!" he thundered. "You want to die on the road, and get me into trouble. Get up into the waggon this instant! Look here, you fool! Stop!" he shouted to the driver. "Can't you hear when you are called?"

Seated comfortably on the baggage with which the waggon was loaded, and lulled slightly by the slow movement it made, Halya felt herself in Paradise. Paul had given her the baby, and it too was evidently happy. It lay peacefully in her lap, and stretching its cramped limbs was ready to fall asleep. Halya peeped under the shawl that covered his face. The baby-face frowned a little as if he had not made up his mind whether to cry or no; but the motion of the waggon was so pleasant to him it did not seem worth while to cry. A smile came to his soft lips, and he tossed his little hands about cheerily.

Halya's face was all sunshine. Bending over her child she kissed the tiny face and small red hands, and pressed this little helpless being to her heart; the source of so much

A A

happiness, and alas! of so much suffering. Oh, if God would only keep the child safe to the journey's end! It was so near now. To-morrow they would be in Irkutsk.

Meanwhile the column straggled and grew longer and longer. Mironov's patience was quite exhausted. He drove the prisoners on with blows as well as curses. At last they saw before them on the ridge of a low hill a small wooden building, showing black against the grey horizon. It seemed impossible that it could shelter all this crowd of people.

The prisoners almost forgot their fatigue, and quickened their pace. There was only twenty minutes further to walk, and then there would be rest, warmth, and food.

The wind had fallen, and the sky was dark. The horses snorted and pranced as if terrified. A white cloud appeared on the horizon, a little to the north of the étape. The lieutenant and the old experienced pri-soners, who were not a few, glanced at it, and at every glance hurried their pace. The cloud grew and moved, but almost imperceptibly. The air became heavy. In several places over the plains gigantic forms were seen appearing and disappearing. Sudden gusts of wind flew across the misty expanse.

"A snowstorm! a snowstorm!" was shrieked by several voices, and the whole mass of people pressed onwards in the direction where a few minutes before they had seen the dark building. Instantly there was wild confusion. An impenetrable mist surrounded them. The snow fell in flakes, which a whirlwind hurled hither and thither, bewildering and blinding the sight. Paul hurried to the waggon to be near his wife and child; but he was knocked down by some of the running prisoners, and when he struggled to his feet he could see nothing but a few human forms scudding away in the darkness.

"Halya! Halya!" he cried. The roar of the wind was his only answer. Halya could not hear him. She was lying at the bottom of the waggon, protecting with her own body their child from the penetrating cold.

"Halya! Halya!" shouted Paul.

All at once, as if rising from underground, there appeared a file of men holding one another by the hand. They were the

A A 2

political prisoners, led by Valerian. He heard the cry " Halya!"

"Where are you going? Come back! You will lose yourself in a moment," he cried ; " come on with us. In a file one does not lose the way so easily. Quicker, boys! Vania, show yourself a man! And, Vera, you must be a man on this occasion. Courage! we are nearly there."

Valerian's hand caught Paul's, and held it firmly. In a few minutes their heads, bowed down against the storm, struck against the palisading which surrounded the étape.

"The gate is to the left," cried Valerian, whose keen sight pierced through the bewildering snowflakes; "keep close to the palisade."

He could hardly be heard for the roaring of the wind, and the confused noises inside the prison-yard. When they entered it there was already a throng of people, and every moment others rushed in, overjoyed to reach the shelter. Soldiers, drivers, and prisoners, mixed together in a cheerful crowd, happy in their deliverance from a deadly danger. It was impossible to make out the roll-call amidst such confusion and the hurricane fury of the storm. Mironov ordered the prison doors to be thrown open. He only called out the names of the political prisoners, who stood apart and together.

"This is the second time you have saved my life," said Paul with deep emotion to Valerian as they separated.

"It is a life worth saving," answered Valerian simply.

Mironov ordered lights to be kept burning over the prison door, and the sentinels were bidden to call out as loudly as they could from time to time in case any of the prisoners were lost in the tempest, and might wander that way.

"To bed!" he shouted.

Then followed a scene of the utmost confusion. The prisoners struggled, and pushed, and fought with one another to get first into the kamera, in which there were fifty places only, for the accommodation of three times that number. The family kamera, into which the women and children and the married men were scrambling, was a long, narrow room, with a *nari* or sleeping platform down each

side, and a gangway in the middle. The
sleeping platform was about four feet from the
floor, and six feet wide, of bare boards, without
pillow or rug for the rest of the weary frames
stretched upon it after the toilsome march of
the day. But hard and comfortless as it was,
a place on it was ardently coveted, as otherwise there was no resting-place except on the
floor covered with filth. Paul and Halya,
happy in finding one another and their child
safe, made their way into the kamera; but it
was already crowded.

During their long march of several months
the Stundists had made a favourable impression
on many of their fellow-prisoners. They had
made themselves useful in various ways on
those rest days, when the whole band stayed
for thirty-six hours at the same étape. The
criminal prisoners, like the political, had elected
a starosta, whom all were bound to obey, and
Stepan had been of great service to him. It
was this starosta who received the alms collected
as they passed through the scattered villages,
and who appointed the beggars to implore
the charity of sympathising spectators. Paul
and Halya, with their baby, were the most

successful in collecting alms, and the starosta
held them in high favour.

"Halya! Halya!" cried a shrill voice, as
they stood at the door of the crowded kamera.
It was Kilina who called, a big-boned, masculine
woman, sentenced to fifteen years of hard
labour, for a double murder. She was standing
up in a corner of the platform, waving her
hands, and shrieking at the top of her voice.

"I've kept a place for you and your brat!"
she shouted. Paul pushed their way towards
her, and helped Halya to mount the platform,
pressing a kiss on his baby's forehead as he
held him in his arms. Then he looked round
for a place to rest his weary limbs in. The
floor was already covered with people lying
in their drenched clothing, which had begun
to thaw as soon as they entered the warm
kamera. There were few who were eating,
hungry though they were, for at the mid-day
halt the weather had been so bad that scarcely
any peasant women had come to sell provisions,
and the prisoners were dependent upon these
uncertain and casual supplies for their sub-
sistence. But a good deal of vodka was being
drunk. This was bought from the canteen

keeper, who contrived, by bribing the guards, to smuggle in a few forbidden luxuries.

They had been locked in for the night. There was no ventilation, no sanitation, no lavatory or closet. There were the open, unavoidable indecencies of a savage's hut. Immediately under the oil lamp, which fortunately shed only a dim light on the horrible scene, crouched a group of men round a turned-up pail, on which they were playing a game at cards, and passing a flask of vodka from hand to hand, and from mouth to mouth. The starosta was looking on, and beckoned to Paul as he saw him seeking for a spot to rest in.

"You're my best beggar," he said, "yet you won't take any vodka. So I've kept a place on the *nari* for you."

A pleasant smile played over Paul's face; he rejoiced in those tokens of good-will, and thanked the starosta heartily. But his eye fell on the grey head of an old convict, lying almost on the melted filth at his feet, and without a word he roused him and helped him up to the reserved place. The starosta shook his head and swore, but he gave Paul a glass of tea for Halya.

The three Stundists crept silently together
to the foot of Halya's resting-place. From
the first night of their long march they had
made it their custom. They sang together a
hymn, and then with bowed heads and covered
faces prayed each one in his own heart. At
first they had been bitterly persecuted; but
now those nearest to them were, as a rule, quiet
for the few minutes this worship lasted. To-
night was the last of their long and painful
journey. To-morrow they would reach Irkutsk.
They chose for their last hymn the one now
familiar to Western Churches, "O happy band
of pilgrims!" Voices from all parts of the
kamera joined in the familiar words—strange
words to utter in that den of human misery,
and degradation, and crime. Then Paul leaned
his weary body against one of the wooden
pillars, which supported the roof; Demvan sank
listlessly on the floor, and Stepan found a
place where he could crawl under the platform. Night and sleep, haunted by terrible
dreams, settled down on the prisoners.

CHAPTER XXXI.

WOULD GOD IT WERE MORNING!

HALYA stretched herself on the hard bare planks of the platform. She was somewhat refreshed by the tea and the scanty provision Paul had been able to procure for her. The three men had not eaten a morsel. She was still nursing her child; but there was no possibility of bathing its tired little limbs.

"I think Loukyanoushka looks strange," she said to Paul; "all the day he seemed so much better, it was a pleasure to see him. And now my darling is quite poorly again."

"It was the fresh air," answered Paul, sighing, "and there is such a thick smell here. But it is the last night, my dear one!"

The baby was breathing with effort in this overcrowded room. He was discontented and offended by this change for the worse, and felt he had a full right to protest by crying. But he was sleepy, and could not postpone the pleasure of falling asleep in his mother's arms, so he confined himself to a displeased murmur, which soon passed into a peaceful snoring.

"Now, you see, I told you so!" said Paul. Halya was cheered, and lay down cautiously, not to disturb her baby. But she could not sleep. The boy tossed about in her arms, throwing out his little hands convulsively and beginning to cry. She would have got up and walked about with him, but the floor was covered with sleeping forms. Sitting up, she rocked him to and fro, singing to him Oukrainian songs. The baby seemed soothed and pacified.

"Singing always makes him happy," thought Halya lovingly; "he will grow up a singer like his father."

She was herself worn out with fatigue and want of sleep; and as soon as the baby was quiet again she sank back upon their travelling-bag, which served her as a pillow, and fell instantly into the heavy slumber of complete exhaustion. How long she slept she did not know. The consciousness of their miserable condition never left her. A delirious dream

filled her mind with horror.   She was separated
from Paul and was working in the silver mines.
She wore the prison dress and carried a shovel
in her hands; she, a free woman, who had
followed her husband of her own accord.
Near her was a cart, and there lay her baby.
Thick darkness, filled with noises and oaths,
surrounded them.   A figure was coming towards her, she felt rather than saw it.   It
was Mironov; but never had she seen a human
face so full of fury.

"Boys! show this woman how to dig!"
he shouted.

A crowd of men came round her with
hooting and laughter, and flung her into the
hole she had just finished digging.

"Throw in her little puppy too," ordered
Mironov, and she felt her child tossed down
upon her.   Then heavy lumps of earth were
flung in amid hideous uproar.   They were burying her and her child alive.   Heavy clods pressed
upon her chest and throat.   She was suffocating.

"O Lord! receive my soul!" she cried
out, and awoke.

But she did not altogether recover her

senses. The lurid light of the lamp perplexed her; the strange, miserable forms; the thickening atmosphere. The kamera seemed a Pandemonium.

One of the card-players had been cheating, and his companions were giving him a beating. The canteen keeper was trying to separate them by violent blows struck at random.

"Be quiet, you devils! Enough!" he thundered "we shall have the lieutenant here, and others will suffer for you. You might even kill him in this way."

He tore the cheating player from the grasp of his comrades, and kicked him into a corner behind his canteen stand. The players sat down and began another game.

Halya tried hard to collect her bewildered thoughts. By her side the baby was moaning and tossing about. She could not pacify him. His little body was all on fire. She turned his face towards the lamp, and her blood ran cold.

The tiny face was quite blue, his eyes wide open, and his little mouth gasping for breath, like a fish drawn out of water.

"Paul! Help!" cried Halya. Paul was instantly at her feet.

"Look! he is dying!" said Halya, shuddering at her own words.

"How can you say such a thing?" he asked in a soothing voice.

"But look!" she screamed. She rocked him in her arms, held him above her head and tried to make him laugh. But nothing was of any avail. The child cried feebly, and opened his mouth wide to swallow the air that was suffocating him.

Halya felt as if she was going mad. But a happy thought flashed across her mind.

"Valerian can save him!" she exclaimed.

In a moment she was rushing to the door, and stumbling over the bodies of the prisoners, which lay as thick as sheaves on a threshing-floor. She began to knock and call with all her might. The card-players were alarmed, and hid their cards; then showered abuse and threats upon her. The starosta came forward with upraised fist.

"Stop! you vixen!" he roared, "you'll rouse the officers. Get back to your bed."

Paul stepped in between them to receive

the blow intended for Halya. But at that instant the heavy outside bar of the door was withdrawn, and Mironov appeared on the threshold.

"What is this noise? Who is the cause of it?" he asked, entering the kamera.

But the stench was so strong he quickly retreated, and stood with his hand on the door to be able to shut it at the first chance. Halya stepped out into the passage.

"My child is dying, your honour!" she cried.

"But what is that to me?" he asked; "I can't help it."

"Please let Valerian Petrovitch see him," she implored; "he is my only child—a little boy: my first-born. Only let Valerian see him—he can save him."

All these few seconds the door was open; and a fresh current of air streamed into this den, and brought out the sickening smell. But the prisoners were more afraid of the cold than of the polluted atmosphere, because their only defence against it was their damp rags.

"Shut the door! Do you want to freeze us to death?" called out a hoarse voice.

" Shut the door, and stop your flirtation with the gentleman," added another ironically. Halya shut it instantly.

She wrapped her boy in her shawl to shield him from the piercing cold, but she did not think of herself.

" Oh! allow me to see the doctor, little father!" she said beseechingly ; " he is the son of our old landowner, General Nesteroff. He knows us all, and was always kind to the sick and poor."

" It is against the law," answered Mironov ; "an exile must not practise as a doctor."

" Is there a law that a mother must see her baby dying in her arms without help?" asked Halya.

He pitied the woman ; and besides, he wished to please Valerian, who would gladly do anything to help his country-people. Valerian was sent for.

" Why don't you go back into the kamera?" asked the lieutenant ; " you must not stay here barefoot."

" That is nothing," she replied, " the child is a little better here."

When in about a quarter of an hour

Valerian appeared he found the little creature quite revived.

"He is quite well," he said, examining the baby; "it must have been the foul air that made him seem ill."

"But cannot you give him some medicine?" she asked, believing, as all peasants do, that there is a remedy for every ailment; "how shall I pass through the night with him?"

"He wants nothing," said Valerian. Taking Mironov on one side, he spoke to him in an earnest whisper.

"A thousand times no!" protested Mironov in a loud voice; "you will get me into trouble with your requests. I've broken the rules already. This you ask means connivance. She is accompanying her husband, a common criminal, and she must be in the same kamera with him. To change from one kamera to another is strictly forbidden. Go back, young woman," he added, turning to Halya; "you've seen the doctor, and that is all I can do."

He opened the door; but now the stench, after breathing the fresh air, was so horrible to her, she felt as if she were being thrust into a sewer.

B B

"I can't go!" she exclaimed; "let me stay outside all night."

"Nonsense! you'd freeze to death! Get in!" said Mironov, giving her a push, and quickly fastening the door behind her. Paul and Stepan approached her anxiously. But for the first minute she could hardly breathe, and almost fainted. Then remembering her child, she roused herself, and made her way to her place on the *nari* which Kilina had kept for her. Paul, satisfied by her report of what Valerian said, fell asleep again. The child too was sleeping peacefully. Halya sat upon the *nari* absorbed in one thought—how to live through that awful night, 'and escape out of this loathsome den. Her head was dizzy; and incoherent fragments of thoughts and memories whirled through her brain. She felt herself losing her reason. Kilina yawned and opened her drowsy eyelids.

"Why don't you go to sleep, my dear?" she said good-naturedly; "are you unhappy about the baby? It is very hard to go on étape with children. How many of them die, God knows! You are not the first, and won't be the last."

" It is cruel to talk like that," answered Halya, sobbing.

" I don't mean any harm," said Kilina; " I do not wish him any evil. But I say it because I see he is dying."

The lamp flashed up for a moment, and a thick cloud of smoke followed the glare. The baby began to gasp again; opened his eyes and shut them, breathing heavily with his exhausted lungs. Halya watched his movements with an aching heart.

" The morning! Oh, Lord! let the morning come soon," she prayed.

But the morning was far off yet, and the sun did not hasten his rising to come to her help. The window with its thick bars looked like a black abyss.

The small oil lamp, which seemed smothered by the weight of the polluted atmosphere, struggled alone with the darkness. It threw a purple glimmering light upon the dirty walls and reeking ceiling, from which drops of congealed moisture fell from time to time upon the slimy floor, with its throng of human beings in the half-death of sleep. Paul was near her, leaning against the wooden support, with

B B 2

his head falling on to his chest. She had seen a picture of the Crucifixion of Christ, with the thorn-crowned head in a similar position. She wondered, in her bewildered brain, if they had crucified Paul.

Two card-players were still at play. One of them, whose face she could not see, had lost all his money, his rations for the next day, and his prison dress, for which, when he reached Irkutsk, he would get a severe flogging. But still he wanted to go on.

"Enough!" said his companion, flinging down the cards, and throwing himself backwards with a loud yawn. He was Kilina's husband, a small, red-haired man, apparently an artisan.

"One game more, you devil!" cried the loser.

"How many last ones have we had?" asked the other; "it is time to sleep."

"Ah! you cursed swindler! you cheat me, and then—sleep."

The face of the red-haired man was distorted with fury. Without saying a word, he plucked out of his high boot a long and glittering knife, which, in spite of many searches, he had managed to keep in his possession. Halya caught the baby to her breast to save him in any emergency. But at the same time, she wished they would make such a row as to compel the officer to open the door, and bring in a rush of fresh air.

The canteen keeper, however, caught Kilina's husband by the collar, and shook him so fiercely that the knife fell from his grasp.

"Only dare to make a row!" he exclaimed.

"Leave me alone, pig's ear!" retorted the red-haired gambler, replacing the knife in his boot, and contenting himself with muttering oaths and curses. Soon after, all was quiet— if it could be called quiet, when the kamera was full of sounds of human misery, the wailing and coughing of little children, the sobs that women uttered in their broken sleep, the deep groans of men who dreamed of their lost freedom. Outside, the storm continued to howl and roar. The chinks of the log building and of the roof were filled up with snow, and imperviously sealed against the admission of fresh air, or the escape of foul. The lamp could hardly flicker. Halya counted every minute, her eyes fastened on the gasping child lying on her lap.

Suddenly the boy awoke with a piteous cry. Kilina lifted up her head and looked at him.

"He is dying, my poor dear!" she said calmly.

"It's not true! God will not let him die," answered Halya.

The child shuddered, stretched himself out, and lay motionless.

"Now we are better again, darling!" said Halya tenderly, pressing the little corpse to her bosom. The lamp flickered up once more, and died out, filling the air with a horrid smell. Deep darkness reigned in the kamera. The dead child lay softly in his mother's arms.

"Now he has gone to sleep again," said Halya to Kilina, rocking and soothing the baby. By-and-bye she pressed her lips to its little face. It was icy cold, the indescribable coldness of death.

A heartrending scream rang through the kamera. All the prisoners sprang to their feet.

"What is the matter? Who is killed?" called out frightened voices in the utter darkness.

"My boy is killed!" shrieked the unhappy mother.

Kilina slipped off the platform and caught Paul by the arm.

"Take my place," she said, "and comfort her if you can."

Paul sat down beside Halya and gathered her into his arms, and pressed her dear head upon his breast. She shivered and trembled; but she listened to his voice. He talked to her of the old happy times in Knishi, when they were children together, and she lay quiet, sobbing now and then. But when he spoke to her of the future, of the heavenly home which Christ was preparing for them, she grew excited again. The dead child lay between her and the wall.

Paul's heart was torn with anguish. Halya had left all for him, as he had left all for Christ. His love for her was a hundredfold deeper than it had been before she became his wife. He caught a glimpse of the Divine Love. To give up his life for her was little; he was willing to pour out his soul unto death for her sake.

CHAPTER XXXII.

VIA DOLOROSA.

HALYA had lost her reason. Fortunately, however, she was so worn-out with fatigue and sorrow she was not dangerous either to herself or others. She was laid in one of the rough, springless carts, which were provided for the sick and infirm, and Kilina was allowed to take charge of her. Paul, with some difficulty, obtained permission from Mironov to carry his dead child to Irkutsk, instead of laying the little corpse in the baggage waggon. It seemed dearer to him than the living baby he had carried yesterday.

The storm was over by morning. The roll-call was made, and four prisoners were missing; they must have lost their way and been frozen to death on the open plain. But as they were common criminals Mironov was not over-troubled on their account. He did not think it necessary to make any search for their bodies. He marked their names as being

lost during a sudden snowstorm, and left instructions with the étape keeper, in case any
corpse was found when the snow melted, to
notify the fact to the prison authorities in
Irkutsk.

Paul, with his dead baby in his arms,
marched in the column of prisoners, Stepan
and Demyan walking beside him in silence.
His heart was full of memories of the child's
short life. It had been born while he was
in prison; and he had not seen it until the
long journey into exile had begun. But
during that journey what a ray of happiness
the baby had brought into the daily and
hourly misery of their lives! They had watched
it grow with the slow stunted growth of a
nursling whose mother is suffering. But how
bright and quick he had been! He had
laughed and cooed in their faces when they
were most cast down. Only a day or two
ago the little one had tried to call him
" father."

If the child had only been spared one day
longer! The goal of their long march was in
sight, and he would be free to make a home
for his wife and child. Yet it had been God's

will the child should be taken and his wife stricken down. "If this cup may not pass from me, Thy will be done!" cried Paul in his inmost soul.

"Paul!" said a voice of profound pity beside him. Stepan and Demyan fell back a pace or two, and Valerian walked beside him. For an instant the old terror fluttered across Paul's heart, but it was gone as he looked into Valerian's face, and was gone for ever.

"Halya will recover," said Valerian confidently, "and will be as sane as ever. You will have a home of your own in Irkutsk, and I will help you to get a living. I have some friends there who will find you work. Demyan, too, will soon get employed as a blacksmith. It will be exile, but it will not be intolerable."

"No," answered Paul, with a new gleam of light and courage in his eyes as he met Valerian's sympathetic glance.

"We lose Stepan," continued Valerian.

"Stepan goes gladly!" said Stepan's voice behind him; "he goes as the messenger of the Lord to preach the Gospel to those who sit in darkness and the shadow of death."

" Brave man ! " exclaimed Valerian, turning to him with a smile. For a few minutes he walked on silently. At last he stretched out his hand and touched gently the sorrowful little burden Paul was bearing.

" A flower crushed by the heel of a monster ! " he said.

" A flower transplanted into the Garden of God ! " said Paul.

The two exiles looked into one another's eyes with a keen and steadfast gaze.

" I know what you would say," Paul went on : "I live in a delusion. Well, I read in the Book God has given to me that man by wisdom knows not God, and that the wisdom of this world is foolishness with God. I know you are a learned man and I cannot argue with you. But this also I know—that Christ dwells within me by faith. By faith alone I know Him and the Father. I cannot tell you what faith is, any more than I could explain sight to the blind or sound to the deaf. But it is here within me; and by it I can endure all things, as seeing Him who is invisible."

" You are a happy man ! " said Valerian;

" I could almost wish I shared your delusion."

" It is no delusion!" exclaimed Paul earnestly, " it is a truth for which every one of us is ready to die. Look round you! Look at my dead child! Look at the wretchedness, and the crime, and the degradation that is all about us. Look at your own condition— exiled, a prisoner, lost to all you held dear. If there is no God, no Saviour, no life hereafter, what a hell this world would be!"

The words brought back to their memory the fateful day when Paul, addressing his neighbours in the church at Knishi, exclaimed, " What a Paradise the world would be!" Their eyes filled with tears. Valerian caught Paul's hand in a close clasp.

" We are brothers, Paul!" he cried, strangely moved; " let us stand side by side in the future which lies before us."

" You will not argue with me?" said Paul.

" Not a word," answered Valerian, smiling. " I would not take your beautiful faith from you any more than I would snatch a cup of water from dying lips. We will be brothers in spite of our differences."

They reached Irkutsk in the full expectation of passing their last night in the étape
there. Halya was taken at once to the infirmary. But they were not released in the
morning; Demyan alone of the three Stundists
was turned adrift in the strange town to earn
his living as he could. Vania was sent on
towards his destination beyond the Arctic
Circle, to live with savages in their foul huts.
Vera was allowed to quit the étape. But
Valerian and Paul were still kept in prison.

A new blow awaited them. The local
authorities had received instructions from St.
Petersburg, the reading of which evoked shrieks
and wailing from the maddened men who heard
them. Almost half the number of convicts
were ordered to prolong their painful march
to the new and awful settlement of Saghalien.
The division among the common criminals was
made at random; some of them implicated in
the same crime remaining in Siberia, the others
going on to the deadly island. All the political
prisoners, with the exception of Vera and
Vania, were also sentenced to it. Stepan and
Paul met with the same fate Life-long exile
in Saghalien was their doom. Paul was suffered,

as a favour, to see Halya once more; and to bury his child, aided by Demyan, who promised to take Halya under his care until she could follow her husband.

Under these low wintry skies, in the gloomy light, enveloped in ice-mists, and torn from all that makes life worth living, we see them, a long-drawn-out chain of unutterable anguish; the common criminals, the agnostic patriot, and the Christian martyrs; and as we gaze they vanish from our sight along their Via Dolorosa —the Highway of Sorrow.

THE END.

Printed by Cassell & Company, Limited, La Belle Sauvage, London, E.C.

10,195